HEADS UP

A Science Fiction Collection

SEAN MONAGHAN

ALSO BY SEAN MONAGHAN

SHORT STANDALONE SCIENCE FICTION

The Molenstraat Music Festival

Barrens

Aelonee

Little Voices

Designated Driver

Cami, Metta and The Cube

Dangerous Machines

Fubrelli's Ghost

Lydia's Mollusk

Load Bearing Member

A Cultural Exchange

Life Span

The Film Adjuster

Problem Landing

The Chule

Sail Man

Visit seanmonaghan.com for more.

Published by Triple V Publishing

Cover illustration © Grandeduc | Dreamstime

Paperback isbn: 978-1-0671350-1-0

Discover other titles by this author at:www.seanmonaghan.com

CONTENTS

INTRODUCTION

I write a whole lot of short fiction, and I've been fortunate that many of my stories have been published in some major magazines and even won a few awards along the way.

But those magazines only have so much space and I find myself with stories put aside, waiting for a gap to send them off, fingers crossed that they will meet the editor's taste and vision for their publication. Or just that the story doesn't repeat themes of stories they've already purchased (which has happened on occasion with my stories).

And then sometimes I just plain write stories that I kind of suspect won't quite fit anywhere.

Here in your hands you have a mix of the above. Stories that, for whatever reason, don't quite fit out there.

Don't get me wrong, I'm proud of them all, in their different ways.

Thanks for picking up this little collection, I hope you enjoy the contents.

Sean
February 2026

HEADS UP

AUTHOR OF CRITICAL BURN
SEAN
MONAGHAN
FIND THE RIGHT STRAND
CHASING
FOX PALTON

CHAPTER ONE

Haylee Dahlen jerked awake, sitting up on the cold transport bench, trying hard to take in her surroundings. Dark, cool, stinky.

She wrinkled her nose against the stench. A mix of something dead and something that had passed through something alive.

She needed to move.

It was always like this on a jump back. Dissociative and disorienting, and with a touch of a nauseas gut.

Time travel could be a nasty cow. Still, it was working out better than cartography ever would have.

She was good at maps, but a little too obsessive over details.

Taking a deep breath, through her mouth, Haylee blinked to focus. Likely it would take a few minutes for her eyes to come right, and her tummy. As if her whole body had to recalibrate.

Tiny tingles ran through her legs and back and arms.

From nearby came the sounds of voices. Laughter. Shouts. The clink of glasses. That's right, the arrival room was part of a tavern. A floor below, people would be downing ale from tankards, tossing their pennies on the bar and downing more.

Like her mother in those final weeks.

Come on Haylee. Dwelling on the past will not move you forward.

It had taken a whole lot of therapy to reach that point.

Just go on, her mother had whispered hoarsely. *Go on and live out the best life you can. It's all you or I or anyone else have.*

Haylee shuddered at the memory. Things had always been strained with her mother. Right on up, almost, until, sitting at the bedside and her mother had gasped and her hand, clasping Haylee's hand, had gone slack.

Departures. Haylee's life seemed to often be about departures.

Now, she was in a room. Perhaps sixty square feet. Light came around the edges of what might have been a painted or papered-over window. The structure creaked. Perhaps she was on the third or second story.

Victorian England. Technically

Eighteen fifty-five. Right between the first and second industrial revolutions. Beyond the stinky little room's walls, factories would be belching smoke, and machinery would be making its way across the fields improving harvests. Kilns would be running twenty-four hours a day baking bricks.

Diseases rampant, but also with a whole bunch of smart people looking at sanitation and even primitive immunization.

A time when the world changed dramatically.

To a woman from the late twenty-first century, it was going to be both a treat and a torture. Amid her fascination and goggling, she would have to remember that she had a job to do.

A man to track down. A man to bring back to twenty ninety-eight to face trial.

Haylee brought up her watch--well, chronometer, really,

since it could keep track of her displacement through the stream. It was her tenuous link back to home. So long as she was wearing it, she could return pretty much instantly.

Besides that incident back in Byzantine Rome, it had always worked for her. And that other time, she'd been with Carly, and they'd figured it out together.

They hadn't even needed to deal with the last-ditch emergency of the little chip embedded in the back of their necks. From what Haylee had heard, that could be nasty.

The chronometer's face told Haylee that it was a little after eight in the morning on September twenty-third, eighteen fifty-three.

Eighteen fifty-three.

Not eighteen fifty-five.

Well that was just great.

Perfect really.

Tilly, Haylee's grandmother, would tell her that she needed to be less sarcastic, but what else could you do in a situation like this?

Two years early.

Haylee had worked long hours and many years with the teams of technicians and scientists, on making the calibration of the jumps back more and more precise.

In those early days, before her time, the windows had been wide open. You might arrive a hundred and fifty years before your intended date. Or a hundred and fifty later.

Glen Moskow had wound up almost getting run down by a Ford in 1930s Cairo when he'd been aiming to see the final construction of the Great Pyramid of Giza. He'd only missed by about forty-five hundred years.

Instead of watching the placing of the gold cap, he'd landed in a pile of camel dung.

But these days, a two year miss was unusual. Practically unheard of.

There were just sixteen of them now, in the research lab, chewing up inordinate amounts of power for a single jump. All the recent trips from the team had been spot on, really. Not more than a week or so out from their intended arrival date.

Anyway, the Heseldan Institute always targeted earlier ahead of later. Time might be a fluid swirling thing, but on the ground, you were always moving forward. No sense in arriving *after* the event you needed to witness.

This time was different, though. And it all pointed to a likely closure of the institute itself.

Fox Palton, former Heseldan Institute employee, had embezzled a cool quarter million, converted it to gold, stashed it somewhere, and made an escape through the portal.

At first it had looked like the guy was a sap, despite a solid record of research through the eighteen hundreds. He'd been easy to track through the time stream and two jumpers had gone back to get him.

Only to find that he had covered his tracks.

Jessica and Nate had practically had to tear the equipment down to its constituent parts to find where Fox had installed an optical baffler--as they called it--that had made all the details kind of chaotic and loose and unreadable.

It had taken Haylee's patience and eagle-eye to pore over the details and determine exactly where Fox had ended up.

And for some reason Director Stephens had thought that made Haylee the perfect candidate to actually take the trip to retrieve him.

Hardly. But that argument had fallen on ears filled with concrete or some other sound-proof substance. Ears with unresponsive tympanic membranes or something.

So here she was, with two years to kill before Fox would even show up.

Assuming that she had the timing right.

Haylee sighed and sat back on the transport bench. At least she had that, with its locker of useful equipment and currency and toiletries.

As she turned to it, a banging sound made her jump.

"Haylee!" a woman's voice shouted from outside the room. "Haylee? You in there?"

CHAPTER TWO

With a deep, almost deathly creak a small door swung slowly open into the room.

A moment of tension ran through Haylee.

Someone stepped through, silhouetted by dim light from outside.

Haylee recognized her.

Marline. From back at the Heseldan Institute.

Even in the half light, she looked older.

"Here you are!" Marline said. "We have had just a devil of a time trying to locate you."

"I just got here." Haylee shook her head at herself. She knew as well as anyone who worked that the Heseldan Institute that the concept of 'just got here' was moot.

Of course Marline looked older. She would have left perhaps four or five years after Haylee.

Marline had a palm flashlight and she shone it around. The room was in worse shape than Haylee had imagined. Rough board walls, with fluids running down, holes in the roof tiles, some kind of covering on the floor that was peeling up and sagging in places.

Haylee peered up and saw stars through the holes in the roof.

"So," Haylee said. "Things have gone desperately bad?"

"'Desperately' would likely be considered an understatement."

Haylee sighed.

"What's the update?" she said.

"Not here," Marline said. "I can't believe you chose somewhere with an odor like this."

"Kind of hard to not, in Victorian England."

"Yes," Marline said. "You think you're in Victorian England" She sighed. "Well."

"I'm not?" Haylee said.

"Come for a walk with me. Let's get this taken care of."

"Don't do that." It was disconcerting. "Tell me."

The palm flashlight floated away and drifted up near the beams of the ceiling, casting light down. Marline went to the transport table and opened one of the cache doors.

"So," Marline said. "You remember how you all pulled apart the transmitter?"

"Not me. Jessica and Nate."

"Right. But then after they found the optical degrader, and you determined where he'd gone, you were the next one through. Through the transmitter, right?" Marline removed a small package from the cache and placed it on top of the table. A little medical kit.

Then another two packs. A micro tool set, and a two-day rations pack. Like she was making up a survival kit.

"Oh," Haylee said, feeling another tingle. Not from the transition. Rather from some kind of realization.

The transmitter itself was broken. At least it had been broken when she'd used it.

"Busted?" she said.

"Yes," Marline said. "But not so anyone would know it."

"Is that why you couldn't find me?" Haylee looked at her chronometer. *Eighteen Fifty-Three*. Somehow it was wrong.

"That and a bunch of other things," Marline said. She stood and slipped the survival kit pieces into a satchel she was wearing. She was dressed in Victorian clothes--a simple muslin dress, worn leather shoes and a thick woolen coat. It was almost the same outfit at Haylee herself had on.

Regulations. You might be allowed to take all sorts of gadgets and food and medications with you into the past, but you at least had to look the part.

"Come on," Marline said. "We don't have long."

Which was an old Heseldan Institute joke, really. When you were entangled in the business of time travel, you essentially had all the time you needed.

Still, Haylee followed Marline out of the room.

"My calibration here says it's Victorian England," Haylee said. By instinct she tapped her chronometer. Perhaps she would shake loose some wire and it would give her better details. She smiled at herself. A ridiculously finely-tuned piece of equipment didn't just *shake loose some wire* and start working more effectively.

"It would," Marline said. "And it's not far off, but enough that we're going to have to fix it. Germany. Late seventeen hundreds."

"Pre-industrial."

"Yes it is."

"So we can just go back to the Heseldan Institute, can't we?"

"Well, about that now. No."

"What do you mean 'no'?"

They'd come into a short hallway. The floor was rough boards and the walls were stone. Rough too. Shaped a little, and laid without mortar.

"Are we in a castle?" Haylee said.

"Yes. South of Bremen. Just a little garrison fortification, so nothing fancy."

"How did I end up here?"

"As I mentioned, damage to the equipment. The whole calibration was out. By a couple of microns, I imagine. Enough to toss you here."

"I guess I'm glad for failsafes."

However they worked, fluffy logic or accurate-randomness, the failsafes tended to ensure that when a traveler arrived, it was in an unoccupied space. Gavin had explained once, over dinner and drinks and a nice walk in the Kolanski Arboretum, exactly how they had worked and still the concept eluded Haylee. She just accepted it.

It had been a second date with Gavin, which was nice, but then he'd gone missing a few weeks later, somewhere in Flanders in nineteen seventeen.

"We're all glad for them," Marline said. "I still don't get how they work. And I don't get how they work when the equipment's main function doesn't."

They started descending a stairway. Stone too.

"Why aren't we going back?" Haylee said.

"You have a job to do, remember?"

"Yep," Haylee said. "So I'm going to have to wait around sixty or seventy years?"

"I'm sure we can do better than that," Marline said.

"I know. I was kidding."

They would just have to wait until the next cycle and send a ping and the retrieval systems would pull them back. Fortunately those required little calibration.

Gavin had described it as being like a rubber band with a pin in it. You could stretch out the band as far as you liked, but the pin never moved. The return would jerk you right back to the origin.

There were a whole bunch of issues with the analogy, but it still had helped Haylee to understand the concept.

Marline turned a corner and they continued down the stairway.

"Germany," Haylee said.

"Yes it is. Don't worry, we'll get you back to Victorian England soon enough."

The smells improved. Haylee caught the scent of baking bread. They passed by a small stone-walled kitchen, with a glittering wood oven, and a sweltering baker working dough on a wood block.

Haylee stopped to watch for a moment, but Marline grabbed her arm and pulled her on down the next flight of stairs.

"I thought this was a small fort," Haylee said. "How many stories is it?"

"Not so many more," Marline said. "It's narrow, for one. I think your room was an add-on. Propped up on the side."

Haylee could picture it. A box held up by a couple of angled timbers. So many of their trips back involved spending time in structures made before any kinds of building codes had come into force.

Two more flights and Marline led Haylee into what had to be a dungeon. If the fort was for a garrison, then a dungeon made sense. They would have drunks and bandits and brigands to lock up from time to time.

Inside one of the cells stood a bright, shiny, chromed vehicle. Like a nineteen fifties idea of a futuristic flying car.

No tires. It hovered just above the stone floor.

The central cabin had a bulbous glass covering that formed both the windows and the roof.

"What is this thing?" Haylee said.

"I guess there have been a few changes at the Heseldan Institute since you went missing," Marline said. "This is a time car."

"You couldn't come up with a better name?"

Marline shrugged.

"The Chrome Hopper," Haylee said. "Oh! The Chromed Chronoslipper."

"Please don't do that."

"The Silvery Steed of the Timestreams."

"Haylee. You're supposed to be distraught that you're in the wrong time and the wrong place."

"I was, but then I took one look at this thing. What a honey!"

Marline sighed.

"Get in," she said, tapping at her own chunky chronometer. "Let's take you where you need to be."

CHAPTER THREE

The glassy hood on the Silvery Steed of the Timestreams tipped up, opening so that Haylee and Marline could get in. The name was too much of a mouthful, that was for sure. Maybe it should just be 'time car'.

The vehicle bobbed a little on its suspension. Haylee settled into the comfy seats. They smelled of Simonize, as if it was an obligatory thing.

"Strictly speaking," Marline said, "the time car is not actually here. It's still back in twenty-one sixty-two, but--"

"Wait up a second. That's way after I left. Like, a lifetime after."

"I know it." Marline settled in next to her and tapped at the controls on the console. The glass top whirred as it wound down at them.

"How come?" Haylee said. "Are we traveling to the future now?"

"No. But our successors looked over the mess you made and decided that things needed to be expedited."

"The mess *I* made? What's that about?"

"Nothing now. Since I've found you before things started to get out of hand. I can drop you on Coventry Street and you can continue as if nothing had happened."

"Excuse me? Drop me on Coventry Street? I thought you were taking me back."

"You do still have a job, remember?"

Marline tapped again at the controls. The vehicle began humming.

"Right," Haylee said. "I still have a job. I mean, I know that, but after an error like this, don't we just up stakes and go on back for debriefing?"

"Not in this case. We still need to find Fox Palton."

"We do. You know that it's an old cliché to put a time machine in a car, right?"

"That's what Gavin said. Apparently the irony is not lost on him."

"I bet."

Around them, the stone walls flickered and grew hazy and vanished altogether. For a moment Haylee could see out into the wilds of the twisting, molten strands of the time streams. They glowed with a kind of organic variation and movement.

Then new walls began to fade in and take on substance. They flickered.

With a thump, the vehicle bumped the new floor.

Tingles ran through Haylee's body, from her toes to her scalp.

Again the room was dark, lit really only by the glow of the console lights from the Silvery Steed of the Timestreams.

"London?" Hayee said, looking over the rough walls. Not so very different from that lean-to room on the German castle.

"Yes," Marline said.

The canopy on the Silvery Steed of the Timestreams began winding open with a creaking and a grinding.

Marline opened up the vehicle's glove compartment and rustled around in the papers and sundry. She pulled out a chronometer and handed it to Haylee.

"This should do better than that other one you've got. But keep them both."

"Both?"

"Yes. Just in case." Marline handed her the satchel with the survival kit packs. "Get going."

"Get going?" Haylee frowned. "Get going where?"

"Your job, remember?"

"But what about my transport table? I need the resources in there." The table had clothes and food supplements and tools. Indispensable when visiting other times.

The survival kit packs were useful, but really for emergencies only. Or small forays away from the table.

"You'll be fine. You've done this before."

"With a transport table and all its gear! Not with just a little bit of first aid and a busted chronometer."

"You're resourceful. Come on, hop out. I can't stay here in this for long."

"You should come with me."

"I have another job. A list of them, in fact. Hop to it."

Haylee got out. Reluctantly. She stood beside the vehicle.

"You weren't sent to help me, were you?" she said. "You came off the books. They'd already given up on me."

"Well... yes. You didn't report in. Then I found a note in your file about it. Also, the crew from twenty-one sixty-two came by. Gave me this." Marline patted the side of the Silvery Steed of the Timestreams. The bodywork echoed.

"No one else knew, did they?" Haylee said. "At the Heseldan Institute."

Marline shook her head.

"You'd get in trouble if they found out."

"You bet. Fired, most likely."

"Who did I--*whom* did I offend?"

"No one. But the Heseldan Institute went through some changes. Darren left as the head and Bettina took over."

"Who's Bettina?"

Marline looked at her strangely.

"Marline?" Haylee said.

"I'd better go."

"Who's Bettina? What's happened?" A sickening feeling ran through her. Marline was older. Bettina was someone Haylee didn't know. Haylee herself had wound up in the wrong place.

It wasn't adding up.

Or rather, it was adding up to a number she didn't want to know.

As in a number that told her she'd wound up in the wrong timestream.

"Do the job," Marline said. "I'll come for you if I can. But once you find Fox, it will all go back. Exactly how it should."

"Why do I not feel confident?"

"You'll be fine."

Marline tapped at the console controls and the vehicle's glassy roof began winding down. The chassis began humming and the stink of ozone overpowered the background odors of Victorian England.

The vehicle shuddered.

Vanished.

Haylee sighed.

Well, she'd always been trained to be resourceful. Perhaps now was the time to put it to the test.

CHAPTER FOUR

Outside the building where Marline had abandoned her, Haylee found a bustle and a busy-ness she hadn't expected.

It was raining. Late afternoon. The cobbled street was slick and shiny with water. A horse clopped along, towing a polished wooden carriage with a driver sitting high and two people inside, behind glass, safe from the weather.

Across the street, a man in patched and rough clothes shoveled horse manure into a wooden bucket. Ten yards away stood a hand trolley, wood like the bucket, filled with more excrement.

Welcome to Victorian England.

Not the wealthiest parts, but there were plenty of towns and suburbs where life was rough and the work was back-breaking and long and kind of demeaning.

Haylee checked the chronometer that Marline had given her.

Eighteen fifty-five. September twentieth. Exactly where she needed to be.

Assuming the chronometer was correct.

Haylee closed her eyes and took a mouth breath.

Compared to just about anyone here, she had come up in a life of privilege. Even just the dental and medical care that she took for granted exceeded anything they had. Air conditioning and central heating. Running water. Electricity. The list was huge.

And this was one of the things she'd been trained on. Empathy, but not getting caught up in it.

From somewhere along the street she heard laughter. She looked along and saw two women grinning at each other. Both had children in their arms and others about their skirts.

Whatever Haylee might feel maudlin or guilty about, there were still people living happy lives here. A little hardscrabble, no doubt, but still good.

She started off along the street. All along were brick and wooden buildings.

After the fires, they had actually imposed some building codes. A lot more brick and a lot less rough and dry wood.

Windows shone at her. Pigeons alighted on sills and bobbed their heads. A break in the clouds suggested that the rain, light as it was, might end soon.

She wasn't in a familiar spot, though. Before leaving, she'd drilled with glasses and sensory systems in the simulation room, getting a feel for the locations.

Back in the transport table, she'd had a map that she could have followed to get to Fox Palton's location. Haylee had memorized the map--just the way that her brain worked--but mostly just for the few blocks around. From her arrival location, through to where Fox was hiding out.

Knowing the general layout of London was critical, and really as long as she could get herself through to the Thames, then she could easily find her way.

Being lost was only temporary.

She watched her footing on the rough cobbles, though, to be honest, the street was paved better than she'd expected.

There was smoke in the air, of course. Horses and carts. Stray dogs and cats. Pigeons and sparrows.

The air was alive with the sound of everything. Primitive machinery and the animals and people.

Haylee found herself running in places, and drawing frowns and stares from passersby.

She slowed. Decorum was called for.

She went by the open frontage of a woodworking shop. The scent of sawdust and shavings was suddenly quite pleasant in amongst the collection of nasty smells she'd been making her way through. Near the front stood a tall wardrobe, stained dark, with quickly-carved decorations and a oval mirror.

She caught a glimpse of herself. Her hair was tangled and her clothing askew. She should have chosen something a little finer, really. These were hardly more than peasant rags.

Continuing on through street after street, Haylee could sense she was drawing closer to the river.

She crossed a canal, with boats and brackish water. Farther along, beyond the bridge, a simple lock was operating, with men and donkeys drawing a barge through the open upper gates.

Soon after, she reached the Thames. Right away she could orient herself amongst the bridges and the Tower of London.

Twenty minutes later she was right outside the little boarding house where her information had told her that Fox Palton would be hiding out.

It was almost as if everything had gone to plan. That she hadn't wound up in near-medieval Germany and been plucked out by Marline and her time car. Terrible name.

The boarding house was three stories high, with windows and little balconies and ivy growing up across the bricks. A black cat stalked along one of the balcony railings, intent upon a starling on the next.

The house's front door was up a pair of steps, and there were narrow steps leading down to a basement door too. Water lay in puddles on the flagstones below.

A sign on the door read *Tarnelle Boarding House. Weekly, Monthly. No Vacancy.*

The Heseldan Institute used remote techniques to make time block imagery of locations so that the operatives could pore over the pictures and have a sense of where they were going. What they were getting into.

So this door, and its sign, were familiar.

The door was unlocked and Haylee stepped through into a small foyer with worn patterned wool carpet and a tall side table with several letters and papers scattered on top.

Haylee picked them up. None were addressed to Fox Palton. The other names were unknown to her.

Perhaps this was a bust.

Fox's room was on the third floor, and Haylee pushed her way through the second door, which was ornate, with a remarkable sectioned glass window, and into a narrow, dim hallway.

A skylight over the stairs partway along allowed in the gray, thick-weather light from outside.

On the second floor, a couple were arguing. More like he was drunk and she was trying to keep him from entering the rooms.

It was tempting to intervene, but Haylee was well-schooled on cause and effect and the potential impact on future events.

You never knew.

The stairway's railing was worn smooth and slick from the

passage of hundreds of hands. Haylee's footfalls echoed around her.

The third floor had a short landing, with two doors at each end, and one in the middle. Rooms at the front and back, and, perhaps, a bathroom in the middle. Running water and indoor plumbing were becoming the norm now, though likely any bathing set up on this floor would be limited to water gathered from the roof.

There were numbers on the doors, and Haylee knocked on the door with a 4.

At the same time, she tried the handle.

Locked.

So either he was out, or he was security-conscious.

"Fox Palton?" she said. "Fox Palton? I have a message for you."

No response.

She knocked again.

"You won't find him there, love," said a voice from along the short hallway.

Haylee looked and saw a slim, tall woman, dressed in a suit. She had thick dark hair, and shiny leather boots. The suit was a dark blue. Pinstripe.

Out of keeping.

A woman in trousers in this day and age. And the pinstripes seemed unusual. Haylee couldn't remember when they'd come into being.

"Where is he then?" Haylee said.

"He'll be down at his boat shed, most likely. Running his experiments." The woman's voice was thickly English, of course. Perhaps from the north, though. She ran words together and dropped consonants. *'e'll be downat 'is bo' shed, most likely*. It was soft and kind of beautiful. A lovely rhythm to it.

"Experiments?" Haylee said.

"He considers himself an inventor of sorts. He's made a little money on a few things, but clearly not so very much that he's moving to a mansion in the Cotswolds."

"Inventions?" Haylee said, a feeling of dread running through her.

Someone from the future bringing in technologies could really unsettle the time streams.

The woman turned. She had a leather shoulder bag and she was holding a key. She must have been leaving and been about to lock up.

"He's not particularly adept," the woman said. "He showed me some kind of light that works from metal strings. He was winding a little metal pepper grinder connected to it by the strings. The thing glowed a little, but he seemed to have to wind a whole lot to get even that. Seemed like more work than it was worth."

"I'm Haylee," Haylee said.

"Delta."

Odd name. But Haylee left it.

"Pleased to meet you," she said. "I'm here to ensure that Fox doesn't do any damage with his inventions." It seemed to be the best way to put it.

Delta turned and locked the door to her room. She came along toward Haylee, moving with the elegance of a dancer.

"To stop him?" she said.

"Exactly."

"You?"

"Yes me. I've known him for a long time, but when he fled to London, we were worried for his safety."

"'We'? Who is this 'we'?"

"I work for an Heseldan Institute." Haylee thought fast. "We help inventors develop their ideas."

"I see. Things sure are changing fast nowadays. I can barely keep up."

Delta came up to Haylee. Delta stood a half a head taller than Haylee, and she had a broad, warm smile.

She leaned in close.

"And we both know," Delta whispered, "that it's barely a trickle compared to how things will go in coming years, don't we."

"What are you talking about?" Haylee said.

"I see how you're dressed, but likewise I see your teeth and your skin."

And I see yours.

"You're another time traveler?" Haylee said, realizing she'd blurted it without thought. Breaking an Heseldan Institute rule.

Never mention time travel.

Delta's eyebrows rose.

From below came a clattering sound. Someone shaking at the front door.

"We should get out of here," Delta said. "Come with." She turned and headed around to the stairway. With her long legs, she ascended quickly.

Haylee stood at the door a moment.

The clattering increased. A loud bang came. Followed by someone shouting.

Calling for Delta.

"If you don't want to get caught up in this," Delta said from the stairway landing, "you might like to follow."

CHAPTER FIVE

From the third floor, the boarding house's stairway continued, though narrow and rickety, right up to a rooftop access door.

Delta had a key for the door.

Below, the bellowing continued, combined with the sound of heavy, fast footsteps on the stairway.

"Who is that?" Haylee said.

"Just some guy?"

"What did you do?"

"Couldn't tell you. Some guys, they just take exception." Delta jammed the key into the door's keyhole and turned. The mechanism clicked.

"Some guys," she said, "you look at them wrong and they get all riled up. Real quick."

"Victorian times, huh?"

"Men all over. Or rather, *people* all over."

"Okay, I get that."

Delta pushed open the door and stepped out into the rain. It had gotten heavier in just the short time Haylee had been in the building.

"This way," Delta said, stepping around with the door, and ushering Haylee along a narrow set of flagstones that lay slightly raised between the valley of two roof peaks. Water ran down the roofing tiles, gurgling and bubbling.

As Haylee strode on, Delta turned and locked the door.

Haylee slowed and turned.

"Keep going," Delta said. "Right to the end. Make a left turn. There's a tricky little spot where you have to drop to a balcony, but then we can cross to the next building and hustle on down to my safe house."

"You have a safe house?" Haylee was starting to feel like an amateur here.

"This is a long story. I can explain it all when we're there. Move it. I don't like the rain any more than you do."

Haylee turned and hurried on, watching her footing on the slick, wet flagstones.

Ahead lay the jumbled roofs of London. Tiled with slate or clay. Some that were boards and some that might have been iron. There were numerous church spires standing above it all, and the chimneys of factories, and, quite wonderfully, the scaffolds around the growing tower of Big Ben. She wasn't that very far from it.

Haylee reached the end of the flagstones and looked over the edge.

There was a balcony ten feet below.

Surely Delta had been joking about that being their exit.

From behind came a rattling and more shouting.

"I fear he is persistent," Delta said, coming up to Haylee. "And somewhat annoyed."

The door burst open. A man leaped out. He looked around.

"Go," Delta said. She swung herself out like some movie superhero and landed on the balcony's deck. From inside the rooms there, someone yelped.

Haylee looked back.

Their pursuer was running through the rain. His feet slapped on the flagstones.

"Haylee!" Delta called.

"It's Fox," Haylee said. "Fox Palton."

She stood and moved in to face him.

He scowled at her, deep lines across his forehead, and bunching at the bridge of his nose.

He brought up a weapon. Some kind of little black gun.

"Wait," Haylee said. "Just wait. I only need to talk with you."

She saw the flash a split second before she felt a poker-prick punch in her chest.

Then she was tumbling back over the roof's lip.

Tumbling into darkness.

CHAPTER SIX

Haylee came to in the dark, aching and tired.

There was someone nearby.

"Hello?" she said. Her eyes were beginning to focus. A plaster ceiling. Wooden board walls.

"Hey there." Delta. A warm wash of relief ran through Haylee. "You're awake."

Haylee was lying on something hard, and Delta's face appeared and looked down at her.

"Hi," Haylee said. "Feel like I got shot." Her shoulder and chest throbbed.

"Because you actually did get shot."

"And you caught me?"

"Kind of. More like broke your fall as you tumbled to the balcony."

"Thanks."

"You're welcome. So that was Fox Palton, huh?"

"Yes," Haylee said. "I recognized him. From the... photographs."

"Right. Something not quite invented yet."

"Yeah." Haylee rolled her shoulders. Her clothes itched.

"Well, here's the messy thing," Delta said. "That wasn't my Fox Palton."

"Excuse me?" Haylee sat up. Twinges of pain ran through her shoulder and chest.

"You should stay lying down." Delta put her hand on Haylee's good shoulder.

"You're right." Haylee lay back. The bed was soft. Better than any bed from Victorian times should have been.

Her eyes were beginning to pick out details in the room. Papered walls, with a framed piece of dark art hanging on one. A long bench with bowls and other items. A window with drapes.

"Where are we?" she said. A twinge ran through her from the wound. Fox Palton had actually shot her. Was the bullet still inside?

What kind of weapon had he used? Certainly not something from Victorian England. Maybe a World War II Luger?

"You're in a safe house," Delta said. "This is my exit room."

"It's dark. Wait, what do you mean, exit room?"

Delta looked away, toward another framed painting. "Where I return to my own time."

"Your own time. Which is?"

"Twenty-one ninety-eight."

"Oh."

"That's your time too, isn't it?"

"Exactly. But you're not from the Heseldan Institute, are you?"

"We're called the Talvis Academy. Training and exploration."

"Based in?"

"Queensland, Australia."

"I've never been. Hot and dry?" It was good talking. It took Haylee's mind off the pain. Although it was kind of mild. Perhaps Delta had given her something. Or perhaps it was just natural endorphins.

Haylee had never been shot before. Had no idea how it was supposed to feel.

"We're actually up in the Atherton Tablelands. Cooler, but still a little dry. Out of the way. You're from Washington State?"

"Spokane."

Delta puffed out her cheeks. With her lips she made a kind of trumpet sound.

"What was that?" Haylee said.

"Exasperation." Delta looked away a moment. "Look." She focused back on Haylee's eyes. "As I said, that wasn't my Fox Palton, but he was yours."

"Different time streams."

"Yes."

"Crossed over." Haylee started to sit up again.

"Wait." Delta put her hand on Haylee's good shoulder again. "Here's the thing. You've been shot, and I'm going to have to fix that, but it's going to take a couple of hours. And I don't know that we have the kind of time."

"Time is the one thing we do have."

"Not when we're from different streams. That adds a whole level of messiness to it. We're here in the same stream, but we're both assuming that it's our own."

"Oh." A tingle ran through Haylee as she considered it. "I could be in yours."

"Right. Or I could be in yours. Or we could both be in someone else's."

"I thought that was not possible. Failsafes. Gavin described it as like a set of parallel rivers. You can't accidentally end up in a different river."

"Right. But what if it's like a set of roadways in a city? Really easy to get across from First Street to Second Street."

"Oh, yeah. You'd just cut across Marshall Avenue. Or Washington Avenue. Or Clara Spartley Boulevard."

"Any number of ways."

"Suddenly I feel like we've been toddlers playing with the house wiring."

"I know it," Delta said. "I could take my exit here, and you could do whatever it is you do to get back home, but *would* we end up back home?"

Delta went to the bench and opened up a cupboard built into it. She started pulling things out.

"What a mess." Haylee closed her eyes thinking things through. "We still have to find Fox Palton. *Both* Fox Paltons. Right?"

"We do."

"But I'm hurt, right? Probably worse than I think. I need a doctor."

"I can take care of that. I have the equipment. But it will take a couple of hours."

"Meanwhile, he's making his getaway."

"Exactly."

"So I... wait. Why was he shooting at me?"

"I guess that's a question for him."

"When we find him."

"Yes." Delta turned to Haylee, holding a white, lunchbox-sized canister.

It had a couple of sharp points.

From outside came the cry of a bird.

"This," Delta said, "will only hurt a little."

She set the canister on Haylee's injured shoulder.

Delta had lied. It hurt more than a little. Way, way, way more.

CHAPTER SEVEN

Two hours later, Delta took Haylee out to a little bakery which had some seating, and also served tea.

There were other customers. Mostly men, but some couples. Some of the men frowned at Haylee and Delta as they sat at one of the tables.

Haylee's shoulder throbbed, but in a good way. Not like the painful, stinging it had been earlier.

The smells of the bakery were just heavenly. Remarkable.

"I think they've borrowed this from Paris," Delta said, pronouncing the city's name as *Paree,* as it should be. "That's a far cleaner and much more sophisticated town. England is still barely over the coal mining era."

Tea came in fine white cups, with fat white scones, crisp and brown on the jagged tops. The young waitress set down a small ceramic pottle of butter, and two knives. She nodded, wiped her hands on her black apron and hurried away.

"What's the story with your Fox Palton?" Delta said.

Haylee broke open her scone and slathered on the butter.

Ordinarily she wouldn't allow herself something so *carb-rich* but time travel tended to relax your attitude to calorie control. She knew it was a flaw anyway, so it was good to have an excuse.

Even if the health control measures in this time were just about non-existent.

"He stole some data," Haylee said. "Damaged our time equipment in his getaway."

"Intentionally?" Delta picked up her cup and sipped. Her pinky finger extended away from the handle, which made Haylee smile.

"Intentionally," Haylee said, popping the piece of scone in her mouth. It was stunningly divine. Unexpected in this era.

"Like a getaway plan?" Delta said, setting down her cup. "So you wouldn't follow?"

"Apparently."

"And yet that's an inherently flawed plan, isn't it? You could take just about as long as you liked to fix it, and still send your operative--you--to exactly the moment to where he'd come."

"I know. But there were data breaches and erasures. We only had the vaguest notion of where he'd gone. And then, even after the repairs, I ended up in the wrong time. And in Germany instead of England."

Delta frowned. "But then somehow you've made it here?"

"I had help."

"Help?"

A tremor ran through Haylee.

"Marline," she said, fiddling with the scone. "One of our other operatives. She came to my rescue."

Haylee popped the scone morsel in her mouth, musing on the moment when Marline had shown up.

"Came to your rescue?" Delta leaned forward. "Say more about that."

"This isn't therapy."

"Isn't it?"

Haylee smiled. "No. But that was an unfair question."

"Had a lot of therapy have we?"

"Little bit. After my mom died I was adrift for a long while." Haylee swallowed, mouth suddenly dry.

She took a sip from her tea. It was bitter, but good.

"Time travel?" Delta said.

"Yes. Mom took her own life when I was..." Haylee swallowed again. Licked her lips. Took a breath.

"No rush, right?" Delta said.

"It's a whole other thing, but essentially, I was just a week out from my twenty-first birthday. Had a trip to Vegas booked with my friends. I could legally play the slots and the tables. Mom threw herself in the Colombia River. I didn't make it to Vegas, but I did toss in my cartography` career trajectory and joined up with the Heseldan Institute."

Delta nodded sagely. Exactly the body language of Sandra, the therapist, who had helped pick up the pieces so many years after.

"So yes." Haylee took a big piece of scone and popped it in her mouth. Too doughy, but she chewed and talked at once.

"Time travel is obvious, right?" she said. "When you break it down. Or at least when Sandra helped me to break it down. I was on a search for a time before my mother's suicide. And there was no way I was going near the water, not after she'd drowned. The Colombia spills right out into the Tranquillus Ocean."

Delta frowned. "The Colombia River? From Washington and through Oregon? That's the Pacific Ocean right there."

"Washington sure, but then along the state line between Washington and Altacali."

"Tranquillus Ocean? How about that? Different time streams and different names."

Haylee took a breath. This was getting hard. Besides dredging through those memories of her mom, the whole time streams thing was taking on some new meaning.

"Pacifick Ocean?" she said.

"Pacific." Delta smiled. "Not so hard on the final 'c'."

"Uh-huh. Our worlds are very different."

"Perhaps not so different. But I am wondering if your little trip to Germany was part of a ploy."

"A ploy?"

"Was it too convenient? You said Marline came to your rescue. We have a 'Martene' on our staff. She's not much at rescues, I fear."

"Relevant?"

"You tell me."

Haylee took another piece of the wonderful scone. Around them other people occupied tables, having quiet conversations. Scones and croissants and sliced bread with jam and cream. All kinds of teas.

"You know," Haylee said. "Marline was older than I remembered. And she had a thing she called a time car. A vehicle I'd never seen before. A Silvery Steed of the Timestreams, was what I wanted to call it."

Delta leaned back.

"You were in the wrong spot," she said. "Marline shows up, older, with a new device, and then what? She took you home?"

"Here. She brought me right here."

"Something is fishy," Delta said. "Very fishy."

"I," Haylee said, "am starting to see that now."

CHAPTER EIGHT

Fifteen minutes later, they had the makings of a plan. It involved breaking into Fox Palton's rooms and locating any documents.

"Not much of a plan," Haylee said, dabbing her finger at the crumbs of her scone. She was very tempted to purchase another one. She had plenty of currency.

"I agree," Delta said. "Not much of a plan, but it's better than no plan at all."

"Only just."

"Yes." Delta took a final sip from her cup. "But it had been my plan for some time. I've been observing Fox for a couple of weeks now. Trying to figure out *his* plans. I really needed a second operative, with a communications device. They could tail him when he was out, so I could break in and be gone before he came back. If he was going to return early, my colleague would let me know."

"Do you have a communications device?"

"Unfortunately not. But I do know something of his routine."

"Does his routine include following you up onto the roof and firing wildly with an era-inappropriate weapon?"

"Huh." Delta rubbed her chin. "No. No it does not."

"So his routine is out of whack."

"Yep."

"That's going to make it tough."

Delta sighed.

"One of us could keep a look out," Haylee said. "Watch for him. Just from the stairway."

"Do we draw straws on that? On who will actually watch and who will search."

Haylee shrugged.

"Do you trust me?" Delta said.

"I... sure." Haylee smiled. "And before you say it, that slightest of hesitations there just gave me away, didn't it?"

"It's mutual. I mean, I like you well enough. You seem grounded, and a good operative, but I did just meet you. And moments after that, Fox Palton was shooting at us."

"To be fair, you were already down on the balcony, so he was shooting at me. *And* he did actually hit me."

Haylee rubbed her pectoral which was still tingling from the wound. Whatever kind of tech was inside that little magic box Delta had used on her, it was little short of miraculous. Would that they had marvels like that in Hayee's own time stream?

"Touché," Delta said. "How about we chance it and we search together?"

"Now?"

"Can you think of a better time?"

"Nineteen fifties America for the middle class."

"So funny. He is usually out around about now. Visiting a gentleman's club in Wilchester."

"Then why are we here at all?"

"Hot tea and delicious scones."

"You're very English, aren't you?"

"Through and through." Delta stood. "Let's be on our way."

CHAPTER NINE

The air was cooler and a late morning fog was settling over the city.

Haylee's lockpick kit admitted them to Fox Palton's rooms on the second floor of the boarding house.

"You're quite the dab hand at that," Delta said with admiration as Haylee stood from the now-unlocked door. "I'll have to get you to teach me *some day*."

Haylee smiled. It was an old joke at the Heseldan Institute. *Show me your pressed flowers some day*. Because days for time travelers were just a jumble so often. 'Some day' could be any day, past or present.

It was kind of a dumb joke, really, but it was reassuring that Delta's Talvis Academy was perhaps not so very different from the Heseldan Institute.

The door swung wide with a quiet squeak from the hinges.

Right away an odd smell hit Haylee. A mix of some kind of pine, with the odd ozone she was used to in the institute.

Ozone from electrical activity.

As if Fox Palton had been running his own experiments, or had some out-of-keeping equipment stored or in use here.

At least, out-of-keeping with the era.

Haylee led the way in, through a narrow vestibule. The walls were papered and a row of hooks protruded just above head height on the left.

Beyond the vestibule lay a wide room, with tall windows on the far side giving a view of the windows of the next building over, but still admitting plenty of light.

A large rug lay in the middle of the room, with a small settee and a low table. Beyond, against the right hand wall, an iron bed frame held a simple mattress with a fat pillow and a colorful crocheted throw across the top. On the wall above hung a poorly executed painting of a sailing ship ablaze, as if some third-rate artist was trying to cash in on J.M. Turner's popularity. Turner had only been dead a few years now.

"Some place," Delta said, turning to the right and into the nook partly hidden by the vestibule wall. There was a bench with a basin and a big jug. A towel lay in a raggedy pile.

In the left hand corner, near the windows, stood a roll top writing desk. Huge. So big that it seemed impossible that anyone might have gotten it through the doorway, let alone hauled it up the stairs.

The roller on the desk was closed.

Haylee went straight to it. Lifted the roller. It rattled a little.

Outside, on the sill opposite, a pair of pigeons cooed. One chased the other and they both spread their wings.

"There's a razor," Delta said from the bench. "Plastic and multi-bladed. Bars of soap and tubes of toothpaste. The guy is breaking so many rules. So many rules."

It wasn't the half of it.

Inside the desk, taking up most of the actual space, lay a

chronometer, a multimeter and a bunch of other equipment that Haylee didn't recognize. Lots of dials and readouts. Wires connecting them all together.

The chronometer was actually in pieces. The casing had been removed and many of the wires led to the circuitry within.

Beside Haylee, Delta whistled.

"I'd like to think he's just a hobbyist," Haylee said. "Or that he's somehow stuck here and trying to figure out a way to get back home."

"You're very generous," Delta said. "You think well of people. I like that about you. Even when the person in question is a conniving, low-down dirty rat."

"Oh I'm convinced of that. But perhaps he is stuck. Trying to figure out a way to get back."

"And maybe all this is why there are *two* of them."

"One from your time stream, and one from mine. That still doesn't explain how it could be that you and I are here now. Clearly from different streams."

The distinct time streams had been barely observed, and remained mostly theoretical. Some of the advanced teams at the institute were looking at ways that people might cross over so that those other streams could be explored.

From what Haylee had heard, those exercises had made little headway so far. Very little headway.

No one had yet come up with a device like the chronometer that would simplify things.

"Listen to me," she said. "The chronometer is hardly simple."

"What's that?" Delta said.

"Just musing aloud."

"Keep going."

"Well, I wonder what happens if we turn this on."

Delta grabbed Haylee's wrist. Pulled her hand back from the cobbled-together device.

"I wasn't going to!" Haylee said.

"It surely didn't look like it. You strike me as someone who just presses a button to see what it does."

"How else do you find out?"

"You read the manual."

Haylee wrested her arm from Delta's grip. "Do you see a manual lying around for this thing?"

Delta snorted. "Well, maybe he has some notes."

"We should find him and just ask."

"Ask? He's not going to tell us."

"We could wait here. Catch him with red hands as they say."

"'Red-handed'."

"Funny way to put it."

"Yours is a funny way to put it."

In the corner of her eye, Haylee saw a change in the light. From the doorway.

Movement.

She looked around.

Marline.

Standing there, staring at them.

Holding a weapon not so very different from the Luger or whatever Fox Palton had used to shoot Haylee.

"Who are you?" Marline said. "And what do you think you're doing in my room?"

CHAPTER TEN

Delta held her hands up at shoulder height and took a step away from the roll top desk and the strange mess of devices and wires.

"Martene," she said. "I did know you were... wait, you're younger."

Martene. But Haylee knew her as Marline. And this woman looked older than the Marline that Haylee had left behind in twenty ninety-eight.

"Younger, yes," the woman said. Martene. Martene who looked like Marline, but now seemed younger than the Marline that Haylee knew.

And definitely younger than the Marline who had brought the time car.

"What's going on here?" Delta said. "Are you helping Fox Palton?"

"He's helping me. We're both in the wrong place."

"Time?" Haylee said. "No. You're both in the wrong time *stream*, aren't you? And it's unrecognizable to you."

"Who are you?" Martene said.

"Haylee. I know a woman about your age, named Marline. Looks just like you, but... well. Time streams, you know."

Martene frowned.

Delta said, "You're not the Martene I know."

"I guess not. Because you're sure not the Naomi I know."

"Naomi."

"You're the spitting image, I have to say."

"And you don't know me at all," Haylee said.

"Nope."

"And I don't know Delta."

"That's your name?" Martene turned to Delta. "Not Naomi."

Delta looked at Haylee. "It's not even close," Delta said.

"Time streams diverge," Haylee said. "We know that."

"Theoretically."

"And the longer since the divergence, the bigger the change."

"And sometimes they knit," Martene said.

"This is getting into way bigger things than I deal with," Haylee said. "I'm just an operative. I go where they send me. I gather information including photographs, videos and sound recordings of Mayan temple building. Of the collection in the library at Alexandria. Of the rehearsals of Shakespeare's plays."

"Likewise," Delta said. "Whoever Shakespeare is, but the same. I don't deal in that technical research side of things."

"Right. Like why there are multiple time streams."

"And how they can cross over."

"And create messes like this."

Martene looked back and forth between them.

"Did you practice all that?"

"Nope," Haylee said. But it was fascinating. As if they had known each other since childhood and had the ability to almost finish each others sentences.

Martene holstered the gun. It was the first time that Haylee had actually noticed the holster.

In fact, Martene was dressed more for the American wild west than for Victorian England. Stitched cowboy boots and denim trousers and a loose, flowing blouse with a bandana tied at her neck. The only thing she was missing was a ten gallon Stetson on her head, or whatever they called cowboy hats.

"Well," Martene said. "Are we going to work together on this, or go our separate ways? I mean, you've broken into my little apartment here."

"Yours?" Delta said. "No, it's Fox Palton's."

"It *was* Fox's. He got started on that, but he vanished. I took over the little lease to keep the landlady from prying, and to hold the space until Fox returns."

"He didn't vanish," Haylee said. "At least, *one* of them didn't vanish."

"He shot Haylee," Delta said.

"Shot you?" Martene said, stepping closer. "When? Where?"

"A few hours back," Haylee said. "Right here--" she touched her pec "--and up on the roof." She nodded at the ceiling.

"You've got a portable hospital with you? One of those micro-jobs?" Martene peered at Haylee's blouse.

"Yes," Delta said.

Haylee undid two of the little bone buttons on her blouse and pulled the left side across to show the scar. She was wearing a modern sports bra and the strap had been damaged by the bullet, but the bra was still functional, even if it had never been especially comfortable.

"Wow," Martene said. "You need to get to a real hospital and get that taken care of."

The scar was still healing, and still covered in a gel scurrow bandage that was still working with enzymes and proteins to rebuild Haylee's skin. But Martene was right. The fix was temporary and needed real medical intervention at a medical institution.

"I know it," Haylee said.

"He actually shot you?"

"You would have shot us."

"Me?"

"Your gun," Delta said, "is about the same as his."

Martene patted the gun's grip.

"I call this," she said, "'Like-for-like'. If he had himself a Colt, then that's what I'd carry. Likewise and Uzi or an M-14."

"Hardly the stuff of Victorian England," Haylee said.

"What's an Uzi?" Delta said.

"That, my friend," Martene said, "is a very nice little Israeli weapon."

"Israeli?" Haylee said with a sigh. "That's a manufacturer?"

"Israel is a country, but let's not discuss that. Right now we have the time streams issue, don't we?"

"We sure do." Haylee looked again at the torn-apart and rejoined machinery. "And is this the source of it?"

From below came the sound of the rooming house's front door. Martene had left the door to Fox Palton's room open, and sound carried in the hard walls and floors of the building.

"Lots of people come and go," Delta said. "It's that kind of place. I'm concerned that he was doing this in here and I didn't know about it. It was my job to watch him."

"Slippery characters," Martene said. "Every one of them I've ever met."

"You've met many?" Haylee said.

"Eight, so far. Eight Fox Paltons. Also some that were named Felix. Petterson and Paterson and Parton. Eels, every one."

Meaning they were slippery.

"Eight!" Delta said. "This is a mess. How can there be so many in the one time stream?"

"I didn't say they were in the same time stream," Martene said. "I just said that I'd met eight. And, I should add, that includes just one here, but I have a feeling there are others."

"At least one other," Haylee said. "Armed and dangerous."

Martene *tsk-tsked* with her tongue. "Yes. I know it."

"We need to do a reset," Haylee said, closing her eyes and trying to picture it. "We need to return them all to their own times, and their own time streams."

"A reset?" Delta said. "And how do you propose doing that?"

"I honestly have no idea." She looked at the mess of equipment lying in the roll top desk. "But I think we can start here."

CHAPTER ELEVEN

The three women quickly concocted a plan. Firstly, they removed the equipment from the roll top desk and decamped to the room that Delta had rented along the hallway.

Haylee relocked Fox Palton's door. Delta had left a motion sensor inside so they would know when he--whichever one--returned to the room.

"You're assuming that he will return," Martene said as they set up the equipment on the little coffee table in Delta's room.

The space was similar to Fox Palton's, save that the windows faced out into the street, making it much noisier.

The decorations were different too. In a way they reminded Haylee of her own old college dorm room. The poster for a book fair was like the vintage Raphael Milner poster Haylee had, the rack of little red and green hardback books like the old battered paperbacks she'd so treasured.

Haylee had essentially nothing with her, but both Delta and Martene were well-resourced with equipment and tools from the distant future.

Somehow they all worked quietly together, testing and checking and running simulations on the rough device Fox Palton had constructed.

Martene had never quite dared to touch it, but mentioned that with the other two in the room, her confidence was kind of brimming.

"As if I'm reassured."

"No longer marooned?" Haylee said.

"That's it. In a word. 'Marooned'. When I never had to be."

Delta's little portable computer had an expanding display that stretched out to better than dinner tray-size. The processors worked fast on analyzing the device.

Haylee went for a walk to a local bakery and headed back with rolls and fresh eggs and spinach and kale.

It was surprising to her, the condition of the food. Almost better than she would find at Albertson's or her local co-op.

It was amazing too, to get out into the Victorian air. It was smokey, but it had a different tinge to it from the air back home. Perhaps it was less petrochemical.

People were out and about, from all walks of life. Dustmen and chimney sweeps and lamplighters, dapper gentlemen and women in cinched bodices under their flowing dresses and children in caps and shorts and leather shoes.

Flocks of pigeons swooped and sparrows darted in at the sidewalk for crumbs and bugs and seeds. Carriages and wagons creaked and inside the glass-fronted stores, machinery whined and groaned.

It would have been so much better to have come here without the whole *mission* to bring back Fox Palton. Just to come and spend some time with a notebook and a surreptitious camera and gather her impressions of the time.

When Haylee got back to Delta's room, Delta was gone, as was the makeshift machine, and Martene was lying, bleeding and unconscious in a curled-up heap in the corner by the bed.

CHAPTER TWELVE

It took more than a full day for Martene to wake.

She lay in the bed, stretched out, wounds dressed by Haylee who had gone out several times for supplies. Bandages and salves and tinctures.

Fortunately she had found more money in one of the bench drawers. Sovereigns and crowns. Currency was confusing, particularly because it was different to what she'd been expecting in her mission preparation. Pounds, shillings and pence was what she'd been told. A complicated system, little above bushels and pecks for weight.

And it wasn't as if there was a CVS on some nearby corner, with a Walgreens right across from it. She visited an apothecary, who was quite possibly a shyster, but fortunately some basic twenty-first century knowledge of chemistry and medicine went a long way to gathering fluids that were beneficial.

"You looked after me?" Martene said, waking as the sun began to set across the roofs of London.

Startled by the words, Haylee stood from the small dumpy

sofa where she had been making notes and trying to figure out her return to twenty-one ninety-eight.

"I did." She went to the bed. "You were hurt badly. Bleeding."

"You dressed the wounds with what was on hand." Martene looked tired, but she smiled. "Then you went out and got medical materials."

"How do you know?"

"I can feel the dressing, and I can feel the pain relief in my muscles. Laudanum?"

"It wasn't easy to get."

"I know of a dozen places. If I get addicted, I'm blaming you."

"I know some good programs back home. Rehab."

Martene laughed, but then said, "Opioids are a serious business."

"Sure, I know it." Haylee picked up the little brown bottle from the tray beside the bed with the other bottles, pottles and cloth-wrapped leaves and such.

"That's a lot!" Martene said. "Concentration?"

"This is Victorian England. The concentration could be fifty percent, or five or point five."

"Let's hope point five. Did you inject it?"

"I talked with the apothecary. I placed a drop on the wound each time I changed the dressing."

"There's just one wound?"

"One bad wound." Haylee touched Martene's left knee where there was a cut that stretched from the bottom of her thigh to the top of her calf.

"Right," Martene said.

Haylee smiled to herself. Martene's voice was similar to Marline's. And she looked so similar.

Martene was missing a small scar that Marline had on her

right ear following surgery from an earring that had been ripped out. Martene's eyelashes were fuller and her cheeks were thinner.

They both had essentially the same body type. Big shouldered, small busted and long legged. Attractive.

"And then scrapes and bruises," Haylee said now. "It must have been quite the bust-up."

"Fox Palton showed up. Kicked in the door. Charged me with some kind of razor. I guess I kicked at him as I turned."

"I get it."

"I felt the blade go in. Naomi--Delta--gathered up the equipment and the pair of them fled."

"And essentially we have no idea where they might have gone?"

"Give me a couple of days."

"I don't know if you'll be walking in a couple of days. Maybe if we had a hospital. Or one of Delta's little micro kits we could... wait. You have one, don't you? Or something like it?"

Martene smiled and nodded.

"Nearby?" Haylee said.

"Technically and physically, yes. But temporally, no."

"When?"

"Sixteen thousand years ago."

"Oh. Ice age?"

"One of the biggest. There's a land bridge to Europe and a glacier tongue that comes within fifty miles of London."

"Okay. And how do we get there?"

Martene reached up and tapped Haylee's chronometer.

"With this," Martene said.

"It's just a tracker. Not a time machine. In theory I can call in help. I sure can't time travel with it."

"It's a tracker," Martene said. "And a communications device. We just need to ask the right person to come and help."

"The right person?"

"Yes. How about *your* Marline? My analogue."

"Marline?" Haylee smiled. "No. Even better. Not *my* Marline. The other one."

"The other one?"

"The one with the time car."

CHAPTER THIRTEEN

Why would Marline call the thing a time car? The Silver Steed of the Time Streams was just so much better.

The trouble was finding her, and it, amongst so many crossing time streams.

"I think I know how," Martene said. "I mean, inevitably, her and I are linked."

"Really?"

"Sure." Martene was sitting on the bed now, with a small cup of tea. She'd revived somewhat. "I mean, why not? We're analogues of the same person. There must be some kind of a connection. If we're in the same time stream."

"At the same time."

Martene shrugged.

"So what do you do?" Haylee said. "Close your eyes and think about her? Like you were trying to mentally teleport or something?"

"More like I fire out signals from my chronometer and see if there's a response. The way those things work, it should pick up if there are other chronometers in the time."

"That's not how mine works. Mine just has a tenuous thread link to my own time. Ready to pull me back when I'm done."

At least that's what Haylee hoped. She'd never quite been able to wrap her head around it.

"Right," Martene said. "Where is my chronometer anyway? I hope it's just that you took it off me while I recovered?"

"I didn't take it off you. I don't remember that you had one."

"Well, that's odd. Do you have yours?"

Haylee held up her arm. The chronometer had been reconfigured to resemble a simple wooden and leather bracelet so that it was effectively unnoticeable.

"What is that?" Martene said. "Did you get that from some artisan here?"

"It's from home. No sense in wearing a glistening piece of glass and plastic and steel here in Victorian England. This I can explain away. A gift from a relative in the south of Italy or something."

"Smart. Can I take a look?"

Haylee unstrapped it and passed it over to Martene.

"Clever," Martene said, admiring the way that the pieces slid across each other to reveal the casing and display which hid the solid state components within.

"We're going to need some equipment, aren't we?" Haylee said. "Stuff that's not really available in this time."

"What do you mean?"

"We need to build a machine like the one Fox Palton built."

"You mean to track Marline?"

"Isn't that the plan?"

"It is. But I wouldn't know how to build such a machine."

Haylee smiled. "Nor would I. But I probably know enough so that I could build half a machine."

"What are you saying? What use is a half a machine?"

"I'm figuring that you would know how to build the other half, right?"

"I know some. But we're talking about finely-calibrated systems here. Glass coils and gold filaments. Things tuned within microns."

"But Fox Palton had built something that looked viable."

"Emphasis on the 'looked' rather than the 'viable'."

"Does it make things worse if we try?"

"It might!" Martene just about yelped. "The time streams are clearly a mess right now. Maybe it's all because of Fox Palton's stupid fooling around with things!"

"We're smart people here, right? They don't send dopes back in time. They only send people who are resourceful and cunning."

"Funny. We're cunning, I suppose." Martene sighed and closed her eyes. "All right there are some facts we know."

"Such as?"

"This Marline found you, correct?"

"Yes. When I'd wound up in Germany in the late seventeen hundreds. A long time back."

"Wrong place, wrong time."

"Exactly." Haylee wondered where she'd heard the phrase before.

"And she still found you," Martene said.

"Yes, we went over that."

"But how? Through your chronometer, correct?"

"I would say so, yes."

Martene handed Haylee's chronometer back to her. "So maybe we don't need to wire anything up. We just need to take a closer look and find the setting that will make her come running."

"If we were somewhere else and sometime else, maybe. But right now..." Haylee gazed out the windows. A black cat was stalking along the peak of the roof opposite. From the distance came the sound of bells.

"Right now what?" Martene said.

"Right now is when I'm supposed to be. So there's no reason for my chronometer to ping up that I'm lost. No reason for that kind of automated emergency call."

Martene clicked her tongue. "All right, but it must have more than that, huh? Can you not actually send an emergency call?"

Haylee puffed out her cheeks.

"I've never used it," she said. "Never needed to."

She'd only done eight missions to the past so far, and the rest had been all very straightforward. Observations in Dublin in nineteen twelve, the Florida fires of nineteen eighty-nine, the two thousand and one Hawaiiki cyclone that that devastated so many of the Tranquillus Ocean islands.

Dangerous to an extent, but no more than expected.

She'd come through them all just fine.

But this had been the first time that she'd been tasked with bringing someone back. She had the training, of course, but still, she'd never been trained for it going quite this sideways.

Haylee sat on the sofa's arm and widened the chronometer's display. She brought up the menus. *Analysis, Recording, Displacement, Time Count, Utilities.*

Inside of *Utilities,* she found the *Communications* sub menu, and inside that the *Emergency Recall.*

Why was an emergency recall hidden away in a sub menu?

Maybe to give people pause. To make sure that they didn't just arbitrarily or accidentally call themselves home.

"Go home," she whispered, finger over the *Emergency Recall* icon. "Go home and start it all over again."

"It was nice meeting you," Martene said. "Thanks for your help with my wounds here. I hope it all works out for you."

Haylee didn't move her finger. Just kept it right over the icon.

"What are you doing?" Martene said.

"Thinking about it."

"There's nothing to think about. This is clearly messed up beyond recognition, right? Crossed time streams, multiples and duplicates of people. Of me. Fox Palton gone rogue and wild and causing all kinds of damage."

"If I go home, then I lose you."

"You only just met me." Martene's eyes kind of shone. She rubbed at her knee, which was probably not a good idea.

"But you," Haylee said. "You're the only one who knows what's going on."

"Your people will know back home. They'll have the resources to help fix things."

Haylee moved her finger away from the icon. She closed the menu.

"Not if I travel back through the wrong time stream," she said. "I don't even know that I'm in my own time stream at all."

"Is there a way to tell?"

Haylee closed her eyes to think a moment.

"Yes," she said. "Maps."

"Maps?"

"Maps of the world." She opened her eyes and fixed her gaze on Martene. "We need a cartographic library."

CHAPTER FOURTEEN

The building that housed the Royal Society of London stood stark and heavy against a darkening sky. Artisanal brickwork, with perfect mortar, and attention to the cuts where angles had been made, where circular and arched windows had been installed, where niches and pillars stood.

A set of wide steps led from the cast iron fences along the frontage, up to a pair of thick wooden doors that looked unbreakable, even by Hannibal and his entire army of elephants and rhinos.

"I'm not sure how this is going to help us," Martene said, standing at the base of the stairs and looking up at the doors. Despite her injury, she had insisted on coming along.

Haylee was glad, frankly. Even if this Martene was from another time stream, she was the closest that Haylee had to someone she knew.

Already people had vanished. She sure didn't want to be left alone here.

"I'm not sure either," Haylee said. "But we have to start somewhere. If the maps match what's in my head, then I can be confident that I'm in my own time stream."

"You know, you can't. Not really. I'm Martene, and there's a Marline who looks like me. From your time stream. What if there's another Marline who's just the same, but from another time stream?"

"I think you make a good point, but then again, would it really matter?"

The door opened a moment after they'd knocked and a small, gray-haired man peered at them over the top of half-moon wire-framed spectacles.

"The drapery is three doors down," he said, pointing to his left. "And Mrs. Jelden's Cookery and Manners School is one block over. Behind. If you go around Coventry Street, then--"

"We're here to look over the maps," Haylee said. "We're not lost."

"Maps," Martene said. "Not cookery or fabrics."

The man frowned at them. He smelled faintly of cloves.

He bent his head a little to look beyond them.

"Are you here with a gentleman?" he said. "Perhaps in the carriage?"

There was no carriage. An old rag and bone trolley went by, hauled by a man in worn shoes.

"A gentleman?" Martene said.

"Victorian times," Haylee said. "Women were very restricted in what they could do."

Martene's eyebrows rose.

"You sir," she said, "will admit us at once. The Royal Society is a publicly owned organization and its resources are available to all."

"You, Ma'am, are mistaken. The materials are available to

men of good standing. A man with credentials. Without such credentials, even a man would not be admitted."

"Really?" Haylee said. "Try this for credentials."

She bent her shoulder in and shoved the door open.

The small man staggered backwards.

"You won't get away with this," he said, straightening his tie and trying to regain his composure. "I'm not the only one here."

"Get the others, then," Haylee said. "Go on. But we are trapped here. In danger. *Immediate* danger. And we need to see the maps to get on our way."

The man frowned.

"Danger?" he said. "What kind of danger."

"A man with a gun," Martene said. "Perhaps two men."

"A musket?"

"Brand new and highly accurate."

"Following you? You need to leave immediately. I shall call the constabulary."

Haylee pushed the door closed from the inside.

"He's not following us," she said.

"But," Martene said, "he will be able to find us."

"So show us the maps."

"Now."

"If--" Haylee stepped closer to the man "--it's not too much trouble."

"Or even if it is," Martene said.

The man rubbed his right shoulder.

"All right, then," he said. "Come this way."

CHAPTER FIFTEEN

The floor space of the Royal Society's Map Room was impressive. Perhaps two thousand square feet. All under thick arched beams, with skylights and long tables and shelf after shelf holding flat maps.

"I was picturing scrolls," Martene said. "All in long carboard tubes."

The air smelled of paraffin, and there were a few well-burned candles, on stands and shelves, their wax drips running down in long tiny pillars. Some of the candles were lit.

The small man, whose name they'd discovered was Mr. Drumblemeyer, guided them to a heavy, dark globe suspended within a scored brass fitting shaped like a C, with the correct inclination.

At least they were on an Earth that hadn't shifted on it axis.

"London," he said, spinning the globe. "England. France, Prussia, Italy."

"Well that was quick," Haylee said.

"What was?" Martene said.

"There's no Prussia where I come from."

"Prussia has changed a whole lot, though. Germany, which split in two for a while."

"Split in two? How?"

"After the war, the Russians and the Americans basically divided it up. Similar to North and South Korea."

"Oh." Haylee had heard of Korea, but it was really just a mainland province of Japan now. There was no North or South to it.

Clearly she was not in her own time stream.

But still, they needed to look more deeply.

The key thing for her was the name of the Tranquillus Ocean.

"America" she said to Mr. Dumblemeyer. "How does it look on your globe here?"

Mr. Dumblemeyer turned the globe slowly.

"There's some wild country out that way for sure. Boston is nice, and they're building railroads west, but they're always fighting with the indigenous people."

"Yes," Haylee said, looking closely in the dim light.

"What do you see?" Martene said, bending in with her.

"Mexican Territory," Haylee said. "But that's what it would have been called before the sales and the establishment of Washington and Altacali and the other states. Idaho and Calientos."

"So, it's hard to say."

"Yes. But there's a Tranquillus Ocean."

"Not the Pacifito?"

"No."

"Interesting."

"Yes, but still not my time stream."

"Well, we knew the maps were a long shot, didn't we?"

Haylee closed her eyes again.

There was something more to it. She had to trust her senses here. Her intuition.

"Where are we?" she said.

"You do that a lot, don't you?" Martene said.

"What?"

"Close your eyes and leave them closed."

"Helps me to think. The Map Archive in the Royal Society of London, eighteen fifty-five."

"Right. Where we are. Now."

"Exactly. I trained in cartography."

"There's your problem right there. You studied it, and so it's your natural inclination to imagine that the solutions to the problems can be found here."

Haylee didn't speak. She kept her eyes closed. Visualized the whole room. Visualized the building. Visualized London.

"They're just maps," Martene went on. "Originals. Or copied by hand."

"Germany," Haylee said. "Show me Prussia."

"The Prusso-Hungarian Empire?" Mr. Dumblemayer said. "I believe we do have some maps of those areas, though my skills at locating them will be limited."

"What?" Martene said.

"I am but the doorman. The butler, if you like. A dogsbody and filler. I know a little about everything, yet remain an expert in none. We do have a librarian, but she is not due until later in the day."

"A woman?"

"Ahem." Mr. Dumblemayer cleared his throat. "Yes."

"Good to know. Good to know."

"Best guess," Haylee said, eyes still closed. "Best guess about where they might be?"

Mr. Dumblemayer's eyebrows rose.

"Go look," Martene said. "I'll look too. Haylee's onto something, even if she can't articulate it."

"Good," Mr. Dumblemayer said. "I'll look here. Here, I think."

"Great. I'll look in the next rack? Haylee?"

"Still thinking," Haylee said.

"Fabulous. You do that."

"It's important!"

"I know it. I trust you on this."

"Thanks."

Haylee had arrived in Germany, in the late seventeen hundreds.

But that was according to the other Marline. The older one. Not from her own time stream.

Haylee had seen that she was clearly in a castle, but hadn't gotten a look at anything much. Stone walls.

No German countryside. No towns. Not even the kitchen or living quarters in the castle.

Had it even been real?

"Prussia!" Martene said. "How about this?"

Haylee opened her eyes to see Martene laying out one of the large map sheets across a table.

The sheet was around four feet square. The edges draped over the sides of the table.

The sheet was off-white, and had clearly been hand-drawn, and colored. Ink lines indicated borders and rivers and roadways. Forests in green and mountains in brown and white. Careful blues for rivers and lakes and the Gulf of Finland, though it was labeled 'Latvia Water'.

There were villages and towns all over. Munich and Berlin and Copenhagen in big, easy to read letters, but dozens of tiny places in text that was barely legible.

South of Bremen, Marline had said. *Just a little garrison fortification, so nothing fancy.*

"Bremen," Haylee said.

"Bremen? And how do we find that?" Martene peered at the map. "We're going to need a magnifying glass," Martene said.

"I have one," Mr. Dumblemayer said. He seemed to have warmed to them, at least a little. He went to a credenza near the door.

A moment later he handed Martene a heavy magnifying glass with a carved wooden handle. She used it to look more closely at the map.

"Bremen's a larger town, isn't it." she said. "Or am I thinking of Hamlin?"

"Hamelin," Haylee said. "As in the 'Piebald Piper of Hamelin'?"

"'Pied', but yes. The very one." Martene leaned back from the map.

"Perhaps if I knew," Mr. Dumblemayer said, "what it was you are looking for, I could help."

"A time car," Haylee said. "Near Bremen."

"A time car?"

"Well, strictly speaking it's a Silvery Steed of the Timestreams."

"A Silvery Stee--"

"Haylee," Martene said. "We just need Bremen, that's all that we're concerned with here. Anything else will come after we get to Bremen."

"Get to Bremen?" Haylee said.

"Are we not going there?"

"I suppose that we are."

"Well, we just need to find it. Only there are hundreds of names on the map."

"But there's a gazetteer," Mr. Dumblemeyer said. "And the map has a grid." He pointed to a row of numbers across the top, each sectioned off with little spiky lines about an inch apart.

With a list of the towns--the gazetteer--they could find the grid reference and find Bremen.

Perhaps this was actually coming together.

"A gazetteer," Haylee said. "Would you mind getting it for us?"

"Ah, no," Mr. Dumblemayer said. "See, it's under lock and key and Mrs. Wilson has the key."

"Mrs. Wilson being the librarian?"

"Quite."

CHAPTER SIXTEEN

Mrs. Wilson arrived as Haylee's eyes were growing tired from searching for Bremen across the map in the gloom. It was entirely possible that she'd already seen the name and just glossed over it in the process. Numb and tired.

Martene had spent the time hunting through the stacks looking for other maps of Germany. Most of the maps, though were of England, with a focus on London and surrounds.

Map-making back in Victorian times would have been a whole other effort to those of the late twenty-first century. Barely any automation. Even though there were printing presses, most of the maps in the Royal Society of London's library were hand-drawn.

Mrs. Wilson was a tall, slim woman, who wore a gray flannel dress and had her hair short. Her dark brown eyes were crisp and alert.

"Bremen?" she said. "Germany, or Prussia. Well, we can take a look."

She unlocked a door in the wall, between stacks, and slipped into a storeroom, returning a moment later with a hefty dark green book. Haylee was impressed that Mrs. Wilson could lift it.

Mrs. Wilson set the book onto one of the tables with a thump.

"'B'," she said, flicking open the cover and leafing through the pages.

The was a lot of white space on those pages, with numerous annotations jotted in.

"Badminton, Baldon, Belden," Mrs. Wilson said. "Blecker, Blyton, Bristol." She turned the page and her eyes flicked up.

"Bremen," she said. "Map G.L.-thirty, reference F.-fourteen."

She pushed the book aside and went to the racks, from where she retrieved a large sheet map. The sheet made quiet, papery sounds as she draped it over one of the tables.

From somewhere, she'd gotten a wooden pointer the size of a pencil and she moved it across the row of separated letters across the top of the map.

"D, E, F," she said, and began running the pointer down. "Ten. Twelve. Thirteen. Fourteen. Bremen."

Mrs. Wilson looked across the three others. Mr. Dumblemayer had stayed with Haylee and Martene.

Haylee looked closely at the map.

The town was no more than a small square.

"There's a castle," she said. "To the south. A small, old garrison fortification."

"Perhaps," Mrs. Wilson said.

"I don't see it on the map." Now Haylee squinted.

There were sprawling lines. Some solid, some dotted, some dashed. There were rivers and lakes, roads and what had to be train lines. Areas of forest and patches that could have been farmland.

The map would have a legend, of course, but she was well-versed enough to understand the basic conventions.

No little castle.

Nothing to indicate that it might be there.

"Do you have something on a larger scale?" she said.

"You would have to go to Bremen," Mrs. Wilson said. "What we have here is very much focused on London. This map itself is really just ephemera as far as we are concerned."

"Bremen," Haylee said, looking across at Martene.

Martene shook her head.

"Oh," she said. "No. Not a chance. Coming here was an indulgence, but traipsing off across the landscape of Europe in the eighteen fifties, forget it."

"There will be a train, won't there?" Haylee said. "Out to Dover, then a ferry to France. Another train from there."

Martene blinked. "You've lost your mind, haven't you?"

"There are trains, I know it."

"Since the eighteen thirties." Martene put her hands to her face.

"Stay here if you like," Haylee said. "I'm going to Bremen."

CHAPTER SEVENTEEN

After the creaking train from London and the rickety ferry from Dover, the train leading across France was sheer luxury. The carriage smelled sweetly of leather and wood polish. The seats were all finely upholstered with delicate stitching, and the brass fittings on the seats themselves, and the overhead racks, the sconces and the door handles, all had leaf and vine motifs, as if some magician had somehow alchemized living grape vines into metal.

The train rattled over bridges and chugged on into stations, blaring the whistle. The smoke from the engine swirled.

Martene had worked out a route that had them changing in Amiens to a road wagon that would take them to Reims, and from there another train that ran all the way to Frankfurt.

In twenty ninety-eight it would have been easier to go via Amsterdam, but then in twenty ninety-eight they could have just taken a personal hover directly from London to Bremen. In twenty minutes instead of three days.

"You know how insane this is, don't you?" Martene said as

the train chuffed and groaned, pulling out from the little station in Ardres. "On a hunch."

"In a way," Haylee said, "that is the story of my professional life. Hunches."

"Really? You strike me more as someone who is thorough and grounded."

"Really?" Haylee smiled to herself. "Clearly you need to spend more time with me. I am so not that."

"Oh."

"I get my reports in late, I forget to fill in cells in the spreadsheet, I forget to go home at four o'clock because I'm caught up in whatever I'm doing."

"Model employee."

"Hardly."

They talked on as the train rode through wooded hills and across tinkling streams and sluggish rivers. Haylee was surprised by the level of infrastructure already in place.

Different time steam, though, she reminded herself, though now she felt an urge to learn more about those early railway networks through Europe in the mid-eighteen hundreds.

Haylee slept and ate sandwiches and drank tea and slept. They reached Bremen soon after first light. A porter directed her and Martene as to where they might find lodgings.

The boarding house was functional and the woman who ran it was matronly. As well as German, she spoke some Italian, so with Haylee's smattering of German, and Martene's little bit of Italian, they were able to converse with her.

A room for the night, with breakfast in the morning. English pounds were not going to be accepted, but the woman directed them to the bank in town. She would hold the room while they made the exchange.

As it turned out, the bank was enthusiastic about taking their pounds, and gave them marks and pfennigs in exchange. Plenty enough for the room and to even purchase the hiking gear they'd decided they needed to reach the old garrison castle.

And a visit to the town's new public library was sufficient to provide them with the maps of the local area--really just hand drawn trail guides for local walkers.

One of the walks led to an abandoned castle. The garrison.

It had to be.

Haylee used her chronometer to photograph the map, and the librarian gave her a strange look.

"Researchers," Haylee told her, unsure if the word *forscherin* was correct, but the woman nodded.

"Enough?" Martene said.

"We can come back and try again if it's not," Haylee said.

"We don't have unlimited resources. We'll run out of money."

"So we get jobs."

"Oh, you're just a riot."

The boarding house smelled of roses and spices, and come morning, pastries and fruit were available in the little dining room, along with coffee and more tea.

The other travelers talked in loud German and Martene, listening in as they sat at their little table, deduced that a pair of them were hiking south into the hills later in the day.

"How could you deduce that?" Haylee said. "You don't speak German."

Martene shrugged. "Just the way they're talking, and I picked up a few words, and the way they're dressed too, I suppose."

The men would have been in their forties, and they wore shorts and long socks and heavy leather boots.

It didn't take much from Haylee, in her stilted German, for them to invite the two women to join them on the walk.

"I saw the way they looked at you," Martene said, when

Haylee sat back at the table. "Eyes up and down your figure, like they were speed-reading a sign." Martene's eyes flicked toward the pair.

"They're fine," Haylee said. "Just men, and they're happy to have the company. I got no sense of any risk for us. Not like that."

"We'll see," Martene said, and finished off her breakfast.

CHAPTER EIGHTEEN

An hour after breakfast, the four of them were on their way. Martene hitched them all a ride in a market wagon returning to a farm. A rough wooden contraption with straw caught in its joins and iron springs that creaked and squeaked as if they might seize at any moment.

The men's names were Herbert and Dieter, and it turned out that they spoke some English.

"In the breakfast room we were nervous," Herbert said. "Of making mistakes in your language."

Haylee smiled. "Making mistakes is all part of learning a language. *Denkst du nicht*?"

Herbert grinned back and nodded and his eyes checked out her boobs again. Sheesh.

The countryside was wonderful. Filled with flowery meadows and thick stands of trees. The rutted roadway had wooden bridges that led across rushing streams.

It was mid-morning before they started onto the real mountain trail. And they weren't mountains so much as big hills.

A chill ran through Haylee when she saw the remains of the stone castle perched atop a steep incline. Sheep wandered through the fields around it.

The path led up to the left, skirting the steepest part of the hill. The smells of the countryside and the woods hung in the air, rich and pleasant. Such a wonderful change from the train, and from London.

"There is someone in the castle," Herbert said, pointing. "They are waving."

Haylee saw the person. Up on the parapet. A woman. She was wearing a tight, dark gray top, with a hood, hiding her hair.

Marline.

At least, someone who looked like Marline.

Haylee found herself running. She moved quickly over the rough trail. A startled bird flew, twittering from a bush.

"You know," Martene said, keeping pace with Haylee, "I'm still skeptical of all this."

"I know. And we are folk with few options."

Haylee saw that Dieter and Herbert were hanging back. Whispering to each other.

"Is there some problem?" Haylee called.

"We are thinking," Herbert said. "About our travels and experiences."

"About places to which we have been," Dieter said.

Their English seemed a little better.

"There are stories about these ruins," Herbert said.

"Strange goings-on," Dieter said. "Lights at night, sounds of the dead."

"People who never return."

Martene snorted. "You never mentioned this earlier?"

"It is only now that I realize what is this place," Herbert said. "Bad."

"We will take another route," Dieter said.

"You could wait," Haylee said. "We shouldn't be very long."

"What," Martene hissed at her, "are you saying? Let them go if they need to go."

"I..." Haylee trailed off. She thought Herbert was kind of cute, but then he had been leering a bit. And there was no way to even spend an evening with him over a glass of wine.

"Haylee?" Martene said.

"You and me," Haylee said. "We've come this far. Let's see what's up there."

CHAPTER NINETEEN

Heavy rain clouds were building from the south, beginning to obscure the sun. Though it wasn't raining yet, from the vantage on the side of the hill, Haylee could see haze across the forests and fields.

The ruin seemed bigger now that she and Martene had reached the stone base.

A fat tower that was perhaps three stories high, with rampart walls a good fifteen feet from the parapets to the ground. An arched entry.

Small, though, as far as castles went. For a garrison to keep watch, rather than as a refuge for a whole town when the Vandals or Picts or whoever came storming through.

"It's in better shape than I expected," Martene said, looking over the walls. "A few stones missing here and there, but nothing to suggest total collapse."

She looked away across the hill, in the direction where Herbert and Dieter were still making their way along the old path.

"Don't tell me that you miss them?" Haylee said.

"Well... I was enjoying their company. Nice guys. In a way. Roving eyes, but that's guys for you."

"Shouldn't be."

"No." Martene looked over at the castle. "Dare we go on in?"

"That's why we're here."

Marline appeared in the arched doorway. Spitting image of Martene, save for the outfit and the hairstyle.

"Didn't think you'd make it," Marline said. "We need to hurry."

"We do?" Haylee said, starting forward. This was the other Marline. The one with the time car.

"Fox Palton has gathered more of himself. He's looking to create time streams where he's nothing but wealthy and powerful."

"Critical mass?" Martene said.

Marline looked her over. "How do you do that with your eyes?" Marline said.

"My eyes?" Martene said.

"Some kind of mascara or eye shadow. It's very subtle."

"A little kohl," Martene said. "Seffora. It's nothing fancy."

"I'll have to try it." Marline looked Martene up and down, clearly approving of her doppelgänger.

"Don't we have to hurry?" Haylee said.

"You bet," Marline said. "As Martene said, critical mass. Once he's infected too many time streams, there'll be no stopping him."

"So let's get to it. Do we have a plan?"

"I was hoping you might have one." Marline turned and headed through the doorway. Haylee followed.

"Not yet," Haylee said. "Do you have your time car?"

"You mean my Silvery Steed of the Time Streams?"

"That's the one."

"Yes, of course. That's why we're here." Marline went on into the dark of the castle. The air was cool and dank.

"We need to use it," Haylee said. "The Silvery Steed. To get to him."

"When are we going?" Marline started down a narrow stairway. It was vaguely familiar to Haylee. It had only been a few days, and perhaps a hundred years, since she'd been here.

"We're going to Fox Palton's birth," Martene said. "From each of our time streams."

"No," Haylee said. "We don't need to resort to infanticide. But you're right about visiting him in each time stream. Before he started forming these megalomaniacal ideas."

"And how do we do that?"

"Victorian England," Haylee said. "Right before he showed up to shoot at us."

"I think," Marline said, "that the moment you're talking about comes after he formed those ideas."

"Agreed. But it's the one time that I know about, where I know exactly where and when he is. If we take him, we can start asking some questions."

Martene sighed. "This is going to be real tough."

"I know it," Marline said. "But we do have one advantage?"

"What's that?"

"My time car," Marline said. "It's from Haylee's future."

She went into the same dungeon room as previously, and there stood the Silvery Steed of the Time Streams, in all it's chrome and glass and polished finish. It hovered just above the stone floor.

"From Haylee's future?" Martene said. "So from my future too?"

"I guess," Marline said.

"It's at least from after Fox came back," Haylee said. "And started riling things up. Chances are that he doesn't even know about it."

Martene sighed again. "I guess we can but hope."

"We can do more than hope," Haylee said. "We can be in action."

"All right," Marline said. "All aboard."

CHAPTER TWENTY

The Silvery Steed of the Time Streams carried Haylee, Marline and Martene down the line to twenty seventy-five. That was Marline's best guess as to a time when Fox Palton had begun his development into someone threatening numerous time streams.

"Psychotic," she said as the whorls of time travel shimmered around the vehicle. "Or something like that. I'm not a psychologist."

"We could have him committed and assessed," Martene said. "At least that would impede his progress."

"We need something better than this all," Haylee said as the shimmering faded and twenty-first century London began to ease in. They were on a rooftop.

The Cucumber and the Broccoli stood tall nearby. Funny how once the idea of London's buildings resembling vegetables had taken hold, architects had begun embracing the idea.

"Better?" Martene said. "Tell me what you're thinking."

"Find me," Haylee said.

"Find you? You're right here." Martene's eyes widened. "You mean the you in this time stream!"

"Yes. There are already two of you. Already who knows how many Fox Paltons. If there are three of you, four of me, and so on, won't we be able to have a better shot against him?"

"Reinforcements," Marline said. "I like your thinking." She tinkered with the Silvery Steed of the Time Streams's controls, shutting it down from the jump.

"We still haven't even figured out how to find him," Martene said. "How do we find you?"

"Phone," Haylee said. "We just need access to the directories and the phone services."

"That sounds academic," Marline said. "Down on High Street."

Fifteen minutes later they were out in the clean and fresh air of autumnal London shopping arcades and parks and residential areas.

The first little store declined cash, and the woman behind the counter grinned and asked about their accents.

"A little bit of everything," Haylee said. "Perhaps my chip card will work."

"Sure, let's try that." The woman pushed the glass reader across a counter varnished with dozens of kinds of scratch tickets. Cash might not be useful, but people still craved money.

The card didn't work at all.

"We need to go to a bank," Marline said. "Talk to them there. Show them thumbprints and so on."

"If we can find a branch," Martene said. "This time stream seems devoid. I didn't see a single one in our walking around."

The woman frowned at them, and checked the glass reader.

"Maybe there are no banks," Marline said. "But if we can find a post office that'll do the trick. One of the venerable English institutions that continues on in most time streams."

"You've been to a whole lot of time streams then?" Haylee said as they left the store.

"Eight, so far."

"Meeting yourself?"

"Never." Marline looked at Martene. "At least not until now."

"How many time streams are there?" Martene said.

Marline shrugged.

"Heisenstein theorized," Haylee said, "that there might be billions, trillions, quadrillions. And beyond. Numbers that defy the human imagination. Numbers without names. Numbers that..." she trailed off.

"What?" Martene said.

"I don't know how I knew that."

They were making their way down High Street now, heading toward Oxford Circus, which wasn't a circus at all.

"Well," Marline said, "I didn't hear about that from this Heisenstein, but rather from Ella Rosenthal, who suggested that time streams can diverge and converge. Perhaps you've converged with another Haylee from another time stream and *she* knew about that."

"Well," Marlene said. "That just makes my brain melt."

They stopped at a crossing. Pod-like vehicles sped back and forth, seemingly heedless of each other. Lights flickered around their skirts.

She'd only been a kid, but this was not like the twenty seventy-five that Haylee remembered. More like a fanciful futuristic movie version. What would twenty ninety-eight be like in this time stream?

Could she be a merged version of two Haylees? Was that possible? Had anyone ever even theorized that it was possible?

Wouldn't she feel different? Shouldn't there be some noticeable change?

Perhaps that was the thing. Time streams diverged and converged and no one was any the wiser. It was only over recent years that researchers had been able to reach back through time, and any thought of separate time streams had really only been theoretical.

The idea of crossovers from one time stream to another was wholly new. And now the idea that she herself could be the convergence of time streams, well, that was just boggling.

"All right there?" Marline said as the traffic came to a stop along the crosswalk. "You seem a little vague."

"She's daydreaming," Martene said. "Or perhaps considering the implications."

The three of them walked across. The motors on the vehicles hummed.

Marline soon found them a post office and was able to finagle her way to obtaining a currency chit. A temporary thing that seemed like a rip-off to Haylee. The credit would last a week, and any that remained unused was forfeit.

"I have the cash," Marline said as they left. "Even if it's from the accounts of the Marline of this time stream."

"Who might be a Martene," Martene said. "And I would be young enough that I didn't really have an income. All the money in my account would have come from my parents."

"We'll put it back," Marline said. "As soon as I figure out how."

Martene sighed. She was getting well practiced at that.

Soon they were at another little store and had a phone with full access to directories. Worldwide.

"I'm eleven," Haylee said when they headed out, looking for the nearest public library to have a less-exposed space to make their calls. "In this twenty seventy-five. Eleven years old. My current self going to be no help."

"Yes, but I'm eighteen," Marline said. "And in tip-top shape, and with a box of attitude you could build a skyscraper with."

"Yep," Martene said. "Likewise. Got myself into a world of trouble."

"We should have gone to twenty ninety," Haylee said. "The institute was just getting started. I'd finished my formal studies and was getting into the work. You were there. One of the early explorers."

"Except that Fox Palton is here and now and innocent," Marline said. "We need to put a stop to him in the now."

"We could have gone there and come back. Twenty ninety, and brought another one of you back to here. Now. Twenty seventy-five."

"Because we're not actually *trying* to mess with the different time streams. In fact we should be doing as little as possible to damage them, or create cross overs."

"We need," Martene said, "to bring Fox Palton to heel."

"Yet you're bringing in yourself from this time stream?" Haylee said. "That's nonsensical."

Marline pointed ahead along the street, where a sign hung from one of the frontages.

Peltham Junction Library.

The library's interior was small. Mostly there were gathering spaces, with easy chairs, and tables and lots of full net access displays. Rooms along the back wall with glass walls, people inside studying. On the left were rows of shelving with paper books, and people browsing. On the right, a little café hummed and chugged with a barista busily making fancy coffees. The glass cabinet filled with spanakopita and croissants and donuts made Haylee hungry.

"We should eat first," she said. "Keep up our strength."

"Food?" Martene said. "At a time like this?"

"We can talk just as well at a café table as anywhere else in the library."

"Of course."

Haylee made her way through and ordered a latte and an everything bagel with cream cheese and egg. The others ordered too and Marline paid with the new chit.

"Fox Palton had the right idea," Haylee said as they sat at one of the few free tables. "Take some money from the future, deposit it in the past, then go back to the future to collect the cash."

"You're meaning about me taking money from the account of my past self in an alternative time stream, don't you?" Marline said. She had a croissant and she took a bite, spilling pastry flakes back across her plate.

"I do. If time's so malleable, then can we change the way it works? Can we create more abundance for everyone? Can we, I don't know, stop the assassination of Archduke Ferdinand?"

"Who?"

"The Archduke of Austria. He was assassinated in nineteen thirteen, leading directly World War One."

"World War One? In nineteen thirteen? For me that nineteen thirty-two." Marline frowned. "Thirty-two or thirty-three. When the Japanese bombed San Diego following their annexation of Hawaii."

"Wow," Haylee said. "That's really different."

"I guess. It feels normal to me. History."

Over in the library, someone burst out laughing, and someone else dropped something metallic that clattered to the floor, which led to more laughter.

"How do those the divergences begin, then?" Haylee said. "When some slight thing triggers bigger changes?"

"If the *Titanic's* course," Martene said, "had been just a fraction to the south, the ship would have missed the iceberg entirely."

"Exactly," Haylee said.

"*Titanic*?" Marline said.

Haylee gave a half smile. "I forgot," she said. "I thought that you and I were from the same time stream, but we're not."

"No."

Haylee closed her eyes. Tried to picture the whole situation.

She leaned back into the chair.

Around her there was quiet conversation. The sound of the barista bringing out their drinks. Setting them on the table. The sweet and succulent scent of the coffees.

"It's all braided," Haylee said. "Like the old rope for tying up a cargo ship. Layer upon layer. But that's only a three-dimensional representation of it."

She took a deep breath. Kept her eyes closed.

The other two didn't speak.

"And," Haylee went on, "it's far larger and more complex and more interlinked than we could ever imagine."

It was like a map. Like a layered map.

She smiled to herself as things began unfolding for her.

A map. But a map was just a single layer.

The surface. But really a surface was just a boundary between two things. Between the solidity of land and the fluidity of the air above.

But geological maps laid out the levels below. The strata of eons. The building and breaking of stone over billions of years.

Slice down enough and every slice was a map itself. A guide to how time had changed things.

And that was just in three dimensions.

"When I was a child," she said, her eyes still closed, "I was on a trip with my parents. In Oregon. We had one of those cars you could drive yourself and my mother liked to drive. Her own mother had been a competitive bitumen speedway driver. Had made some good money. My grandmother. She had a real disdain for vehicles that drove themselves. I didn't get it. Why not just let the car take you where you need to go? Why do all that extra work? Might as well have a horse and cart."

"Haylee?" Marline said. "Where is this going?"

Now Haylee opened her eyes.

"We saw a raccoon," she said. "It darted out into the road. And the car took over from my mother and slowed down enough that the raccoon scampered away unharmed."

"Roadkill used to be a thing," Martene said. "But not anymore, right?"

"My grandmother told me a story of how she'd been driving that same road, in a twenty thirty-one Mustang, which hadn't had any of that 'fancy whiz-bang stuff' and she'd seen a racoon too. And she'd slowed down on instinct and that raccoon also scampered away."

"So everyone needs to be a race driver to save raccoons?" Marline said. "Is that what you're saying?"

"Not at all. I'm saying that if things had been fractionally different, there would have been a different outcome."

"Branching of the time streams," Martene said. "Just like in all the theoretical time models that every other PhD candidate is writing."

"Fox Palton is the raccoon," Marline said. "Is that the point?"

"I suppose," Haylee said. "It's taken me a while to come around to that."

She reached forward and picked up her latte. It was steaming and frothy and just plain delicious. Maybe she should just stay in this time stream, here in twenty seventy-five London.

"We don't run him down though?" Marline said. "Do we?"

"Not at all," Haylee said. "Quite the opposite. We find that moment where he *wasn't* run down. Metaphorically. And tie things up. Bring it all together."

"Stop the fraying of the braids, you mean?"

"Fair analogy."

"So how do we find that moment?"

"I think we're already there," Haylee said. "Marline's instincts were probably right. As soon as we find him, we're home free."

"The trick, though," Marline said, holding up the chit, "will be actually finding him."

Haylee smiled.

"Actually, I don't think we need to find him. We just wait for him to find us."

Martene smiled.

"Just like back on the roof top."

"Exactly," Haylee said, and she took another sip of her latte.

CHAPTER TWENTY-ONE

It didn't take long. Not long at all.

Haylee, Marline and Martene had left the library and returned to the rooftop where they'd left the Silvery Steed of the Time Streams.

The rain had stopped and London glistened in sunlight shining through gaps in the patchy clouds.

There was a security guard standing by the vehicle. He wore a dark gray uniform shirt, with black slacks and a black cap. A row of little satchels and holsters and clips held an array of equipment on his waist belt. He was taking notes, facing away from them as they approached.

"This is some classy car," he said without turning, as the three women approached.

"It sure is," Marline said.

"I can't help but wonder how you got it up here."

"It's a long story."

"I'm sure." He turned.

Fox Palton.

He looked much younger.

Of course. The Fox Palton from this time stream.

He gave an odd smile.

"He told me you would be coming. Two or three people. Probably women. Possibly with some strange equipment." Fox Palton glanced toward the Silvery Steed of the Time Streams. "I figure this counts."

"What do you know about time travel?" Haylee said.

"Haylee!" Marline said. "Let's ease into it."

"Not much," Fox Palton said. "But it strikes me that I'm about to learn a whole lot more."

"When did he come to you?" Haylee said.

"When?"

"Haylee," Marline said.

"It's all right," Martene said, touching Marline's arm. "I see where she's going with this."

"You do?"

"I hope so."

Haylee took a step closer. "Just in the last couple of days, was it?"

The younger Fox Palton looked back and forth, across the three of them.

"You know, he looked a whole lot like me. Like an uncle maybe, but it was just because he *was* me, but older. But then, not me exactly, apparently." Fox Palton scratched at his thin stubble. "I was skeptical. As you should be, right? But then I'm looking at the two of you." He gestured at Marline and Martine.

"Sisters, I would guess," he said. "Under normal circumstances. If I met you in the lobby downstairs and you were here for an appointment, I would just think that. But it's not a familial resemblance, is it? The two of you are the same person. From different points in time."

Fox Palton cleared his throat and he stepped forward.

His right hand went to the butt of his weapon.

England, and they still only carried non-lethal weapons. Even the cops, so a security guard would definitely have something simple. It was probably a gel-pellet pistol. The pellet's charge would incapacitate the receiver for a few minutes. Long enough to put cuffs on them.

Not pleasant at all, from what Haylee had heard.

"Not different points in time," Haylee said. "From different time streams entirely."

Fox Palton's eyebrows rose in surprise.

"How about that?" he said.

A flock of pigeons wheeled overhead, flashing the white undersides of their wings. From the distance came the sound of a siren.

"He's looking to disrupt things," Haylee said. "God-emperor or whatever. You're just another cog in the machine."

"From what he told me," Fox Palton said, "*I* would be wealthy beyond measure, right here in London."

"Wait," Marline said. "What's *this* Fox Palton doing here in London at all?"

Fox Palton frowned at them. Right away Haylee saw the early signs of those grooves that would form in his forehead.

"It goes back further," Martene said. "Doesn't it? Somehow he's manipulated *earlier* time. Planted copies of himself around the world. Just to make our job harder."

From behind them came a laugh. Then a male voice said, "Don't think too much of yourselves there, ladies."

Haylee turned, with the others.

Fox Palton.

Older. And much older than he'd been when he'd shot her. Somewhere in his mid seventies probably.

Thin white hair. Lines across the leathery skin of his face.

He was slim, though, and wearing a kind of gray, almost silvery suit. Double-breasted, and with wide piping down the sleeves and trouser legs.

"You're the key one, aren't you?" Haylee said, taking a step toward him. Behind, the roof access shack stood, door open, vents humming.

"Key one?" Fox Palton the elder said.

"Haylee," Marline said.

"The lynchpin," Haylee said. "You've been awaiting the opportunity to neutralize us."

He laughed.

"We must be a real threat." Haylee took another step. Her feet crunched on the rooftop cinders.

Her mind whirred. Whirled.

Was this a critical moment? Or just another side track in whatever was going on?

Did it matter at all?

People would live out their lives no matter what. In each time stream.

Or would they?

"What is your ultimate goal?" Haylee said. "What is the point? We live, we die. All of us. There's no turning, no changing. All we have to do it live out our best lives."

"Yes, of course. I've heard this before."

"I had a feeling." Haylee sensed movement behind. Marline and Martene coming up in support?

Or the other Fox Palton. Creating a pincer between them.

"You're an odd thing," Fox Palton the elder said. "Haylee Dahlen. Kind of unreadable. A whole lot less than this pair. Marlena, Marlene, Martene and all those variations. But you, you're always Haylee. It's fascinating.

"And you're always Fox," Haylee said. "Fox Palton. That's intriguing too."

Movement behind her again. Haylee could hear someone breathing.

"I suppose that is a little intriguing," Fox Palton the elder said. "It has made things straightforward on my part."

Haylee whipped around. Darted her hand out. Before she'd even properly looked.

She grabbed the younger Fox Palton's gel-pellet gun.

Spun.

Fired.

Fox Palton the elder twisted. He dodged the pellet.

Just as Haylee had suspected.

She raced forward.

Shoulder charged him.

Fox Palton grunted.

The pair of them landed hard in the cinders.

Then Marline and Martene were there. They grabbed him. Tugged his arms around.

Haylee squirmed out. Found herself looking right back up at the younger Fox Palton.

He had some other kind of weapon. A spray can.

He squeezed the cap.

Stinging liquid whipped across her eyes.

But she still had the gel pellet gun. Blind, she squeezed the trigger.

He yelped. She heard him thump down onto the roof.

With her eyes still stinging, Haylee lurched to her feet. She knelt on his chest.

The poor guy was still spasming from the gel pellet. From his belt she grabbed his cuffs.

She flipped him over and cuffed his hands behind him.

Looking around, she saw that Marline and Martene had Fox Palton the elder bound with something. His own belt.

"Nice work," Haylee said. "Nice work."

"You too," Marline said. "It was almost as if we'd planned it."

"Maybe we did," Martene said. "But in another time stream."

"You mean a convergence?"

"Yes."

"Or," Haylee said, "maybe we're just all really good at improvising."

Both Martene and Marline laughed.

Haylee got to her feet.

"Come on then," she said. "I guess we need to get this all wrapped up."

"That we do." Marline hauled Fox Palton to his feet.

And Martene grabbed the younger one and hoisted him up.

CHAPTER TWENTY-TWO

The arrival table back in the institute felt suddenly familiar as Haylee blinked and found herself back in twenty ninety-eight.

The ceiling was a soft, luminescent white, and the air smelled faintly of vinyl. It was reassuring.

The world had not fallen apart in her absence.

But her neck ached something terrible. As if someone had been burrowing into it with prong. She reached around and rubbed at it. Tender, but the skin was unbroken.

The emergency return chip. They'd activated it.

"Hey there," a voice said.

Marline.

Younger than Haylee remembered her.

Or rather, she was back to the age she'd been when Haylee had left. Not that older Marline who'd shown up with the Silvery Steed of the Time Streams.

"Hi," Haylee said. "Data?"

Her chronometer would have uploaded every detail the

moment she'd come through. Analysis would have already begun.

Would it mean that this Marline did not take a Silver Steed of the Time Streams back to meet her in that German garrison castle?

"Nothing," Marline said, taking Haylee's wrist with a gentle grip. "You don't have your chronometer. We don't know what went on."

Haylee stared at her wrist. What had happened to the chronometer? Where had she lost it?

How had she not even noticed?

Marline looked around at the glass walls, into the dimness of the control booths where all the session's technicians sat, busy at their consoles, faces lit by the glow of their displays.

"But I'm here," Haylee said. "Safe."

"So it would seem. You're going to need a whole lot of debriefing, I guess."

"Fox Palton?"

"Neutralized, apparently. You did well."

"I had a little help."

"You can tell us all about it."

"Good. You..." Haylee closed her eyes and visualized the rooftop again. Two Fox Paltons. A Martene and a Marline who were the same person from different time streams.

"I what?" Marline said.

"What's your name?"

"Ah, there. We're getting into the crux of things."

Haylee opened her eyes.

Marline looked just as she remembered her.

But was it another person entirely?

Had Haylee arrived in a different time stream? Had she

crossed over in all that confusion and wound up somewhere else?

"Marline," Marline said. "I'm Marline. And you're the Haylee I remember. The interesting thing is that..." Marline turned to look at the control room. She gestured, beckoning someone through to the arrival room.

Through the glass, in the dimness, someone moved. A woman. She'd been standing against the back wall.

"Another Marline?" Haylee said.

"No. Another Haylee."

The woman came through from the control room, an odd half-smile on her face.

Her hair was shorter, but her eyes sparkled.

A chill ran through Haylee. It was like looking at a photograph of herself. A hologram.

"Hi," the woman said, her voice sounding just like a recording of Haylee's. "I'm Holly."

"How...?" Haylee said. "I thought..."

"I know."

"It's disconcerting," Marline said. "Isn't it? Like when I first came across Martene."

"Not for me," Haylee said, feeling a warmth building inside her. "This is great. It just shows how much more scope there is to our work here."

"You know," Holly said with a smile, "that's what I was just thinking."

AFTERWORD

I just plain love time travel stories, but they can be a tricky thing to get right. When I was starting out in the world of professional writing, an editor returned a time travel story to me with the kind note to the effect that 'why didn't they just go back to before the incident and do it differently?"

It was a good question. Time travel stories do take a lot of fine-tuning so that the answers make sense and questions (like the above) are answered within the text.

And when done well, time travel stories can answer the question effectively—whether by things just falling apart with every iteration, or with some structure to the mechanism that means that travel is not straightforward. Witness the classic movie *Back to the Future* and the power requirements for their DeLorean (which immediately answered the question—and effectively became a key part of the premise of the movie).

Another favorite of mine is the old Richard C. Meredith novel *Run, Come See Jerusalem!* which is so convoluted and so pacy that it's just a joy to read. To my mind, that book is extremely finely-tuned.

I can only hope that I have done justice to the genre here, in what is essentially an adventure story, and a story that grew legs in the writing as I discovered more and more of the story that required unfolding and tinkering.

Thanks for reading. See you next time around.

Sean
December 2025

SEAN MONAGHAN

AWARD-WINNING AUTHOR

LOST IN THE MAZE

ERR: INTERNET DISCONNECTED

CHAPTER ONE

A cool wind whipped along the tarmac street, bringing dead leaves and air that felt like it had come directly off the remains of the glaciers hundreds of miles away.

Darryl Landrie carried his beat-up rollscreen along the sidewalk, head tucked down into his collar. He wore a long woolen overcoat over plain blue jeanics, t-shirt and sweatshirt. His MacQuarrie work boots were a decade old and looked it. Far too much time stomping around old worksites and mountain trails.

He stopped outside a Racey's. In better days the place would have served coffee with human baristas and a smile and some good conversation. Now it was little more than a kiosk with a few stools at a long wooden bench. People kept moving nowadays. As they did around him right now.

The endless sea. Faceless humanity. Every one of them reading articles about how to avoid being lonely, how to plan for the next phase of their career, how to find and hold love.

There was a line of them in the Racey's. They filtered up to the silvery dispenser. It read their retinas and determined their beverage of choice. They didn't even have to refocus from whatever newsfeeds were cluttering their eyeballs.

The line moved on. At the end, they took their cups and exited back to the street.

The air reeked of coffee and cinnamon and chocolate. Faint piano music played from overhead speakers. A recent popular song, reimagined for this space.

As if anyone would listen. Ears already tuned to other worlds.

Darryl joined the line. Hushed solo conversations spilled through the air. The young woman ahead talking to a friend about some squirrelly guy who'd run up bills in her name. Darryl only caught a few of the breathy words.

A middle-aged man joined the line behind Darryl. Glancing back, Darryl saw him eyeing up and down. Running quick assessments of Darryl's place in the scheme.

Yeah, good luck with that one buddy.

The coffee machine hissed and pushed odors into the air. The line moved on.

Soon it was Darryl's turn. He kept his eyes narrowed and he vocalized. Asked for a cappuccino.

A tiny door wound open on the machine's face. Right below the eye reader. A flat soft panel inside.

"Some guy de-retinaed," the man behind Darryl whispered. "Yes. Holding things up here."

Because an extra few seconds were so valuable. Darryl lifted his hand and pressed his thumb against the panel.

The machine clicked. The tiny door closed. Darryl moved along.

He retrieved his coffee, in a warm pot-plant-shaped cup, and went to the the stools and bench.

No one noticed him. The music played on. The machine kept making coffees.

No one else needed the thumbprint panel.

The bench was actual wood. Grown wood, from a forest. The stool was comfortable, though bolted to the floor. Darryl sat on the stool's edge and dropped the rollscreen on the bench top.

The screen unrolled and activated. Out to the size of a hand towel. The top left corner flickered with a cluster of busted hexels. Just some rot. To be expected, really. Rollscreen this old, near impossible to get repaired. Unless of course you wanted to go down the nano road and, well, that just opened up a whole mess of other issues.

He tapped in the middle, let the screen's display read his palm print. The numbers came up and he tapped out the four digit ID.

The screen gave a pretty Samkia swirl, and a little burbling chime.

An image faded in. Rembrandt. Looking old and wise, a fat hat on his head.

Darryl waved and snapped his fingers. Rembrandt faded off and Darryl's work appeared.

Movement next to him. The smell of paprika.

Darryl turned and smiled.

Melainey. She had her hair plaited with strings of tiny glowing cowries and an old iguana automatoon clung to her shoulder. The iguana opened its mouth and licked its upper lip with a wet tongue.

"You should leave that thing at home," Darryl said.

Melainey leaned into him him from behind, pressing her body against his back. Head against his neck.

"I can hear your heart—" she said, with the slightest hesitation "—beat."

"Well, that's nice. Are you getting a coffee, or did you just come to bother me?"

Darryl and Melainey had grown up through egg farm together. All the learning lessons and regridding systems they should have had ingrained. Melainey still had full wetware connections.

"Coffee," she said, glancing at the line. "That's a nice idea."

"Yes. You'll be able to order in two point five seconds."

"I know how the connections work," she said. "I'm immersed every second of every day."

"Not like these poor suckers."

Melainey sighed. "I guess not."

Back in '22 or '23 the two of them had spent six weeks at an Ashram. Banks of the Ganges, chapatis and rice and cheese for meals. Back before the purges.

Melainey had come out with a real facility with her mental switch. Everyone had them. The ability to shut off the feeds. Just that Melainey had learned to put hers to use.

And Darryl? He had his comms surgically removed. That explained the scar on his temple and the slight issues with his peripheral vision.

Blurry shadows. Often. The shape of birds, trees or like someone with a raised knife. Darryl would turn his head to look and they would be gone.

Melainey stood. She walked across and joined the line. Her order would be in already—she would allow the retina read only for confirmation that she was the one who'd ordered.

Darryl worked on his flat rollscreen. The data feeds still came through, though it took a lot of work from the screen's processors to cut it down to something that it could actually display.

The left hand top corner of the display flashed red and blue. Just a circle the size of an old-style quarter.

The police.

Keeping an eye on him.

Darryl put his attention on the feeds.

Water levels in Baja were rising again. Nano milk vats in New Zealand had suffered another terrorist attack, fifteen million liters of the stuff had drained into Lake Karapiro. The Austrian Chancellor had survived yet *another* assassination attempt.

Pretty hard these days to plan something like that. Just thinking about it too hard could throw your numbers up on the socmeds feeds and you'd find yourself rubberroomed and dealing with a shrink who might well be passive-aggressive and facing divorce over an income sharing situation.

At least, that's what had happened to Melainey's brother Cameron. Read up too much on Guy Fawkes and imagined blowing up the modern-day British Parliament.

Cameron found himself stuck in an isolation prison outside of Brighton. Up on stilts above the waves. Feeds all blocked by meshes and active suppression.

Didn't sound like such a bad thing to Darryl.

Melainey came back to the bench and sat. "Pity these stools are fixed," she said. "We could cosy up."

"Yeah." They'd done enough of that kind of thing over the years. Probably for the best that there was some separation between the stools.

Melainey looked over the display. "You got work?" she said. She sipped from her coffee. Surprisingly it hadn't come in a takeout cup, but rather a crisp white, bowl-shaped cup with a small handle, and a saucer.

"Gardening for Mrs Entwistle. She doesn't like the way the ouba tears up her herbs. Also, I'm cheaper than a real gardener."

"Nice." Melainey kept peering at his display. "Not in any trouble?"

"No more than comes from being disconnected." Darryl sipped from his own cup. "People frustrated that I'm slowing things down."

"Committed any crimes?"

Darryl peered through the window, looking up into the sky. There were tall buildings around, six or ten story glassy tenements and office buildings. Despite everything people still liked to work in offices.

People walked by on the sidewalk. Vehicles crept along. Some traffic snarl somewhere slowing things down.

"Darryl?"

"Yes."

Melainey sighed. "What did you do?"

"Nothing."

She pointed to the flashing blue and red corner of the rollscreen. "And so what is that?"

"Glitching." He pointed the the other corner with the busted up hexels.

"You think that because I'm retinaed that I don't know the difference between a rollscreen's broken section and a police surveil?"

Darryl said nothing. He picked up his coffee and sipped. It was good. Strong and warming. Waking him up.

"You're not saying anything," Melainey said.

Darryl looked around. The line continued. A steady stream of new consumers. "None of them are saying much."

"Watch their lips." Melainey turned too. "Plenty of them are having conversations. You know, answering questions from their friends."

"So how's work with you?"

"Well, they've got me designing systems that will get more people into the void. As in people like you."

"But you called it a 'void'."

"Well, you got a better word?"

"No. I like that."

Outside, a police bubble pulled up. Its fat wheels angled hard so that it could roll right in against the curb. The door unfurled and two cops stepped out. Both in dense black uniforms, their peaked caps covered in an array of antennas. Both cops wore reflective wraparound glasses. Specifically designed to hide their retinas.

"Huh," Melainey said.

"You call them? I thought we were friends."

"I didn't call them." She squinted at him. "But why would you think that I did? What have you been up to?"

Darryl sighed. Harmless little things that people took exception to.

Melainey peered into his rollscreen some more. She tapped at spots, letting data and images wheel into place. "You sure have got a lot of ancient movies on here."

"Documentaries," he said. "History, mostly."

The cops reached the entry. If they were here for Darryl, this would be the moment to exit through the other door. With the other departing customers.

He stayed put.

No sense in calling attention to himself. Anyway, the data streams were so filled nowadays, if they knew something, they knew it.

The cops strode inside, casting their glances around the place. They joined the line.

"Documentaries," Melainey said. "Kind of things that are banned?"

"Not banned. Hard to find." Darryl forced himself to look at the rollscreen display.

Both cops had glanced their way.

Unusual for people to have a full-volume conversation. At least in this kind of place. Maybe at home in the evening, shutting everything off and slowing down.

But here, out in public, quiet was the way.

Everyone's onboards would pick up even subvocalizations and convert them into messages and data. No one needed to raise their voice. Not really.

One of the cops whispered something to the other, then turned and headed for the bench.

"Uh-oh," Darryl said.

The cop was slightly taller than him, but slimmer. She had milk coffee-colored skin and a straight nose.

"Darryl Landrie," she said. Her syllables were clipped. She might have grown up in one of those Swedish-Finnish enclaves. The pole cities keeping above the bogs.

"I'm Darryl Landrie," he said.

Even with her glasses on, her eye roll was obvious.

"I ought to run you in just for that," she said. "Smart Alec talk. Back to a cop."

"You're a cop?" I said. "I don't see any ID."

She sighed. "If you were properly retinaed, you would see my ID right there in your feeds. I could run you in for that too."

"Couldn't." Darryl glanced over at his rollscreen and brought up the *Sustainable Arrest Procedures Bulletin*. A quick wave and drumming of his fingers called up the lines on police required to display a physical ID to the non-retinaed. "There," he said.

Another sigh. "If I had my way, you wouldn't be able to get away with that kind of nonsense."

Darryl said nothing.

A moment later the cop's partner joined her. The partner was male, stocky, and a few centimeters shorter than her.

"Who are your friends?" the male cop said. He handed her a coffee. Same kind of cup as Darryl's.

"Some guy," the female cop said, "who thinks he doesn't need to play by society's rules."

"That a fact?"

"That is a fact, yes."

"Not even close to a fact," Melainey said. "There are no 'society's rules'. There are laws and there are mores."

"Mel," Darryl said.

"Well, *that's* a fact. Laws which are unambiguous and clear. Mores which are more like guidelines."

"Guidelines," the male cop said. He took a sip from his coffee. His nose wrinkled as if the beverage tasted bad.

The female cop removed her glasses. Her eyes were a deep, deep blue. Almost an impossible blue. Very unusual.

And familiar.

"You're Inga Devlin," Darryl said.

They'd trained together at a martial arts academy outside of Poughkeepsie six months before he'd met Melainey.

Darryl had never had much to do with Inga, but still, he should have recognized her.

"Yes, I am," she said.

"I'm sorry," he said. "Memory's not what it used to be."

"He ID'd you by name?" the male cop said. He took another sip. Wrinkled his nose. "Can we run him in for that?"

"Nope," Melainey said. "And right now, we're pushing up against harassment."

Inga Devlin blinked. "You got problems with the gangs?"

Darryl shook his head. "No." There were some out there

hacking back through their feeds and fixing to look like they were off-grid.

They weren't.

No way to retain connection and be invisible. You had to be like Darryl. No connection at all.

"Come on, Devlin," the male cop said. "We've got fish to fry."

"*Bigger* fish to fry," she said.

"If you say so." The cop headed for the exit. He glanced back over at Darryl, Melainey and Inga, and gave a shake of his head. The door threaded open for him.

Inga reached over and tapped Darryl's rollscreen. "We could use your help, you know. With your skills. And no connection. Could be just what we need."

Data appeared on the display where she'd touched. Her police ID, and full contact details.

"Get in touch," she said, and stepped away. In moments she was out the door and getting back into the police bubble.

"What was that?" Melainey said.

"Cops."

The bubble's tires angled the other way and it fed itself back out into traffic. Disappeared.

Inside the Racey's, the line had all but gone. Just two people now. Rush over.

"Darryl?" Melainey said.

"Yes."

"Explain please."

"What's to explain?"

"Please. You flirt with the woman with me sitting right here."

"Oh."

Two things. How was that flirting? She was a cop.

Second thing. Why would it bother Melainey?

Oh.

"And wipe that goofy smile right off of your dumb face there. Sheesh!"

Melainey pushed herself from the stool. "Why is it that I bother, again? Please, tell me."

"The Ashram."

"Oh, my word. You still think all this is about meditating and getting in touch with yourself?" Her voice had gone up both in pitch and volume.

The last customer at the dispenser looked around at them.

Another customer stopped and the entry and backed out.

"Great!" Melainey said. "Now this is all over the feeds. Thank you very much, mister!"

She headed for the exit. Stopped. Came back over. Picked up her cup.

Drank, draining it. Set it back down with a clunk.

Stalked off toward the exit.

Darryl looked at his rollscreen. Inga's contact details hung there in the middle.

Personal contact details. Not just her police details. Her home address. Her online links.

And that had upset Melainey. Which would make sense if Melainey was attracted to him. But surely they'd been through enough together to know that all that was behind them.

Surely.

Darryl reached to delete the details. It was straightforward to delete numerous things from the rollscreen. It had limited storage and he kept right away from the effectively infinite storage back through the feeds.

A little text data didn't take up much space though. Nothing really, among the petabytes in the rollscreen's memory.

Nothing meaning he would have have to delete some ancient photographs or movies, or text files, or any of the analytics systems. Not that he ran any of the analytics anymore.

With a wave, he saved the information into a separation retrieval sector.

He sipped at his coffee as another customer came through the door. A middle aged woman in smart workout clothes. She gave him a suspicious glance and went to the machine.

Darryl sighed. Maybe it would all just be easier if he reinstated his retinals. Join the world of the living once more.

Or the world of the barely-living.

He rolled the screen and left the Racey's. An icy rain had started up. Drizzle, really. Darryl hurried home.

CHAPTER TWO

Darryl's apartment was a local universal basic. Three rooms, all set up and paid for by the state. The walls were white and the furniture was modular. Everything was a little rough around the edges.

The bedroom was in back, windowless. A display even older than his rollscreen showed a depth image of a park in Barcelona. As if he was overlooking all of Gaudi's ancient, whimsical tiled walls and gardens. There was approximately one foot of floor space around three sides of the bed.

The bathroom was approximately nine square feet. The toilet bowl and cistern folded away into the wall so he could take a shower.

The kitchen, dining, living room was large enough that the three functions were separate, though his dining table was little larger than a breakfast tray and the living room had barely space for his two dumpy armchairs.

The main window, floor to ceiling, wall to wall, looked out

over an actual park. A cluster of baseball diamonds, popular with kids in the weekends and adults in the evening. Sometimes the too-frequent *thunk* of aluminum connecting solidly with cowhide, together with the cheers of enthusiastic parents and other family, could get a bit wearying.

But it was nice to see people having genuine fun. Out in their bodies, pitching and swinging and running. Racing and diving to make a catch or steal a base.

Heartening, even. All was not lost for the human race.

Darryl made himself a kale and spinach salad, with roomeat —the new thing from the Australian vats—together with crispy dimple fries. The smell of those was divine.

Rather than using the dining table, he sat in one of his armchairs and watched one of the games. Teenagers. *Blue Sox* against the *Trojans*. The *Blue Sox* were up eight to three in the fourth. Their pitcher could virtually send bullets at the poor batters.

As he ate—the kale was very fresh and tasty—Darryl's rollscreen chimed.

He ignored it for a moment. But he really didn't get calls that much. Who made calls anyway when you were always connected?

As he finished up his salad, the rollscreen fell silent.

Out in the park a pinch hitter came in. The girl was a regular. She could turn a game.

The pitcher hurled high for ball one. The small crowd groaned.

The rollscreen chimed again.

It was Inga.

Inga the cop.

Inga the cop with whom he'd trained in martial arts.

He'd been lousy at martial arts. Karate, Judo, Kung Fu. Even peaceful, blissful Tai Chi. Slow reactions and awkward movements.

He had, however, enjoyed the training camp.

And part of that had been Inga's company.

And now she was a cop.

He tapped the rollscreen to answer the call.

"Now you're stalking me?" he said.

"Stalking?"

"Old term." Not really in use now you could know where anyone was any time. "It means following someone around without them knowing."

"Ha, ha," she said, but sounded nervous.

Maybe she *had* been flirting with him.

Back at martial arts camp she had been with some guy out of Spain. He'd rolled his Rs and switched around his verbs and nouns. Something like that.

Swarthy and muscled and with eyes that smoldered.

Also, very good at all the martial arts.

"You there?" Inga said now.

"You can't tell?"

"I'm off the retina. Taking a break. Got to when you're cop. Ha, ha."

It was half-laugh, half-vocalized. He'd forgotten that she did that. Quirky.

"I wonder what that's like," he said.

"What what's like?"

"Being in among the void and then coming out."

"The void?"

"That's what Melainey calls it. Being switched on to your retina all the time."

Silence.

Darryl waited. Had he done that intentionally? Mentioned Melainey.

Because it sure was odd having Inga calling him up. Perhaps he should just come out and ask her.

"Darryl," Inga said before he spoke. "There's a coffee shop opened up near your place. More like an old-style place." She was speaking very quickly now. "They still have the automatic baristas, but lots of tables. Posters on the walls and sometimes live music. You know, musicians with actual instruments."

"And you're telling me because?"

A beat. Then, "I'm asking you out, bozo."

"Oh. Yes."

"Also, you can explain Melainey and 'the void' and all that to me."

Now he was silent.

"Darryl?"

"You mean now, do you?"

"Sure. I mean, yes. Now. If you like. I could meet you there in fifteen?" She gave him the address. It was no more than two blocks away.

"All right," he said, not even sure if he would go. What was the obligation? Nothing? She'd called him.

"Oh. Good. See you there."

"See you there."

The rollscreen faded as the connection broke.

They did have a history. Of sorts. Maybe he should just meet her.

Out in the park the pinch hitter was on third. Chomping at the bit. The new batter got a hit.

The ball went high. Very high.

Everyone sprinted. The ball was caught, but she'd made it home already.

People cheered.

Darryl picked up his plate and carried it to the sink bench.

Maybe, if he was going out, he ought to get changed.

CHAPTER THREE

The place was called *The Exchange*. It had glass windows painted black on the inside. A drum-shaped retina-read bouncer barred Darryl's way in.

Should be used to that kind of thing. If you didn't have decent retina connections, there were all kinds of hoops and roadblocks to actually getting things done.

"Please wait," the bouncer's synthesized voice told him.

"You need a thumb scanner," Darryl told it, knowing there would be no response. "My thumbprint is on record."

"Please wait."

Traffic hissed past. A low-flying corporate jet whizzed across the street, hover units braking for a helipad landing somewhere nearby.

The bouncer admitted a young couple wearing matching ripple vests. Right after they'd gone in, a woman in jeanics and glowing purple boots came to the door.

"You duh guy wih no ID?" she said. She might have been

Polish. Lot of Poles leaving the continent with their economy surging.

"I've got ID," Darryl said, holding up his thumb.

"Funny guy."

"Yeah." He lifted the rollscreen. Still rolled. The the exposed portion of the display showed his linked ID.

The woman shook her head, but she bent and looked at the display, letting her retina query the databases. She stood upright and after a moment stepped aside, waving him in.

"Cahn't be too careful," she said. "Not dese days."

"Nope."

Inside, *The Exchange* was dark and smelled of beer.

There were circular tables around the main area, mostly occupied. A long bar took up the wall space along the left, people clustered in front. Background music. The hum of conversation. Deep maroon curtain across the back wall.

It was like one of those old-style jazz bars from last century. Darryl had seen plenty of pictures and movies. A speakeasy?

Not hidden away, though. Not some deeply secret place out back of a launderette or stationery store.

Darryl stayed just in the entry. A small vestibule to the left had a coatcheck. Automated, with a retinal watch.

He saw her then, sitting near the middle of the room.

She'd changed outfits.

Well, of course. Now she was wearing black, but nothing like a uniform. The trousers glistened in the sparse lights. She had a halter top that hugged her figure, and translucent or sheer or something long-sleeved cardigan over top.

Very lightly dressed, really, for the evening. The place was about as cool as the outdoors. Why did they even bother with a coatcheck spot?

"Hey," Inga said as Darryl came up to the table. "You're here."

He nodded. "You asked me." She looked really good. She'd done something with her hair, though when he'd seen her last she'd been wearing her cop hat. Her dark hair was down just to the bottom of her ears. The tips bleached blonde, with those microscopic lights coruscating, giving subtle shimmery patterns.

"You can sit," she said. "Instead of gawping."

"I was gawping?" Darryl sat. "I guess I'm surprised."

"Surprised?"

"We go way back, but it feels like there was a real separation of paths there. You've gone on into law enforcement, while I'm basically a bum."

"Law enforcement," she said, drawing the words out. "Just say cop. Also, you're not a bum."

A waiter came by. A silvery sphere the size of basketball, with three thin rods for legs. It got around very well. A display asked them what they'd like to drink.

"We could just order from the bar," Inga said, glancing around. "Talk to a real person."

A young woman with dermal displays on her cheeks wiped at the bar top with a cloth. It seemed very primitive.

"That's kind of the point, isn't it?" Darryl said. "Actual human interaction?"

"Yes."

"I don't. This thing is kind of cute." He looked at the waiter. Similar kind of tech to his rollscreen. Simple systems.

"'kay then."

Darryl ordered a Pilsner Wite, Inga ordered a Mercury Volatile.

Thank you, the waiter's display flashed. The waiter scuttled off.

"What is a Mercury Volatile?" Darryl said.

"You'll see."

Darryl shifted his seat. It made a scraping sound on the floor. A waft of slightly warmer air washed over him, actually making him shiver.

The curtains at the back of the room fluttered and wound open. They revealed a low stage, with musical equipment set up. Microphones and speakers, stools and guitars on stands. Blue and red lights played across the things for a moment. Someone testing the lighting.

"It's very... something here," Darryl said. "Sorry, not being very articulate. Very minimal. Simplified."

"That's the appeal."

Darryl looked around the room again. There were maybe twenty people. Including the woman at the bar. "Not so much appeal. How many people live here? Few hundred thousand? And how many showed up tonight?"

"That," Inga said, leaning across the table, "is also part of the appeal."

The young couple Darryl had seen entering earlier went up to the stage. They picked up a guitar each and sat. The guy stood and adjusted his stool.

They plugged cords into the base of the guitars and tinkered with dials on the speakers. Amps.

The woman began strumming chords. She leaned into the mic and sang in breathy whispers.

You swirl like candy she sang, words just audible in the whisper.

I fill your vortex

You ask will I still be there

The guy joined in, playing a bass counterpoint rhythm to her strumming.

And he sang too.

Deep baritone. Not even words, just gentle moans and hoots.

A chill ran through Darryl. Not the words, or the guitar. Not alone anyway.

The combination. Reaching inside him. He felt teary.

The waiter came back, a robotic arm delivering their drinks to the table.

Darryl barely noticed. He was tied to the performance.

"Pretty good huh?" Inga said, leaning in close to him.

"I... yes."

The song wafted and wound, *swirling* into him. It ended with the gradual removal of parts. The woman eased away her singing. Decreased her strumming. The man's sounds grew quieter and quieter.

Left with just the plucked deep notes. And then, one last one, hanging as he leaned back and let the string resonate.

The audience clapped.

Darryl joined in, barely aware of what had just happened.

The woman whispered a 'thank you' and started with the next song.

"Fabulous," Darryl said. "I didn't know there was..." he trailed off. *So much beauty left in the world.* Sounded way too corny.

Inga sipped from her drink. Through a straw. It had layers. Deep red at the base, orangey-white at the top, with a transparent layer filled with glitter in the middle.

"Want a taste?" she said. She turned the glass, pointing the straw toward him.

Close. Real close.

It was kind of nice. Very nice.

"Thought of being a musician," she said. "Thought of being a painter."

She held the straw just a little closer.

"Policing ended up being the way I went."

"You would have made a fine musician," he said. Did he really say that? What was his basis for it? "Or a painter."

He really was very awkward at this.

"Try it." She held the straw right there.

He found himself taking a sip. *Mercury Volatile* was right. The liquid blasted its way into his mouth as if hyper-aerated. He could practically feel it penetrating the roof of his mouth. Clawing its way into his tongue. Crawling down his throat like a snake on adrenalin.

And it wasn't half bad. That experience. That taste.

"Wow," he managed.

On stage the duo were building up the song. More beat to it now. Both rocked their heads and tapped their feet.

"So," Inga said, taking her drink back. "What have you been up to in the decade since I last saw you?"

CHAPTER FOUR

Darryl took a bubble taxi sixteen blocks to the doctors' surgery. A white, rippled building that looked more like a screwed up piece of paper than a habitable building. Perhaps that was the point. Who used paper at all now, let alone screwed a piece up?

The frontage was a series of oval sheets of glass set into the scrunches and spikes of the walls. An arched sign above the largest oval read *Michelson, Choudhary, Mbutu, Physicians.*

Darryl used his thumbprint to pay the fare and the taxi darted off into traffic. In the foyer he joined the line for the unretinaed. The doctors' was perhaps the most likely place to find clusters of such unfortunates. Just like himself.

The others, in the line for those with implants, moved faster, and they all looked healthier. Barely in need of a visit here.

Healthier, but with distant expressions.

Darryl had burr on his foot. From bad shoes or something. It wasn't clearing up and the data feeds from the rollscreen were no use.

The people around Darryl had lined faces and clear eyes. Some of them coughed and some of them limped. They were thin, or fat, sallow skinned or blotchy skinned.

A middle-aged man stood behind the stone counter, taking notes from the first person in the line. A woman wearing ragged mesh and plastic strips in all kinds of colors. She had a boldly tattooed face.

The air was tainted with a hint of disinfectant. To be expected, really. The place probably had microbots swimming over the walls scrubbing everything back to elemental particles.

After a moment, the receptionist man indicated for the tattooed woman to go wait in the next room over. "The doctor will see you soon."

"Fat chance," the woman said. "I'll be here all day." She lifted a fat chunk that might a been a brick of some kind.

No.

A paperback book.

Darryl smiled. He should have recognized that. Antique and popular among the unretinaed. She'd come prepared.

Eventually it was Darryl's turn at the counter.

"You again?" the man said.

"Me, what?" Darryl peered at him. The older man was unfamiliar. The age Darryl's father would have been, had he lived. "I haven't been here for... months. I don't recall you."

"Well, I remember you." The guy got a twinkle in his eye. He glanced at the display built into the counter. "Thumbprint please."

Darryl touched his thumb to the little plate set right in the middle of his side of the counter. The plate and counter were cold, as if they had refrigeration plates built in.

"There you are," the guy said. "Darryl Landrie."

"You read my name off your display."

"Yes. I remember you, but not your name."

"Right."

"Yes. Fine. Can you confirm your current physical address, please?"

Darryl told him, and answered another couple of questions. The display set up listened to his answers and checked against the information on record.

"That's all fine," the guy said. "Your appointment is scheduled. Please wait over there. The doctor will be with you soon."

Darryl lifted his rollscreen. "I came prepared."

The guy managed a smile. "You all think you're so original."

"Yep." Darryl headed into the waiting room while the guy dealt with the next person in line.

The waiting room had animated images of ducks flying. Some in wide Vs high over mountains, others flapping across a water's surface heading for take off. The images were really simply part of the wallpaper.

People sat waiting in steel-framed chairs. About twenty, taking up half the chairs, more or less. The carpet was crisp and new. Plenty of money in the medical establishment for renewal.

Darryl sat across the room from the woman with the hefty paperback. She had it open, the cover curled back around the spine. Her gaze bored at the page.

An orderly came out and called for a patient.

One of the retinaed people glanced up, but it was a non-retinaed who stood and headed over. Maybe a similar name. Anyone with a connection would get their call that way, not from something as primitive as someone actually saying their name.

Darryl had been there over an hour when someone came and sat by him.

Melainey. The sweet scent of paprika. The iguana glared at Darryl from her shoulder.

"Well," she said. "Well."

"Melainey? What are you doing here?"

"Me. I got a regular physical. Annual. What are you doing here? Catch something from your new girlfriend?"

Melainey seemed annoyed. What had he missed?

"She's not my girlfriend," he said.

It had been a week since he and Inga had gone to *The Exchange*. They'd spoken a couple of times. It was nice, but still... he didn't have the words for it.

But he was feeling nice. Had to be brain chemistry, right? Enjoying her company. Looking forward to seeing her again.

So different from when they'd first met. And she smelled so good.

"Not your girlfriend," Melainey said.

"That's right."

"But you keep seeing her."

Darryl took a breath. "Three times. Including calls. Might see her again. Might not."

One of the retinaed stood and headed for the door where the orderly had appeared earlier. The carpet gradually recovered its smooth shape after bending to the weight from her shoes.

"Three times," Melainey said. "She's retinaed?"

"We—"

"Of course she is. She's a cop. It's obligatory. Has to be connected."

Melainey was jealous! That's what was going on.

Darryl closed his eyes and looked at the ceiling. It was coated with subtle, wafting cloud shapes. Was that supposed to make people feel more well? What did they call it? Helix Health Care? Wholistic? Something like that.

"We should go for a proper drink sometime," he said. "You and me. This place *The Exchange* is pretty amazing. They have these musicians who are like angels. And drinks you just wouldn't... what?"

Melainey stared at him.

An orderly called his name from the doorway.

The woman with the paperback book glared.

"You went there with her, didn't you?" Melainey said. "With Inga?"

"Darryl Landrie," the orderly called again. "Please, the doctor is ready to see you."

Darryl stood. "Sure. I didn't know it existed..." he trailed off.

The look on Melainey's face told him that he should have stopped speaking long ago.

"All right," he said, still speaking, somehow unable to stop. "I've got my call now. We'll talk later. Yes?"

Melainey didn't reply.

Darryl headed for the orderly. He glanced at the woman with the tattoos and the paperback. She sneered at him.

It was hardly his fault he'd been called first.

CHAPTER FIVE

A few days after, Darryl was back working. He dug in bulbs along the front walk for a woman named Mrs Cavendish. No first name. She had to be close to a hundred. Retinaed.

Not fancy work, but satisfying. Back to nature, blah, blah. But there really was some truth to that concept. He always felt better working with plants.

The walk was some kind of grown plastic-concrete that self-repaired, exploiting capillaries that took material from the waste stream. The bulbs were daffodils and jonquils. They would look pretty come spring, smell nice.

If they came up. Might be too late for them to bed in well for this year. Maybe next year.

If Mrs Cavendish was still alive.

He got gritty dirt under his nails. Insects buzzed him. A robin stood in the bare branches of a neighbor's oak, watching Darryl with a wary eye.

Should be used to wary eyes by now. At least the robin wasn't retinaed.

A bubble cop car pulled up at the sidewalk. The vehicle's top unrolled, revealing two cops inside.

Inga, and the same cop from the coffee shop a few weeks back.

"Hey," Darryl said, standing. "Haven't heard from you for a couple of days." He glanced around at the house before walking over to the bubble.

Inga nodded.

"Just getting my hands dirty," Darryl said.

"You know there's a bot can do that, right?" the male cop said. "You don't need to go near the soil."

"We came from the soil," Darryl said. "No harm in touching it now and then."

"Oh, boy, he's a philosopher now."

"Zip it, Bruno," Inga said. She touched the lip of the door and it unfurled. She stepped from the bubble. She looked really good in uniform. Better than she had back in the coffee shop.

But back then, they'd only just met. Kind of. Now they'd had a date.

"Melainey called me," Inga said, tapping the edge of her eye. Right on the bone. "We had a long conversation."

Darryl's internal organs jostled. He felt queasy.

"You and Melainey," He said. "A long conversation."

"That's right."

Darryl swallowed. "So I suppose the message was... I don't know? Back off? Never see me again?"

Inga nodded. "She sounded pretty ticked."

"Oh."

Inga took a step closer. "You smell earthy."

He held his hands up. "Real Earth."

"We got a call-out," Bruno said from the bubble. "Looks like it might be a bad one."

"A bad one?" Inga glanced over.

"Check your feed."

Inga sighed. She said something barely above a whisper.

Bruno laughed.

Communicating directly, leaving Darryl out of it.

A quiet sound came from the house. The snick of a door opening.

Darryl turned. Mrs Cavendish came out through the front door. Her house had a long veranda at the front, and she came out of the shadow onto the steps. She stared at the police bubble.

"Everything all right there, Mr Landrie?" she said. "You're not in any trouble, are you?"

"Little trouble with my girlfriend," he said, wanting to bite his tongue the moment the word came out.

"Which girlfriend is that?" Inga said, loud. Edgy. "Me? Are you calling me your girlfriend? Or is it Melainey there?"

Darryl turned. "Sorry, that popped out."

Surprise on her face. "So you do mean Melai—"

"I meant you. Of course. Why would—"

"Inga!" Bruno called. "Let's go!"

"Yeah," Inga said, turning. "Yeah."

She got into the bubble.

She gave Darryl an enigmatic smile. Something quizzical in there.

"If I was retinaed," he said, unsure how to finish. What? If he was retinaed she would know how he was feeling? If he was retinaed *he* would understand a whole lot more about the world. About her. About women in general.

He sighed.

The bubble's hood started forming up, and Inga called over, "What do you mean?"

"Maybe things would be easier." He shrugged. "Maybe."

"Nope," she said. "Talk soon."

The bubble sealed up, hiding her and Bruno. The wheels angled and the bubble moved out into the roadway. In moments the vehicle was scooting off, leaving a wake of swirling leaves.

"You should join the police then," Mrs Cavendish called. "Goodness knows they always need more police."

She turned and went back inside her house. The door snicked closed.

Really, they didn't need more police. Every year the media proclaimed how crime of all kinds was down, statistically.

What they needed was more gardeners. Ecology was a mess.

Darryl went back to the bulbs. But he was distracted. Warm.

It was a nice feeling.

Of course, he would have to talk with Melainey sometime.

Something to look forward to. Or not.

CHAPTER SIX

Kaper's Rock was a promontory that looked out over Eagle Lake fifteen kilometers north of town. With a backdrop of steep, stoney hills, and a few old boat sheds along the shore, the lake had been popular for decades.

The old dam didn't generate electricity anymore, but the body of water was still popular for recreation.

Darryl strode up the steep inland face of the promontory. In places the chipped stone steps were supplemented with old setcrete. Bees buzzed around the clumps of wildflowers. The floral perfume was pleasant. The air was much fresher and crisper than back in town.

He found Melainey sitting on top of the promontory. She had a folding seat an a flask of Sprite. Out over the lake a little ground effect aircraft sped along, rippling the surface with its passage. The engines buzzed, like a giant version of the bees.

"How's your signal?" Darryl said. The iguana automatoon was racing around, leaping after bees and other bugs.

Melainey looked around. "I didn't hear you."

Farther across the promontory's wide plateau a young couple lay back on an old tartan picnic blanket. A walker-talker basket stood at the edge, the neck of a wine bottle poking up.

"I got new boots," Darryl said, lifting one foot. "Saffron. Very comfortable. Very quiet soles."

"I've heard of them. You maybe came into some money?" Melainey looked out over the lake and back at him. She picked up her flask and sipped. "You didn't bring anything to drink?"

Darryl took a breath. He walked across the plateau, heading toward the edge. It wasn't a cliff-face drop to the lake, but it was too steep to navigate. Juniper and blackberry competed for light and soil in the rugged slope. The sun was very bright.

"I'm thinking of getting a retina connection," he said. "I mean, getting it re-established."

"You've lost your mind," Melainey said. A scrape sound from her folding seat and next moment she was right next to him. "Just for some woman."

"You have your connection."

"Mmm. It is good up here. The signal is attenuated. In behind the mountains. The system does a lot of extrapolations, but it's still quieter."

"You miss it? Having it right there?"

"Kind of." Melainey took a deep breath, making him look around at her.

She seemed tired.

"You're thinking of disconnecting, right?" he said.

She managed a smile. "How come you're so perceptive?"

"You shouldn't do it."

"Says the guy who's thinking of going in the other way."

"Can't you just switch it off? You're good at that."

"It's getting harder."

Darryl stared off into the distance. The ground-effect aircraft was nearing the northern end of the lake. The aircraft tipped up, nose lifting, banking right. After a nicely parabolic sweep, the aircraft settled in close to the surface again and sped south.

The couple with the picnic blanket burst out laughing at some private joke.

"It's lonely," Darryl said. "I didn't realize it, but that's what's been going on."

"Loneliness?"

"No one's lonely anymore, are they? Not unless they come up here for some disconnect." Darryl glanced around at the couple. They'd stopped conversing and were now wrapped in each other, limbs entangled. "Even then, there are still connections."

Melainey followed his gaze. "Oh, leave them alone."

Darryl turned to watch the ground effect aircraft again. It was a single seater, the pilot lying low, almost prone, inside the small cockpit.

The lake was a few thousand meters long. It took the aircraft less than a minute to sprint end to end. Flying slow, really, riding that cushion of air, however that *worked*.

"I'm lonely," Melainey said. Her voice was very quiet. "The world bustles on around me. People don't notice."

Darryl looked at her. Her eyes glistened. A single tear ran down her cheek.

He wanted to pull her into a hug. Hold her close. Was that some kind of deep-seated thing. Like he needed to protect her from a harsh world?

Was that deeply human?

But he couldn't move. What if she misunderstood? What if she thought this was him now taking a step toward them becoming lovers?

"You all right?" he said.

He had Inga to think about, after all. Feeling closer to her. Thinking about joining up. See what it was like on the force.

Maybe he was ready to make a change.

"Melainey?"

She sucked in breath and turned away. Took a step closer to the edge.

The aircraft lifted again. Banked. Sped off along the lake. North.

"Remember when we were learning Tai Chi," she said. "You were so lousy at it?"

"Thanks for the reminder." After the academy, he'd gone to local classes. At least it had been good to get out of the house.

She took another step. The buzz of the aircraft shimmered through the air.

Melainey lifted one foot and spread her arms. Some Tai Chi move. He couldn't remember the names.

"I was envious of you," she said, balancing, arms out like the necks of swans. "You just kept going. You enjoyed yourself. You didn't worry about getting it right. The rest of the class were so obsessed. Striving so hard to be perfect. They weren't having fun. They just worried what Tam Miko thought of them. What the rest of the class thought."

"So I was the class clown?" Tam Miko had been the instructor. An ancient and wiry Japanese woman, with short-cropped ink-black hair. She'd spoken in clipped sentences, instructing the group.

She'd died a few years back. The rollscreen had let him know.

"You were very endearing," Melainey said. "You were striving. It was sweet."

She set her raised foot back on the rock. The couple had

finished with their activity. They'd separated and were packing up the blanket and other items.

Out on the lake, the aircraft's wing caught the water. The aircraft went cartwheeling. A puff of vapor and some kind of pod burst away. Rocketing high.

As the aircraft came to a stop and began to settle in the water, a chute opened on the pod. It hung on cords and steered toward the shore.

"Look at that," Melainey said.

One of the couple was speaking now, clearly. Talking to emergency services somewhere. Alerting them to the incident.

"Guess some people have connections way out here," Darryl said, glancing back. But he looked quickly again at the dangling pod and bobbing aircraft. Simply fascinating.

"There's good coverage really," Melainey said, staring out too. "I just shut off."

"Yeah. Thought you might have. Guess it's easier up here."

"We should go. Nothing we can do for them. The place is going to be swarming with people and aircraft soon."

"But your shutting off, that was just a temporary one, right. A time-out. You didn't go do anything foolish now. Did you?"

Some kind of hollow grew in Darryl's belly. Digging out. A void. A black hole.

Melainey didn't say anything.

The pod touched down on a small beach on the lake's far side. The parachute canopy collapsed gently, wafting like lace and spreading out as it reached the water's surface.

The canopy popped off the pod and someone stumbled out.

"They're hurt," one of the couple said.

But the person on the far side of the lake quickly regained their footing. They stood upright. Waved over.

Melainey waved back.

"Maybe we should get down there," she said.

"The lake," Darryl said.

There were public bubbles in a small lot in back of the promontory. One of those could take them around the end of the lake and back up toward the landing site. But there wasn't really a road around there. Would a bubble go off-road if you told it to?

But it was clear from the overheard conversation that help was on the way. A police search and rescue autothopter, with actual paramedics following.

Anyway, it looked like the aircraft's occupant was all right. He or she had sat down on a rock in back of the beach and was just waiting.

"Did you see it?" the other member of the couple said. The one who hadn't been speaking with emergency services. "Did you get footage?"

"Someone will have," Melainey said. "I was disconnected."

The woman looked at Melainey with a quizzical eye. "Oh. Oh, I see. Wish I'd seen it. I can't find any footage." The woman blinked and stared into space. "Nothing."

"Come on," Darryl told Melainey. "We should go."

She nodded. "All right. Yes." She whistled for the iguana and it raced over to her.

They headed back down the promontory. On steeper parts they took each others hands for assistance, but there was nothing more to it than that.

By the time the public bubble brought them back into town, it was twilight.

Inga was waiting out front of Darryl's apartment building.

CHAPTER SEVEN

Inga had brought takeout. White cellulose boxes of rice and egg and stir-fried vegetables.

Melainey glared at her from the bubble.

"Join us," Inga said. "There's plenty."

There was plenty. Even with Melainey, Darryl would have leftovers from his refrigeration for days.

"No," Melainey said. "You kids enjoy. I've got work come morning."

The sky was darkening. Rainclouds coming in. Other bubbles buzzed by.

"You were at the lake," Inga said, leaning into the bubble. Darryl had made it to the sidewalk, Melainey was ready for the bubble to take her home.

"It made it to the feeds?"

"Best thing," Inga said. "No actual footage. The pilot was on disconnect anyway. No hard recordings. But there are a whole lot of extrapolations and artificial footage. It looked quite spectacular."

"Not quite the same as being there."

"I suppose not." Inga stepped away from the bubble. "Nice to see you. I mean, truly."

Melainey opened her mouth as if about to say something. Closed up. Then, "All right." She nodded. "All right. Nice to..." Deep breath. "Nice to know you. Watch out with this guy."

"All right."

Inga stepped back. With a hiss, the bubble pulled back out onto the street.

"Hungry?" Inga asked Darryl, and holding up the boxes.

Up in his apartment they sat on the floor, the boxes open, eating with chopsticks and watching the baseball. Some adults' social league, under lights. More shouting and ribbing than actual playing. Perhaps that was the point.

"If I quit the cops," Inga said, "what would I do for a job?" She looked around his standard issue apartment. "Maybe I'll be a painter?"

"Why would you quit?" Darryl got a floppy piece of bok choy from the box to his mouth. Sticky sauce got on his chin.

"Can't be a cop without a connection."

Darryl chewed. The meal was quite delicious. "Oh," he said, and swallowed. "So you're going to do that?"

"Fool thing to do. My parents would disown me." Inga got some strips of egg, rice sticking to them. She said something unintelligible as she chewed.

Darryl smiled. He got a mouthful of rice, and replied.

Inga laughed, bits of rice and egg spilling from her mouth.

Darryl reached over and wiped some sauce from her lips. She smiled.

Out on one of the diamonds, someone hit the ball out of the park. The watching friends yelped and hollered.

"I like your spot here," Inga said. "Simple, but functional."

"I like it too," he said. "Did you mean something by that?"

"Like moving in, you mean?"

Darryl swallowed. "Well. One thing at a time."

"Well..." Deep breath. Kind of like Melainey there. "I guess that would depend."

"On?"

"You."

"Me?" Darryl's hand stopped partway to his mouth, some broccoli caught in his chopsticks.

"Is there someone else?" she said.

He gave a shake of his head. "You mean connection, right. You mean, am I going to connect up and join the police?"

"It won't matter if you do. I don't think it would change you that much. Plus you'd be able to ask my advice. You know, on policing matters."

"But you'll be a painter. What would a painter know about policing?"

"Oh, funny man." She reached over to tickle him.

Darryl dropped his chopsticks. He shuffled away. "All right," he said. "All right. I give in."

Inga backed away. "This is good," she said. "Good."

Darryl nodded. "And, after due consideration, I've decided..." he hesitated.

"Drum roll," Inga said, using her chopsticks to air drum. But there was worry on her face.

"Decided to stick with what I know. I won't be joining up."

Inga's grin was the biggest he'd seen.

So things were going to work out just fine.

AFTERWORD

I write a lot, which is becoming perhaps more expected in these days of artificially-generated fiction. It amuses me as much as it troubles me. I hope you enjoyed this story, written by an actual human.

I write all the words myself. And frankly, I'm kind of ticked-off at those companies that stole writers' work to develop their models.

Anyway, the reason I mention writing a lot, is that I'm making more of a conscious effort now to get my stories out into the world. I tend to write faster than I can publish. My stack of copy-edited and proof-read manuscripts is much too tall. So, yeah. I'm challenging myself this year—2026 as I write this—to get more stories up and out to readers.

Some time has passed since I wrote "Err: Internet Disconnected", but it's fun to look back on for a couple of reasons.

The first is how I come to write stories. I really don't plot things out ahead of time. I tend to let the stories evolve as they will. Some call this writing into the dark. I think of it like a band improvising on stage. The musicians know where the beat is and can anticipate the changes coming up, but they don't always know exactly where things are going.

So I don't write down story ideas. But what I do note is cool titles. I had seen this phrase—"Err: Internet Disconnected"—come up on my display from time to time and frankly it seemed like a good thing, really. Less internet. Fewer distractions.

But I am easily distracted (hence a pile of yet-to-be-published manuscripts). When I came to actually format and publish the story, I discovered there were *two* stories with the same title.

Now I do find myself doing this more often these days, but I tend to keep better track of things. Mostly it's when I've written a story and it hasn't worked out quite as well as I'd thought, and I still want to explore the themes or what-have-you.

[As an aside here—I recently wrote two stories titled "Abandoned Cars of Chatham Island"—which started out kind of in the same place, with different characters, but then the stories diverged. I have a couple of ideas about how to get those out into the world].

The trouble with the other "Err: Internet Disconnected" is that the manuscript file I have seems unfinished. As if there's another document floating around. Ah, the disorganized life of this writer.

Perhaps I'll find that. Perhaps one day I'll be able to get that story out too. Perhaps I'll even revisit the whole idea in another story at some point and find myself hunting around for a new title.

Thanks for reading, and making it through my ramble here. I hope it was at least a little entertaining.

Cheers

Sean
January 2026

SEAN MONAGHAN

AWARD-WINNING AUTHOR

CAREFUL IN THE COLD

BECCA AND THE GHOSTERS

CHAPTER ONE

High in orbit above the planet where her father had lost his life, Becca Cardatious shivered.

The hollow volume of the empty observation deck was cold. Too cold. The ship's heating had been on the fritz since before they'd left for Hammerhound.

Sixteen paying passengers and every one of them had complained to the captain about the lack of heat. Ten days of transit with temperatures sitting around 8 degrees centigrade.

The *Curlew's Plaintive Cry* was an aging rust bucket with patches of standard gray Braemer's grout over edges and corners, and welded plasteel sheeting on too many decks and walls. It reeked of oil and grease, and of globs of the still-hardening grout.

Still, the ship must have passed inspection to have even been allowed out of port.

Becca had taken to wearing her big thick thermal body coat, intended for on the ground. The thing billowed too much. It caught on the ship's lugs and loops and she would find herself snarled up. On the ground of course, gravity would tug it into shape.

Hammerhound had a higher gravity than she was used to. Something like one point three. She'd been taking Dr. Klon's Muscle Remedy tincture to help strengthen her muscles and cartilage. Disgusting tasting stuff. Three drops a day on her tongue and she would feel like she'd been licking the belly of a sand gecko.

Still, some of the other passengers—most of them—were heading for the Branaman Isles, a tropical haven filled with pools and spas and robot hustlers eager to sell you another extortionately-priced mai tai. Passengers with little more than thin, gaudy shirts and shorts, and ropey sandals. Wide-brimmed hats for the sun.

They seemed to spend most of their time in the ship's small centrifuge casino, tossing around their credits and downing colorful cocktail bulbs. Their vacations had begun even before they had stepped aboard.

Becca, meanwhile, had spent most of the time in her pokey cabin, going over the same meagre set of documents again and again, trying to wring out fresh details.

Now, Becca returned to the cabin, tugging her way along through the cylindrical companionways, trying to avoid getting caught up on the lugs.

Her cabin as a haven, really, with all that she had on her mind.

How she would pay for the trip. How she would feel when she got on the ground.

Thoughts about her father that she kept pushing away. His search for moments to paint. That was all.

She pushed away again. Focused on where she was.

The cabin had a single porthole. For most of the trip it had been sealed with a cluster of bluish pebble-shaped balls—the ship's natural protective coating for the transit through the strange bent physics of the supra-light environment.

Now, though, in orbit, the port was transparent. Hammerhound was gorgeous. Blue and gold and green. Oceans and cloud forms you would expect. Vast tracts of deep, thick forest and wide swathes of rolling prairies.

The appeal was obvious. Extraordinary open acreages and spectacular scenery. A mild climate. At least, closer to the equator.

Of course that ramped up gravity weeded out those with lower tolerances.

Becca's cabin had become more home-like on the trip, somehow. When she'd first come aboard, it had seemed so tiny. Like the old coffin hotels her friend Karl frequented on his jaunts around Europe and the Middle East.

Now, though, it was more cozy and comforting. She would be sad to give it up when it came time to board the dropship to the surface.

She had yet to give thought to her return.

Her two foot walker bag was packed, ready to go, but she kind of didn't trust it. The walker feet were fine for following her around terminals and into transport, but when she made it down to the tundra the thing might struggle. It was certainly adaptable—during the trip, it had maneuvered itself around her hammock and dresser with an agility that suggested monkey DNA in its little brain.

Pulling herself close to the viewport, Becca stared out at the planet. The terminator was coming up. A dark, fuzzy line creeping across the mountains and ocean.

Hammerhound's star, Sharolus, was distant and bright.

Hammerhound's orbit was little more than ninety days, and its day ran to a little less than twenty-two hours.

In the last six years of financial investigative services, Becca had visited thirty-four planets. Mostly core worlds within forty light years of Earth. Her reputation had begun to grow and had begun to precede her. Organizations, both governmental and private seemed to have their books in order when she arrived, though it was often obvious that the work had been rushed.

It was so strange to be coming to a place on her own recognizance. There was no local accountant down there quaking with worry about the state of their company's books.

And likewise, no hotel, no buffet, no eager pageboy slavering to run around after her and ensure everything was smoothed over.

This was all her.

On her own.

Below, the terminator shimmered and crept along. The ship would be passing right over it soon.

Somewhere down there, her father lay in a casket, awaiting her arrival.

It had come too soon.

A chime came from her door.

It was time.

CHAPTER TWO

Becca stretched and rolled her jaw as she stepped from the ticking drop ship. She tingled all over.

The craft stood on high, spindly legs, and the steps down were more like a ladder. Hard to tell whether to go down backwards or forwards.

Some of the other passengers were on the ground already, kind of milling around. The air was warm and tasted of tamarillos. Sweet and tart at once. She'd been warned about it, but the taste wasn't bothering her.

"Hey there!" One of the men called over to her. Six of them, three women and three men, were standing by a low trolley transport. Beyond stood the tall conical roofs of one of the resorts. "Carefree Days" or something. Maybe "Troubles Forgotten". No, it was "Beyond Bliss". Far more positive.

Becca waved back.

"Come on over," he called. "They have welcome cocktails you would not believe." Ben Alexander. A tire and wheel manufacturing magnate from Grallaide. Money practically oozed from him.

"It's all right," she called back as she walked over. "I have an appointment at the library." Thin grass and weeds whiskered around her boots.

Ben laughed. "I might have known, could have guessed. Always with a tab in your hand, never at the pool or the shows. Tucked away in your cabin the whole time."

It was a fair assessment. But unlike the other passengers, she wasn't here on vacation.

What was she here for, though? To bury her father? To see what had happened? How he had lost his life?

Ben strode toward her, arms out wide.

Before she could move, he'd wrapped her up in a fierce hug. It wasn't sexual at all, though he was squishing her boobs. There was a tender genuineness to it.

"I hope things go well for you here," he said. Quiet, but not a whisper. "I do hope you find the peace you so deserve."

Becca shivered and he released her. Stepping back, he grinned at her.

"Thank you," she whispered. "Thank you."

"Of course, of course. Now you make sure to look us up when you make it over to Yelhena."

Yelhena was a market world sixty light years away. Way outside of her regular runs.

"I will," she said, meaning it. If by chance she ever did get out that way, she would make sure to connect with Ben.

But who knew what her life would be like after today? She had taken a leave of absence from her work—something she could not really afford. Her father's trail of debts and angry former spouses stretched far beyond even distant Yelhena.

"I will hold you to that," Ben said.

Becca smiled. Doubtless Ben would. He was a savvy guy. Likely he would have contacts within the Yelhena institutions who would let him know the second her disc scanned at the planet's immigration desk.

"And watch out beyond the fringes of the inhabited areas. This place is like that old Yelhenese morel fungus that's a delicacy."

"How so?" She didn't even know what he was talking about.

"Prepared correctly it's extraordinarily delicious, but the chef has to be careful that none of the toxins from the cap are within the flesh. It's a heavenly-taste abutted with potentially deadly chemicals. Same here. Spas and scoot-skiing close to wilderness that will deceive you. Chew you up."

"Oh." She'd read of the wilds, of course, but had never thought of it like that.

"Listen to me, getting all gloomy! I'm sorry you're here under the circumstances. I hope that you'll find the peace—listen to me repeating myself. Take care!"

He hugged her again. Stepped back. Smiled. Waved.

"Thanks," she said, though she wasn't sure for what.

Ben turned and rejoined the others at the trolley. Some of them waved and Becca waved back. She started off toward the small town.

CHAPTER THREE

The town was a collection of several hundred self-built granite and composite buildings from shed-sized, right up to a small stadium. *Next Game Saturday! Go Blazers!*

Becca found herself standing outside the hospital. Three stories with sweeping blue curves in its architecture. Vapor swept from vents on the roof. A sign near the door activated and welcomed her.

Becca Cardatious, it read, *proceed through corridor three to the morgue.*

Becca shuddered and stepped away, almost stumbling.

For a half an hour, she wandered aimless.

He was lying there. Waiting for her to uplift him. To take him somewhere else. Home?

How could she?

People on the street smiled at her. Nodded greetings. She felt lost and adrift.

A food cart sold her a gyro, crammed with salad and sauce and strips of nutty-tasting meat. It was delicious. Invigorating.

She needed it.

Wiping her hands on the napkin the cart had provided, she walked with more purpose.

Uplifting his body could wait. For now, she needed to know what had happened.

After all, that was really why she was here.

Wasn't it?

She started looking for the library.

CHAPTER FOUR

Hammerhound's library system involved sixty-two separate locations, forty-nine of which were fully automated. Livingston, the town where the landing ship from *Curlew's Plaintive Cry* had set down, had a population of close to six thousand and the library was a three story granite building right on the edge of the town square. Just between the administrative complex—a garish purple and green tower that looked like a stack of dish bubbles—and a silent generating station—a black cylinder draped in copper and gold pipes and valves and huge jack points of all descriptions.

The air was cool and there was a sort background hum of distant machinery. It seemed as if every place Becca went there was sure to be active industry. Sometimes desperate, sometimes struggling, and sometimes surging as if the local resources were pouring themselves into the hoppers, eager to be consumed.

The library's interior smelled of old books—that slightly sweet, slightly musty odor that suggested quiet and reverence.

Becca walked through the entry atrium, boots clicking on the tiles. Rows of shelving stretched away through the wings to the left and right. A few people sat in easy chairs, or at tables, with data tabs or heavy paper tomes.

The reception desk was staffed by an actual person. A woman of about nineteen, with tiger-striped eyebrows and a wide, welcoming smile.

"You're Becca Cardatious," she said, her accent soft and pleasant, drawing out the vowels and hardening the consonants. *Behckah Kahrdayshuss*. It was sweet.

"I am," Becca said. "How do you know?"

"The ship manifests," the woman said, standing. "They all come through here. I noticed your name and realized you weren't a regular tourist. I'm Shana. I'm really sorry about your father."

Shana came around the desk, holding her hand out to shake. The were an awful lot of cultural differences from world to world, but handshaking remained a constant everywhere.

Shana's grip was firm and her skin was cool. She stared deep into Becca's eyes with a warmth and sympathy that was almost disconcertingly genuine.

"I'd hug you," Shana said, " but I don't know if you would stomach that from a stranger."

Becca made no response. Not that she couldn't stomach it, but more like she was still having odd sensations from Ben's hug.

Unidentifiable. Everything was tangled up inside. Hard knots of feelings she hadn't experienced before. Sadness and grief of course, but other things that were new.

Things she didn't have names for. Not yet.

"Thank you," Becca said. "I appreciate it. I'm kind of glad you know about it, I suppose. He was... very private. Very, well, secretive."

"Things happened in those mountains," Shana said. "Things that should have remained hidden and unknown."

Something twisted inside Becca.

"Things?" she said.

Shana shrugged. "The fauna here is not to be trifled with. He's not the first to die. But we're safe here."

"Safe? From what?"

Shana stepped back. "You'll want the documents, of course. All the details on his time here. Everything he left with us. And all the ancillary information."

"He left things with you?" That didn't seem like the man she'd known. Cagey and reluctant.

"I'll set you up in one of the research rooms," Shana said. "It will give you some space. Where are you staying?"

"Staying? I... I hadn't planned that far."

Here she was, interplanetary arbiter and auditor and she couldn't even properly plan a simple trip like this.

"I guess..." She trailed off. There was a tall window beyond, behind Shana's desk, with a view across a flowery meadow. Some kind of jet black bird jumped up from the plants as if frolicking.

"I can arrange something," Shana said. "If you would like."

Becca smiled. "I would like that."

"Perfect. Come along. I'll show you the Persimonous Smith room. You'll like it, I think." Shana turned and began making her way through the library.

CHAPTER FIVE

The Persimonous Smith room sported an oil painting of Smith himself at the door, hanging in a gilded frame. He was severe, with a strip of amber hair across his scalp and a manicured goatee. His eyes seemed to follow Becca as she went through the door after Shana.

The interior was racked with wooden shelves and a long, glistening table through the center. A skylight admitted sunshine, shining through in beams, picking out myriad drifting motes. The air smelled of old books and camphor.

"Smith was the founder, wasn't he?" Becca said. "First settler on Hammerhound?"

"The first to stick it out, really," Shana said. "All those who came with him abandoned the surface within a decade."

Shana touched Becca's shoulder.

"But a history lesson is not why you're here, now, is it? I'm sure you read all that you needed before you came. You just need the space to get into the deeper records and the databases about the investigations."

"Yes," Becca said. "Thank you."

"Good." Shana took another step into the room. "Table please," she said.

The table gave off a light whirring sound and a panel the size of a dinner tray folded up slightly. The panel's face shimmered and formed into a depth display.

"It should have everything you need to access the details you'll be wanting," Shana said. "And I'll be right out front if you have any problems."

"Thank you," Becca said.

Shana slipped away and Becca sat at the table. The chair squeaked as she pulled it forward.

The display was an older model, but it responded quickly to her gestures and questions. It didn't speak to her, for which she was grateful. She still needed quiet, it seemed.

Dates flickered by, and images sat softly deeper in the display, waiting to filter up if she asked for them.

She dredged right back to the details of the days leading up to his death.

Rockfall. It had blocked his access to the pass he used to get to the local outpost. His cabin had a full communications suite, but limited support systems. He still had to make his way through the mountains to the outpost to obtain food and batteries and other supplies.

There were no resources available to clear the rockfall.

The images showed that 'rockfall' was an understated way of putting it. It looked as if half the mountain had fallen. Chunks of rock the size of houses lay churned and tumbled across a swathe that was perhaps a kilometer across in the lower reaches. It had cut a notch through the trees.

The event would have been phenomenal to watch. The sound probably had echoed on for minutes. The forest stood not a chance against the tons and tons of rock debris that had swum through it.

Before she'd found the intrigue of financial instruments and the sleight of hand that some investors could use, Becca had spent a semester imagining herself becoming a geologist. There was something about feldspars and optical mineralogy and the very physical act of being out in the field with a rock hammer and sensing equipment that appealed.

She would have gotten to travel as much, but ultimately it seemed that what she was up to was more about doing good than geology ever would be.

But she did like to think that she still retained a rudimentary knowledge and understanding of these kinds of processes. High mountains subject to freeze and thaw processes. Fractured rock ready to collapse. The very fact that mountains got to be the shape they were was because over millions of years pieces of them kept falling off.

Just like this rockfall.

Becca focused back on the display.

Notes and dispatches from her father. Responses from officials. An attempt to send in an airdrop of emergency supplies.

Another request signed by someone else.

Shana.

Shana Foster.

A shiver ran through Becca.

Shana should have been long gone. A decade or more since her father had managed to slither his way out from under Shana's thumb.

And yet, here was her name.

Signed.

What was going on?

CHAPTER SIX

Shana found Becca a small room in an informal boarding house. The place was a hundred year old stone and plastic building with serrations on the roof peaks and verdant basket planters hanging from the eaves. The man who owned it, Kalv Baker, had built it. Kalv had recently celebrated his hundred and twenty-eighth birthday—and he was busy with replacing one of the plumbing pumps on the bathroom.

"I knew your father," he told Becca, wiping his hands on a rag which didn't seem to budge the oil a bit.

"All right," Becca said, standing near the door. Shana had already departed.

"I'm sorry for what happened. There aren't many of us on the ground here, so it reverberates through the community, if you know what I mean."

"I understand."

Kalv showed her the room and the hookups and systems. There was a fold-down bunk and a small writing dresser. The bedding smelled of lavender, as if he used some special kind of wash cycle.

"Breakfast at seven," Kalv said. "I can whip us something for dinner too if you feel so inclined. Nothing flash. Gene-chick egg omelet and okra and charrots from the garden. If you're hungry."

"I'm hungry," Becca said. She was still processing through the idea that Shana had been out here with her father.

Unbelievable.

Unbelievable, yet true. She'd dug through the data further, and discovered that Shana had been accompanying her father for years.

"All right," Kalv said. "You have things on your mind, clearly. Dinner at eight. I'll come get you."

Becca smiled.

"Sorry," she said. "Yes. Lots on my mind."

"Don't apologize. I'm sorry about your father. He'd been a good friend to a lot of people."

Becca focused on Kalv. He had white stubble and not a single hair on his scalp.

"A good friend to you?" she said.

"Yes."

"We should talk." Perhaps Shana had brought her here intentionally.

"Surely," Kalv said. "I'm about done with this pump, but then I'll stoke the fireplace and pour out some brandy and we can talk after we've eaten."

Becca smiled. "Brandy disagrees with me." It always had."

"Ah," Kalv said. "But this is Persimonous Smith Brandy. A whole other thing. Aged and full and warming. I guarantee you'll like it."

CHAPTER SEVEN

Kalv's fire crackled and sparked. Bright flames flickered. The fire was built in a blackened steel dish three feet across. It stood in the center of his living room, with a wide funnel above, tapering to a chimney that vanished into the high ceiling. The gray lines of a spark-catcher field ran around the lip.

"It's summer now," Kalv said. "And I still need a fire. Come winter, I'll be running it all day and night." He was sitting in a wide armchair and swirling his brandy. The glass caught the glow of the fire.

"You don't have adjusted heating?" she said. Hammer-hound's star was well bright enough to deliver sufficient energy to heat a home. A few well-placed collectors and all of the needs would be met.

"Surely," Kalv said. "And where's the romance in that? This was when our ancestors changed things up. When they began talking and leaving the plains behind. Fire. It's as much a part of us as the ocean."

Becca smiled and swirled her own brandy.

Fire was a part of being human, just that few people had much to do with it anymore.

"Tell me about my father," she said.

"Fool of a man," Kalv said. "Setting himself up out there in the mountains. A thousand kilometers from anyone."

"There was an outpost?" Becca said. "I thought there were others. It's about thirty miles—fifty kilometers?—from his home."

"Automated. Bots and sensors and that's about all. I think some technician goes up there every eighteen months to tighten the nuts and grease the nipples and whatever else needs doing."

"So he had no help?"

"There was a woman."

Becca made no reply. A vague memory of Shana trickled through her mind, hazy and indistinct. Shana in a diaphanous gown, standing on a rocky headland while Becca's father waved photographs.

"And they could call in for help any time they liked," Kalv said. "That would be automated too. Punch a button and a robot flitter would sprint its way out to them."

"But they didn't do that."

Kalv swirled his brandy a little more. He took a delicate sip.

"Why?" Becca said.

"Why? I can't answer that."

She stared into the fire. The fuel was fist-sized black nuggets. Some kind of artificially-produced charcoal. Off in the forests somewhere there would be robots selectively removing trees and converting the fibers to all manner of things. The charcoal was probably a by-product.

"I have to go up there," Becca said.

"After the funeral? Or are you taking his body away? Back to his home world?"

Becca gasped and looked away.

His body.

It all seemed so unreal. He was dead.

"This must be a tough time," Kalv said.

Becca couldn't speak. She took a sip of the brandy. It was strong and warm and seemed bent on curling its way through her tubes rapidly. That might be good. Good and bad at once.

She took another sip.

She stared into the fire. It crackled. Homey and heart-warming.

"If you go up there," Kalv said, "you're not going to like what you find. Not a bit."

"What's that now?" She focused on him.

"You should just claim his remains and get on home. There's nothing up there that will help you find peace."

Becca took a breath.

"I have to go up there," she said.

And after what he'd said, she had to go up there more than ever.

CHAPTER EIGHT

The flitter was a long gray and silver thing standing on the tarmac on a tall, spindly undercarriage set. Like a jumping spider ready to pounce.

Kalv had arranged it for her, producing the documents at breakfast.

"If you have to go," he'd said, "then you need safety and reliability."

The interior sparkled as if it had been polished for hours. Three passenger seats and long strip windows on each side below the wings. Once she was aboard, the flitter lofted and sped away north, engines humming serenely.

The view was nothing short of fantastic. The landscape slipped away rapidly. She was perhaps two thousand feet above the rolling hills.

The front wall of the cabin gave her readings on speed, altitude and estimated time of arrival.

Mach 0.99, 3000 feet, 3PM nominal, 7PM local.

A clock ticked down the time. Four hours.

Her father had been a long way east of where she'd set down. And far to the north. In the tundra and ice and bare plateaus.

Becca checked her personal display for local conditions at her destination.

Below freezing. Sunset at 6.41pm.

Hammerhound's day ran to a shade over twenty-two hours, so near standard hours applied, with midday and midnight at eleven o'clock. Her display had adjusted automatically.

The time whiled away and she tried reading a novel—*Albatross Wake* by S.E. Clementine—but her focus wandered.

Still, when the flitter swung around for a landing, she was startled.

Outside it was growing dark, and the cold seemed latch onto the flitter with a misty grip.

There were lights.

Had the flitter brought her to an installation? Perhaps the very one her father had used to obtain supplies. The one he'd failed to reach at the end.

Despite all her reading, Becca remained unable to determine the exact sequence of events that had led to his death.

The rockfall. Attempts at communication.

Then, several weeks later, the discovery of his body during a response check. He hadn't reported in, so an automated S&R—search and rescue—flier had overflown the area searching for him.

But when the flitter set down, Becca saw that the other lights weren't an installation at all.

They were from another flitter.

Larger than her own. Running lights and light from the cabin.

An open doorway near the nose, with a stairway.
A silhouetted figure standing there.

CHAPTER NINE

When Becca's flitter's door opened, the cold swarmed in and bit through her clothing. Kalv had offered to loan her a coat, but she'd shown him her thermal body coat.

Kalv had laughed.

"What?" she'd said.

"That thing might do you fine around here and maybe a little north, but up where your father was at, well, you might as well be in Bermudas and a button shirt with banana palm patterns."

She didn't know what those were, but it was easy to understand what he meant.

Inadequate.

So she'd brought the extra layers of smart fabric shirts and leggings he'd offered and right now she was glad of them.

The sun was casting mighty shards of light up through the misty atmosphere. Becca had arrived a little earlier than that ETA, and the sun had barely set. At these latitudes, the sunsets could be spectacular.

She'd seen images her father had run out during his time here.

Not directly to her. Only after his death when she'd been struggling, and delving into the records.

Of course, there were a thousand worlds where the sunsets could be spectacular. Many without the chilly climate and lack of infrastructure.

The little flitter's scoop lowered Becca to the rocky ground. It glistened with mica or ice.

The person in the other flitter stayed right where they were, in the doorway. Silhouetted.

Female.

Shana.

Becca started heading over.

CHAPTER TEN

The hull on Becca's flitter ticked and pinged behind her. The steelite cooling from the rapid flight through the air.

"Shana?" Becca called, striding toward the other flitter. Her thermal body coat swayed around her, working to keep in the heat.

Shana made no reply.

The sky was darkening rapidly. The shafts withdrawing and the reds deepening away to black.

"Shana!" Louder.

The silhouette stepped back, deeper into the cabin. Faded away with the blaze of light from within.

Not really a blaze, but the darkness made things relative.

From nearby came some kind of howl. Behind, and to Becca's right.

It was joined by another. Harmonizing. To the left.

The sounds went on and on.

Shana's silhouette reappeared. Holding something.

Three sudden flashes of light burst forth. Accompanied by the crack-boom of some kind of weapon.

As the sounds died away, Shana called over.

"Becca. You should get aboard. Things get ugly right around now."

CHAPTER ELEVEN

The interior of Shana's flitter was wide and open. More like a circular conference room than the kind of cylinder-style of aircraft cabins Becca was used to. Low sofas ringed the margins, with a narrow window running around behind.

Shana punched at some controls and the door whined shut. The air was warm and sweet with the scent of tea and bread.

"You shouldn't have come." Shana stowed the weapon in a wall niche. Some kind of heavy energy blaster. Before the niche sealed up, Becca saw flickering lights along the weapon's barrel. A cooling mechanism?

She didn't know much about weapons.

"My father is dead," Becca said. "I had to come."

"Yep, you tell yourself that, hon', but you will regret it."

"Why?"

"When they're in your head." Shana had moved to a small upright chair across the cabin from the door. She'd folded down a console with a control board and a grid of displays. They flickered like the lights on the weapon.

"In my head?" Becca said. "Explain."

"You'll see." Shana glanced over and focused back on the displays. "Or feel."

"What are you even doing here?" Becca said. "You were supposed to be on Nalla, I thought. Some voltage business you had there."

"I was. Not anymore. When your father contacted me—"

"He would never contact you."

"And yet, he did." Shana tapped and waved at controls on the console. The displays changed. A hum rose from them. Not a background sound, but part of the data she was processing.

"What are you doing?" Becca said.

"Determining if we should stay on the ground, or depart. There's food if you're hungry. I doubt you ate on your flight up. In the little cabinet back there. Fresh rolls and spreads. Some coffee."

"This is what you want to tell me, about food? My father's dead and apparently he contacted you."

"You should let the past lie, hon'. It's not becoming to hash over things again and again."

"He's dead. You're here. Nothing much to hash over. It's all happening right now."

"Get a bite to eat, Becca, and take a seat." Shana worked faster on the console.

Things twisted inside Becca. Shana shouldn't be here. That time with her had been just awful.

Becca sat. Stood again. She went to the cabinet and peered through its glass door. There were sandwiches and instant tacos and flasks of tea and coffee and milky chocolate.

"I had to come," Shana said. "He asked me."

She looked around.

"Right," Becca said. She swiped open the door and took a

tuna sandwich and one of the chocolate flasks. A tab appeared at the top and she twisted it to warm the liquid.

"Will you let me explain?" Shana said.

"I want to know how he died," Becca said. "Can you tell me that? I want to know *why* he died."

Shana nodded. She stood and stepped away from the console.

"We have perhaps fifteen minutes before we can leave safely, so I can tell you what you need to know." She opened the cabinet and rummaged. "At least, I can try to answer questions as best I can."

CHAPTER TWELVE

The tuna sandwich was surprisingly tasty. A good old fashioned standby. The chocolate was sweet and warm and rich. Becca ate and drank slowly while Shana watched her.

"I'm sorry about what happened between us," Shana said.

"Sorry hardly does it. You destroyed my mother and swanned off with..." Becca looked away, unable to speak.

It had happened over the course of a few months.

"You were young. Your mother was on a path of self-destruction already. *Hellbent,* is the term, I think. Striving to find a balance and always overshooting. Or trying to step away from the chemical helpers and finding herself along a dark path of madness. And I'll admit that I could have done more, perhaps, to help her. I *was* attracted to your father."

Now Shana looked away herself. Took a deep breath.

She looked back at Becca.

Shana's expression was hard to read. Sadness? Regret?

Indifference?

"I was young," she said. "Well, perhaps not so young that I

didn't know better, but—and I know it's no consolation—but I would do things very differently now."

"If he was still alive."

Shana remained silent.

Becca sipped from her chocolate. It seemed very appropriate in the cold climate here.

She peered through the long windows.

The light was all but gone, but she thought she saw something move. Hard to tell in the reflections.

"What's out there?" she said.

"You saw it?" Shana said. "I'm going to kill the lights."

She waved and the flitter's cabin fell dark.

Becca blinked and stared out into the last of the twilight.

Shana came up alongside. She smelled of musky sweat and some kind of fruity hair product.

"You loved him, didn't you?" Becca said. Hard to actually get the words out.

"Of course. But I... I was younger than you then. Less worldly. Less—there it is."

Shana pointed into the night.

Something moving out there.

White and ghostly. The size of a house.

Huge eyes.

Staring right at them.

CHAPTER THIRTEEN

The creature seemed to hang just above the ground. Becca's brain tried to parse what she was looking at.

Quadruped? Mammalian?

Had to be along those lines, with all the ghostly white hairs draped from it. It was like those seed pods that burst open, with shredded fibers cast in all directions.

"What is it?" Becca said.

"That, I'm still working on."

"Indigenous life form." Becca leaned closer to the glass. "Big, like an old African ungulate. But hairy. Like a... like a lemur or a husky."

"Not an ungulate. I think it's more like a mastodon, but there's a whole other aspect to it."

"Other aspect? You're meaning that whole *not as we know it* aspect. Something alien."

"Exactly."

"You're *studying* it?"

"Not formally. But this is what killed your father and..."

Becca stopped listening. At least, stopped taking the words in.

This had killed her father.

But it hadn't stomped him to death. Nor gored him with tusks.

It was the alien aspect that had killed him.

"What is it?" she whispered.

"I said I'm still working on it."

"No, not that. I mean... telepathy? I can feel it. Looking deep into me."

The creature stood there staring.

"Your father felt that too."

"It's hurt," Becca said. "You shot at it. You... you hurt one of them. It's sad and angry."

How was she feeling all that?

"It's deceiving you," Shana said.

"No. It's like..." Becca had to breathe. She sat. The seat's cushioning seemed to wrap her up.

"Becca."

"It's as if my soul is drinking up... drinking up its soul. Oh my word."

She couldn't breathe fast enough. She put her hand to her mouth.

The air was thick and tough and filled with fibrous strands. It clung to her tongue, to her cheeks and teeth and throat.

A living thing.

"Becca. Stop. Focus on me."

She looked over.

Shana seemed slow and cadaverous and lined and stolen and broken and tired and wafting away on a sudden tornado of whipping air.

Becca breathed out.

"This is why I had to come," she whispered.

CHAPTER FOURTEEN

Shana leaned back from the window. Outside, the animal continued to stare at them.

"What are they called?" Becca said.

"Locally they're *ghosters,* but formally, they're pharnalle." Shana tapped her fingers on a handheld. "We have to be quiet now and wait."

"Why is it in my head?"

"Quiet now. It won't take long."

The glass darkened until there were only sparse dim reflections from the consoles and devices. The flitter's air circulation systems hummed.

"Shouldn't we be watching it?" Becca said. "Shouldn't we take flight?"

"Best not to watch it. Best to stay put."

Becca could still feel it there, but it was fading.

"How was it inside my head?" she said.

"That's the question, isn't it? When your father came up here he found himself asking the same thing. More. Asking why they were so quiet and slow. Why they watched so much. He was here to paint, you knew that, didn't you?"

"Yes." A crack in her voice surprised Becca.

That was all he'd wanted. Peace. Solitude. An easel, canvas and some quality paints.

"I have some of his pieces now," Shana said. "I recovered them from his home. They're very good, but many are of the ghosters. I... I get the sense that he was becoming obsessed with them."

"But not his doing."

"No. You pick things up quickly." In the gloom, Shana smiled. "I remember that about you."

"And you're secretive and conniving. I remember that about you."

Shana stared for a moment. She looked back at the low glow of her handheld.

"I never meant to be a wedge," she whispered. "I never meant to create the problems I did. I just wanted to..."

"Who cares what you wanted? My mother was heartbroken and you are to blame."

"You father—"

"Yes! My father! Absolutely he shares some of the blame. Of course. He could have been—*should* have been—mature and responsible and lived up to his promises. But he's not here. You are. Besides, I railed at him plenty when he was alive. Believe me."

Shana took a breath.

"We should keep quiet," she said. "We should keep our emotions in check here. They pick up on it all."

From outside came a muted, muffled groaning sound. The ghoster.

Becca could feel it there. In the back of her mind. Ticking away. Burrowing.

Looking for her feelings. Asking her to come outside for some comfort.

It will be all right. We'll make it all so much better. Come out.

Becca stood. Shivered. Took a step.

She stopped.

Focused on Shana.

"It's powerful," Becca said.

"I know it." Shana was on her feet too. She turned toward the cabin door.

CHAPTER FIFTEEN

The flitter gave a shudder.Shana staggered.

Becca felt the ghoster in the back of her head.

Come. Quickly. It's safe.

Not safe with her.

She hurt your mother.

Keep away from her.

More than one voice. More than one ghoster.

Their appeals were so strong. So sensible. So much more to them than just the words.

She moved with Shana. Closer to the door.

Time to go. To go join them.

To join her father.

"How did he die?" she said.

"Die?" Shana said. "Who? What?" She turned a fraction to face Becca.

Shana's eyes were a little glazed. She blinked. As she stared, her left hand reached for the door controls.

Come. Quickly. Safety.

"Where's your weapon?" Becca said.

"Weapon?" Shana said. She seemed dazed. Stunned.

Becca looked around the flitter's cabin. The only light came from telltales on the consoles and the food cabinet. Her eyes were adapting.

Come to us.

How was the voice so strong?

It had cadences to it. Levels of her own voice even.

It wasn't human, but there was a humanity to it. A lilt that was both beautiful and morbidly fascinating at the same time.

Come.

Becca took another step toward the door.

Yes.

"What did he see in you?" Becca said. "If that's not too rude to ask."

She felt like she was a firework cluster firing off randomly. Thoughts failing to coalesce.

"It is rude," Shana said. "But then, you're his daughter. I suppose that you can be about as rude as you like."

Becca found herself drifting toward the door. She felt like she was in a quagmire. Moving through molasses. What even was molasses, besides the saying?

Fractured thoughts. Fragmented.

Come to us. Quickly.

She took another step toward the door. She was almost within reach now.

"I freed him, you know," Shana said. "I gave—"

"You did no such thing."

"I gave him freedom and scope to explore his painting. Something your mother never did."

"Don't bring my mother into this! You were nothing but a soul-sucking leech."

Hush. Quiet now. Come quickly.

"You'll never know any of it."

Quickly. Softly.

Shana reached to the door controls.

Becca took another step.

Shana tapped.

The door hissed and clanked.

Good. Now. Hurry.

Becca took another step. Right to the edge of the opening door.

CHAPTER SIXTEEN

The presence of the ghosters swept into the cabin. A cluster of warm, kind presences.

Welcome. Step out. Join us out here.

But her father had died.

At their hands.

"What happened to him?" Becca cried. She pushed on the door. It was opening too slowly.

"You know," Shana said. Her voice was soft and lost.

Becca looked around at her.

"I wasn't asking you," Becca said.

"They'll never tell."

We'll never tell.

Becca focused on Shana's weapon. Some kind of heavy, chunky pulse rifle.

About a foot long, and as fat as her thigh. Twists and grooves along its side. A thin, trumpet tube stuck from one end. The barrel. There was a fingery electrode sticking out above.

Becca knew the principles. Of course.
But she'd never fired a weapon.
Taking a step away, she scooped it up.

CHAPTER SEVENTEEN

The rifle was heavier than Becca had expected. Of course it would be heavy. Batteries and pulse rounds.

She hefted it and turned to the door again.

Ease, Becca.

The voice was so soft and soothing. The undertones suggested that she should put the weapon down.

Shana stepped in front of her. Shielding the door.

"I can take responsibility for what I did," Shana said. "But I can't take the blame for the way you feel."

"Step aside."

"You don't want to hurt them."

"Me? You were just now blasting at them through the doorway. *Before* they started talking to us. Deceiving us."

We are only truthful. Come. Softly.

Shana shuddered.

"Why were you shooting?" Becca said.

"To protect you. Crossing the ground from your flitter to mine. They would take you."

Into our hearts. Come.

The call was so compelling.

"They killed my father," Becca said.

Shana swallowed.

She stepped aside.

"The trigger button is forward of your right index finger," she said. "Careful with it. There's a kick. The barrel tends to lift with each round. If you're not careful, you'll end up sending a burst into the sky and through the flitter's roof."

"You take it."

"I can't. They're burrowing now. I can't shoot at them. Be careful. Shoot low."

"Low. Got it."

"I'll turn on the flitter's external floodlights. You'll be able to see."

"Thank you."

Becca stepped to the door.

It opened wide.

The lights came on, turning the landscape stark and monochrome.

A trio of the ghosters stood there. Drifting and waving as if loose in a breeze.

Come. You're safe.

She didn't trust them.

She lifted the weapon.

CHAPTER EIGHTEEN

Becca stopped on the first step of the flitter's stairway. She held the weapon level. Tried to aim the muzzle at the feet of the nearest ghoster.

The air was cold.

Becca. Please.

She took another step down.

"You killed my father," she said.

He is with us. Always. We learn so much.

Becca took a breath. Took another step.

"He's dead."

"Becca," Shana said from behind. "Don't hurt them. Please."

The stairway shook a little as Shana stepped down.

Becca felt Shana's hand on her shoulder. An icy, firm grip.

"Destroy them," she said. "Or leave them be."

Come softly.

Be calm.

Rest.

We care.

We are here.

The sense was so overwhelming. So strong.

And yet they'd taken her father.

"What did you do?" she shouted. She took a step closer to the ghosters.

Quiet now child.

Something burned through her then. A hot feeling. Right in the back of her neck. Along her spine.

The rifle fell from her grasp. Clattered on the rocky ground.

"Shana," she said. "Time to fly us out of here."

"I can't," Shana said. "Their call is too strong. I'd crash. It's—"

Becca grabbed her.

Dragged her by the ghosters. Headed for the other flitter.

The ghosters shuffled. Their fur whispered. The bundles shifted and swished.

Go child. Go quickly.

Becca ran.

Stay. Come back. Peace.

Life.

Light.

Oh lustrous beauty.

Stay.

Becca kept running. One voice within that clutter of sound.

She reached her flitter's access ladder. With Shana's sleeve still in her grasp. Becca practically hurled Shana up and in. Dove in after her.

Oh stay. Oh child. Come now.

Becca hauled the door shut. Heard the scraping whirr of the ladder winding in.

Child stay.

"You're not my father," she said.

But the temptation was so strong

Reaching for the flitter's consoles. She thumped the autopilot's home-return button.

The craft gave a deep groan as the engines started.

"We should stay now," Shana said, twisting around for the door.

"Wait," Becca said.

Wait, her father said, somewhere buried within the ghosters' voices.

Then the flitter took to the air.

CHAPTER NINETEEN

It was two days later when Shana sought out Becca. Kalv had given Becca access to his verdant rooftop garden and she was planning on spending the day there making notes on a recorder as she tried to fathom what had happened.

It was good to be among the sweet scents of the tamarillos and heather plants growing almost wild. Hummingbirds darted around, wings blurred.

Shana was sharply dressed in a peach suit, with tiger stripes on the left arm and a black half-hat that shaded her face. She looked more like she was going to a ball than heading to the library.

"How are you doing?" Shana said, stepping through the vegetation.

"Fine, actually." Becca gestured to one of the sling chairs. They were comfy and she was spending far too much time in them.

"Really?" Shana took a seat. "I read your notes and saw the recordings from the flitters. It seemed more like there were shots fired and those creatures were... well, smarter people than me are looking over all that. It sounds like they're about to place a moratorium on travel there."

Like the Yelhena morel. The edges of danger.

"I heard that too," Becca said. "Perhaps no one else will perish."

"So it was a near thing?"

The voices still resonated in Becca's mind. Her father mixed in among them. Perhaps he had found peace.

"It was a near thing."

"And you saved your... stepmother? On the footage it looked as if she was about to walk into the maw of one of those ghosters. You grabbed her."

"Not stepmother." Becca shuddered at the thought. But what would she be then? He father had chosen Shana, in the end. "But I don't know what to call her."

"Well, she's alive, thanks to you."

Becca nodded. And it went both ways. Perhaps. If Shana hadn't shown up, perhaps it would have been Becca herself walking into a ghoster's maw.

"Peace?" Shana said. "Did you find it?"

"I don't know that I found peace," Becca said. "But I found something."

"So you'll be heading away now. Back to the stars."

Becca almost laughed. She'd forgotten really. She had a job.

Taking a breath, she smiled over at Shana.

"I might stay a while," Becca said. "After this, accountancy seems rather pedestrian."

It did. And she didn't know what to put in its place yet, but she would find it.

Even as her father's voice tickled in the back of her mind.

Come. Stay.

AFTERWORD

Thanks for picking up "Becca and the Ghosters". I hope you enjoyed it and found it intriguing and surprising.

This was a story that somehow ended up a long way from where I expected. I knew Becca was looking for answers about her father's death, but the ending even surprised me. Sometimes I feel that my stories lack sufficient character development, so I'm always striving to make more of that.

I like to think that Becca made a shift through the story. That she grew and changed and elevated herself. Perhaps even found something new that she hadn't known she had before.

I wondered if I'd included enough about her relationship with her father. About how things had gone with Shana. As with other writers, I suspect, I find myself second-guessing what to include and what to leave out. Popular writing saws suggest to include just the relevant details, but there are always different schools of thought as to what might be considered relevant and what is not.

Still, thanks again for reading. I hope that you found the

story satisfying. Feel free to drop by the website and say hi—it's the best place to find out about new releases and hear my musings and, from time to time, to find free stories.

Take care.

Sean
January 2025

SEAN MONAGHAN

AWARD WINNING AUTHOR

EXPLORERS OR PRISONERS?

TERRARIUM BLUES

CHAPTER ONE

The glass was pitted and scratched, and Marcy had never seen something so big and solid and transparent.

There was no way through.

Of course.

What crap of a situation. She was going to write her congresswoman, for sure. That's what Marcy's mom would have done.

Serial letter-writer, that woman.

Marcy rapped her knuckles against the glass. She got a knocking sound back, but no sense of how thick it might be.

If you knocked against a thin sheet of glass you'd would hear a kind of chiming. A ringing as those wonderful, clever spreading waves bounced from the margins and interacted.

When she'd been a kid, Marcy's father had bought her a glass chime xylophone. She must have been about six.

Quartz glass. The thing must have set him back a week's salary. Still feeling guilty, no doubt, over cheating on Marcy's mom, and leaving the pair of them right there in Santa Fe.

It had been a glorious thing, that xylophone. It had lifted her spirits with the wonderful, fabulous tones it could make. Just twelve notes, but she'd quickly learned *Mary Had A Little Lamb*, and *Hey Jude*, and *Twinkle Twinkle*.

Twinkle, twinkle, little star.

And here she was, out there among them. Trapped behind this wall of glass with the other members of her expedition.

Marcy put her face up to the glass, cupping her hands around. The glass was transparent, but so thick that the green-blue color had built up so much that she couldn't make out much beyond.

Turning, she leaned back against the glass. She stared back into the murky, dank forest. The air was busy with clusters of tiny black insects. They swarmed like those gigantic flocks of swallows, creating marvelous swirling shapes.

The air was rich with a thick, heavy organic scent. Lush, fast-growing plants, and layers of rot and humus. Fungal growths quickly turning the material into rich nutrients the plants could recycle.

Six days they'd been here. All that original excitement had evaporated.

The ship, the *Puerto Limón*, was wrecked. Their equipment smashed into ten trillion pieces.

Not a good start to exploration of a Goldilocks planet, right?

This had been Marcy's first chance to actually get away from the camp for a minute. The place was wearing on her, that was for sure. Long days, stressed-out colleagues and uncooperative equipment.

Should have stayed back on Earth. There had been that great job going with CubeAntarctic teching glacial rebuilding projects. Some of the stuff they were doing was brilliant. They'd already brought sea levels down by almost six inches.

But nope. She had to chose adventure. Had to throw herself in and just hope someone would toss her a life ring, as her sister would say.

Callie was two years older, and a teacher in Missoula. With a husband and two kids and a nice house with extraordinary views of the Rockies. Yep, when they handed sensible, they gave Marcy's share to Callie.

Which was how Callie had put it.

Marcy put her hands to her face. She was grubby and sore. Hungry too.

Harv had been cooking up this odd kind of nutritional dough. It was sustenance, but it didn't count as food. Not really. Barely palatable. It would keep them alive, but probably it was half the reason for everyone's irritability and grouchiness.

Marcy took a breath and stood again.

It was easy to get despondent.

She'd made her independent little recce and it was time to get back to the camp.

She would face Broll's wrath, momentarily, for going off alone. But frankly no one was making any headway with getting them out of this jam, so someone had to start taking the lead.

There were six of them. Marcy, Harv, Broll, Natalie, Chow and Birjette. Crew of the *Puerto Limón*. A gorgeous vessel. Like a glorious flower that would wrap you up in her lovely petals. Safe and warm and perfect.

Now little more than shredded plastic, splintered glass and rended metal. Shards of her lay scattered across the jungle.

It was only Broll's quick thinking that had ejected the bridge as the ship broke up around them.

The spherical bridge had gently come down, on wide chutes. Inside they'd been protected by a burst of gel. They'd wound up upside down, but that wasn't so bad.

They were alive. Unhurt. And the bridge had a modicum of supplies they could exploit.

Now their little camp was becoming livable.

Now they were starting to accept that they might be here for the long haul.

Now Marcy felt like punching something.

The ship's gym had boasted a punching bag, and a pair of sparring arms for boxing against. Maybe she should be searching the scattered wreckage for those.

"You shouldn't be out here," someone called.

Chow. He could be a little brusk, but he had a wicked sense of humor. Sometimes.

"I needed a break from you lot," Marcy said.

He laughed, still somewhere hidden in the trees. "I know it. That's why I'm out here."

Chow appeared. Bald and rangy, he was a good five inches taller than Marcy. One of the pockets had been torn from his ship overalls. At the left breast. The overalls were designed to be light and easy to work in while aboard the *Puerto Limón,* but really not up to the rigors of camping out in a jungle. If they could find an intact supply pod, then maybe they could all update their outfits.

Thankfully they'd all been wearing decent shoes. High-top hikers with organic, self-repairing soles. The little slippers for shipboard wear would have fallen apart on the first day.

"I don't remember this," Chow said, looking up at the glass wall.

"Nope. But then, your memory is not that great, right?"

"Ouch! There are some prickly plants around, but none as prickly as you."

"Oh, funny."

"That's me. The ship's comedian. This thing is huge." Chow looked left and right. "Has it been here the whole time?"

"I guess so. I looked along the base and there's no evidence of recent work. There are lichens and mosses and creepers growing along the base. A little bit up onto the glass."

"Glass." Chow came closer and rapped his knuckles against it just at Marcy had done. "Pretty huge piece of glass, don't you think?"

"Yep."

"Alien?"

"Nah, I'm thinking it's natural. Like a volcanic dyke or something."

"A volcanic..." Chow trailed off, smiling. "You know what they say about sarcasm and humor, right?"

The lowest form.

"I am but an amateur," Marcy said. "And I defer to your mastery of comic timing and so on."

"Again, you're mocking me!"

Marcy smiled. Even in this situation, they crew could remain upbeat. Or perhaps it was just a way of deflecting and avoiding having to really think about how badly up the creek they were.

"How big do you think this is?" Marcy said.

"We should get some ranging equipment on it." Chow looked up, and left and right again. "Ten meters tall, perhaps? And it runs off vaguely north to south a good kilometer or so."

"A fence," Marcy said.

"Pretty fancy fence." Chow knocked on it again. "It's a little scratched and scuffed. Old. It's been here a while. How come we didn't see it as we came down?"

"Busy with other things." Like ejecting from a vessel that was splintering around them.

"Oh, that's right. But not from orbit?"

They'd spent a few days above Kirchall, the planet, scanning and gathering as much extra data as they could. The scans from the early remote orbiters had been useful, but there was still nothing like getting human eyes on the feeds.

And on the ground.

The whole reason they were here.

"It's big," Marcy said. "I'll give you that. But I think it would be easy to miss. We covered a lot of ground. And then our deorbit went all kinds of wrong."

"It did, it did." Chow sighed. "If only there was some way to use this to our advantage..." He gazed off through the glass.

Thinking.

Marcy shut up and let him do it. Sometimes it was as if Chow had a clockwork brain and it just needed to get all the cogs lined up to spit out an answer.

From the trees came the chirrups of birds. Bright and cheerful. Long, complex songs, mixed in with single bells and clunks and short arpeggios.

Marcy had seen dozens of different birds. Brilliant, fabulous colors, and with long decorative plumes from their tails or heads or wingtips.

It was like an aviary, really, the variations were so amazing.

A chill ran through her.

"We need to map this," she said.

"What?" Chow said, interrupted from his thought process.

Already Marcy was heading back to camp. This was what they did, after all. They were an expedition. They would have had little remote fliers and vehicles to get around and explore, but all of that had been lost in the wreck.

So this would be on foot.

"Where are you going?" Chow said. "I had an idea."

"Walk with me," Marcy said, pushing her way through the damp foliage. "Tell me your idea."

Chow caught up quickly.

"We could move the camp," he said. "Set up in an open space along the glass wall. That way it gives us a hundred and eighty degree protection."

They had no idea yet of the kinds of predators they might be dealing with. The early surveys had made it clear that this was a vigorous and dynamic environment. It was scary to think of some of the gigantic predators that might come strolling by.

Marcy's head went to dinosaurs too often. Good old T-Rex with its tiny little arms more than compensated for by those massive jaws filled with massive teeth.

Save for the Yucatan asteroid, Earth might still be populated by those kinds of killing machines.

"Let's map it first," Marcy said. "Then maybe we can relocate."

Chow muttered something about cartographers, but he followed along.

CHAPTER TWO

It took two days to walk the perimeter.

A six kilometer, by three and a half kilometer enclosure.

More or less rectangular.

They were glassed in.

Twenty one square kilometers of jungle, bounded by a sheer glass wall, a minimum of ten meters high, and possibly as much as ten meters thick.

"It's an impossible volume of glass," Broll said when they gathered back at the camp. "I'm still trying to figure it out." Broll was good pilot, but numbers threw him.

"Close to two million cubic meters," Chow said. "I think it was exuded from a square form. Probably a machine like a road-paving truck, just laying it down as it rumbled along."

"Very evocative," Natalie said. "How does it help us?"

Natalie was the lead biologist, with Harv. All of them were generalists, really, able to fill in on various roles.

"Information is always useful," Birjette said. "We know what we're dealing with. We're in an enclosure. It reminds me of a terrarium. The question is, do we attempt to escape and explore further, or do we stay within?"

As the *Puerto Limón's* captain, Birjette was the one facing the tough questions, but she would still listen to all everyone's thoughts. She still solicited ideas from the crew.

"My question," Broll said, "is whether the glass wall is designed to keep something out, or to keep something in."

From somewhere far off came a deep-throated roar, followed by the squealing of a smaller animal.

"Well that doesn't sound so great," Marcy said.

CHAPTER THREE

A week later, with their camp moved to the enclosure's northwest corner, Marcy saw something through the glass.

On the other side. Moving.

Big. Organic, rather than mechanical.

The glass was probably pretty good in an optical sense, but even the best kind of manufacture was going to have imperfections and irregularities over the space of ten meters.

Marcy smiled to herself. She was coming at it from a human point of view. If these aliens could make a glass wall ten meters thick and six kilometers long, then who knew what kind of manufacturing they were using?

Maybe this was just them being lazy. Perhaps they could actually make glass completely invisible.

Broll wanted to chip out some samples for analysis. Trouble was, no scientific equipment.

They were making regular forays back through the forest to examine the wreckage to attempt to retrieve useful items.

So far they had some water purifiers and the pieces for making a flyer, and various other supplies that would help out with their survival odds. But nothing useful in terms of equipment that would help them with their mission brief.

The *Puerto Limón's* mandate was to conduct orbital and ground surveys with a view to potential colonization of Kirchall.

Technically, now, they were expecting to have to wait at least two months, and probably closer to three, before an emergency relief mission made it out their way.

"What did you see?" Chow said, while he tended the campfire. The area was damp, practically rainforest, but they were doing all right finding and drying wood. A campfire was as much about cooking and safety as it was about making the area seem more homey and cozy. As if they were trying to pretend they were just out at Lake Jollsin for a weekend.

Better times. Marcy and her sister, who was less than a year older, had gone up to Lake Jollsin so often in the summers.

But that was a long time back.

"I guess I saw a dinosaur," Marcy said. "Big lumbering thing. Dark blue with yellow splodges."

"Splodges. Very descriptive."

"How much of anything have you recognized on the other side of the glass?"

"Fair point."

The other four were out on another recce looking for more supplies, and hunting and gathering. Expected to be back an hour before sunset.

Kirchall's day ran to a little over seventeen hours. Sunsets were short and snappy, and the at sunrise, the star practically leaped up from the horizon.

"If we could get a flyer going," Chow said. "We could send it up and over and take a look at the other side."

"That would be nice." They'd talked about scaling the wall too. At some spots around the circumference, there were trees as tall as the wall, and close by. It would have been possible to leap across from the branches.

Sensibly, Birjette banned the idea. Too easy for someone to slip or to slightly misjudge their leap and wind up slamming face-first into the wall, then falling to their death on the ground below.

"If we felled a tree," Marcy said. "You know, chopped it so that it fell just right. We could scuttle up to the top and go take a look."

Chow looked off into the trees. He scanned around.

"You want to try it?" he said. "Now?"

Marcy snorted. "Sure. If we had something to cut with."

Chow pulled a rod from his ragged overalls. It was about six inches long. Shaped like the handle of something.

"What is that?" Marcy said.

"Laser knife. Smart. It knows not to be used as a weapon. But it could cut a notch out of a tree.

"I..." Now Marcy looked into the forest too.

"They'll be hours," Chow said. "I wouldn't worry about it."

"We should run it by Birjette."

"You already know what she'll say."

"I do?"

"Sure. She'll say that she thinks it's a brilliant idea and what a pity we didn't think of it earlier and that we should set to right away and get to cutting."

Marcy snorted. "Like, the exact opposite of what she would say."

"You know it."

"All right," Marcy said. "I know just the tree."

CHAPTER FOUR

It turned out that Chow was a deft hand with the laser knife. The beam hissed and crackled as it cut through the wood. The stink of sap and burning cellulose hung, cloying in the air.

"Disadvantage of a big wall," Marcy said. "No breeze to carry away the smoke."

The enclosure did get windy, from time to time, but it was pretty much always calm close to the wall.

They'd had some massive rainstorms too. They'd had to move their camp the first time, as threads, then streams, then torrents of water had raced through.

Didn't it mean that there had to be an outlet somewhere? Wouldn't the giant terrarium fill up with water otherwise?

Maybe the ground was too porous. Or perhaps the sheer heat of the day made all that moisture evaporate again. That was a big part of rainforests. They were big enough to generate their own weather.

The sky rained, the plants transpired, the water evaporated and it all just rained back down again. Daily.

Surely, though, the enclosed area was too small for that?

And rainforests did have rivers. They weren't entirely closed systems.

"Timber!" Chow called.

The tree creaked and shuddered. It was fatter than Marcy's abdomen, and stood a good fifteen meters tall. There were numerous branches all up the trunk, making it, in theory, easy to climb.

The trees along the margins, by the walls tended to be leafier all up the exposed side. That made sense, really. In the gloom of the forest the trees were mostly be canopy-focused, with few leaves in their lower reaches.

The tree's trunk dropped from its stump. Hit the ground with shuddering, sucking sound.

Birds and insects took flight. Marcy saw something like a monkey, with a long, forked tail, leap from the high branches. It vanished into the trees.

Chow cursed as he backed away.

"What?" Marcy said. She was even farther off.

"Don't know if I got the right angle."

There were few lumberjacks left back home. Mostly forestry management was done by machinery. But back in the day, it had been one of the most dangerous kinds of work. Dealing with a vertical mass that could weigh tons, and trying to make sure that your cuts were precise so the tree fell the right way. Most especially, not on top of the lumberjack themselves.

The tree tipped. Slow at first. Barely perceptible. Then it hit the glass wall.

"You got it," Marcy said.

"Wait."

The tree shuddered again.

Then it began slipping. The bole moved along the wall. Very slowly, but it picked up speed.

Heading toward Marcy.

"Back, back," Chow said. "Into the forest."

The tree picked up speed. Marcy stopped watching and darted back between the trunks. Her feet slipped on the soft ground. She grabbed at branches to stay upright.

From behind came crashing, squealing sounds. The leaves and branches scraping their way to the ground.

Chow was right behind her.

The pitch of the sounds increased. Then, a sudden loud smashing noise.

Something like a peccary ran by her, with three little piglets following along. Any other time Marcy would have thought they were so cute.

The forest fell silent.

"Well," Chow said. "Scratch that, I guess."

CHAPTER FIVE

Birjette was not at all happy about the incident with the tree. Things that, obviously, should have been discussed with the group. Foolhardy, excessively dangerous and with little in the way of clear, useful outcomes.

Marcy kind of agreed, but it was Harv who was able to actually put it into words as they sat around the campfire that evening.

The wood crackled and sparked. On a makeshift wooden spit above, turned some kind of pheasant they'd caught. They had been able to check its flesh for toxins using a couple of their devices.

Eighty-ninety-percent certain it was probably, possibly safe to eat.

But what choice did they have? Eat the alien bird, or just go hungry.

"We can't stay in here," Harv said, nibbling judiciously on the bird's flesh. They had rolled in some logs to sit on. It was almost like being back at Summer Camp.

"Explain," Birjette said. "From my perspective, help is on the way. Months off, I know, but if we can eat and stay sheltered, then we wait. There's no sense in getting ourselves injured. That just compounds the problems."

Harv leaned back and looked skyward. The sun had set, but there were still some streams of light flickering through the sky. The stars were beginning to shine.

"And if help isn't coming?" he said. "Then we could go on eating these fowl and digging up roots for years. But right now, we have the opportunity to examine close up an alien artifact. Something truly odd."

Birjette took a breath.

Marcy nibbled on her dinner too. The meat was strong, but tasty. *Like chicken*, as the old joke went, but really it was more like lizard. Soft and dark, quite succulent. If anyone was going to get sick from it, it would be her. She would happily keep eating.

"My approach," Birjette said, "is cautious. I know. Here we are breathing the air and eating game and local vegetation. Standing in the rain and getting bitten by insects as we sleep."

"Actually," Natalie said, "getting bitten, frustrating as it might be, is a good indication that our biologies aren't too different from the endemic lifeforms."

"But puffer fish," Chow said. "And toadstools. And those poisonous frogs. There are plenty of things in Earth's biosphere that look like food but will kill you deader than dead."

"Whatever that means," Broll said.

"Don't you start, Broll."

"What did I say?"

"Easy people," Birjette said. "We're all in this together, remember? Remember. Yes we're tired. Yes this is frustrating. And we're still a team. We trained together for this. For months.

We knew it might go this way. And we need to rise above and get through this together."

No one spoke for a moment. The fire crackled. From somewhere in the forest a night bird hooted.

"We should go over the wall," Marcy said. "We could build a ladder from two tree trunks. Or even just stabilize a trunk before we felled it. So that it stays upright."

She expected Birjette to object, with a good logical set of reasons why it was too dangerous, unnecessary and a waste of resources.

But Birjette didn't. She stayed quiet. Ate some more of her pheasant.

"So," Marcy said, "Does that mean we have the go ahead?"

CHAPTER SIX

Chow developed an abscess in the sole of his foot. Wet boots. Not a great thing.

One of Natalie's insect bites swelled up like an egg, with the skin turning gray in less than twenty-four hours. There was a school of what had to be larvae swimming around inside, just visible through the taut, translucent skin.

Birjette agreed they should lance the swelling, like a boil. And Marcy, helpful fool that she was, agreed to be the one wielding the needle.

The pustulence burst out like beer from a can dropped from a height. It sprayed across Marcy's face. Nearby, Chow retched and brought up his lunch.

Natalie howled, and passed out.

Harv had darted right in, holding a cloth. He wiped down Marcy's face.

"I'm worried that it might have gone into your eyes," he said. "Or your mouth."

"I'd go bathe," Marcy said. "But I don't know that I trust the water."

They'd discovered a stream that had some pretty pools. Clear and beautiful. They were boiling the water to use for drinking and cleaning. No one was going swimming. Not a chance.

The wound on Natalie's arm had gone ragged and hollow. Clearly the festering was worse than it had appeared from the lump. From the looks, the larvae had been chewing into her muscle, and anaesthetizing her as they did so.

Natalie shuddered and shook.

Marcy shut off some part of herself and set to work with the limited resources of the emergency medical kits. She applied salve and packing and a little automated scurrow bandage that would analyze and deliver medications and healing enzymes as needed.

Marcy bound it all up with an old-style crepe bandage.

She was done, she sat back on her haunches.

Around the camp, everyone was quiet.

"All right," Marcy said. "Birjette, I'm going to go out on a limb here and suggest that it's time to stop waiting around for rescue—that we don't even know is coming—and get on with exploring."

Birjette's face had paled.

"I don't think so," she said. "As we expressed, what if the wall is to keep something worse out? What if the people who made it put it there to protect us?"

"They're not doing a very good job." Marcy pointed to Natalie. "That could have been so much worse."

"So we work harder at protecting ourselves," Birjette said. "That's my role. Balancing the risks and benefits."

Marcy's brother Leo had been in the marines for a decade.

He liked taking orders. It gave him a sense of knowing what to do and knowing where he stood.

"And," he'd said to her one time, "sometimes the orders seem stupid. And I know they're stupid. And I know that they're risky and will have little payoff or whatever. But I still do them. Because of the *things I don't know*. There's always a bigger context. I'm a cog in a gigantic machine. If I question why I'm going around in a circle and then just arbitrarily stop, the machine grinds to a halt. People look at their clock and they don't know what time it is. Or the guy at a concrete pour finds his cement has set inside the truck because the mixer has stopped. Cogs don't question, they just do their job."

Leo was sweet, and smart, if a little insecure. But he'd had some good lessons in letting the people who make the decisions make the decisions.

Even if, in this case, Marcy was pretty sure that Birjette didn't know any more than anyone else trapped on the planet.

"What's the benefit of staying here?" Marcy said.

Chow looked at her, scowling. Disapproving of the challenge to Birjette.

"It's a known quantity," Birjette said. "And frankly the wall is protection. It keeps us in a limited frame."

"I like that," Harv said. "Nasties in here, but they're contained."

"And that dinosaur you thought you saw," Broll said. "I haven't seen anything like that in here. A few small cats and little deer."

"The peccaries," Chow said.

"Yeah, those. No iguanodons or spinosauruses."

"So let's go find them," Marcy said.

Birjette sighed.

"We need to get more established here," she said. "We're

doing a good job of retrieving useful materials from the wreckage. Our camp is looking almost habitable."

She was right. They'd been able to gather all kinds of things from wall panels and insulation and trusses and spars to clothing, machinery and packaged foodstuffs. A reel of two hundred meters of black woven nylon-carbon cord. Already Marcy could imagine a hundred uses for that.

They would be able to last through.

But not if people kept getting sick and injured.

Which was going to happen whether or not they went off exploring.

Natalie had gotten bitten while asleep. Chow's foot had really just been carelessness on his part. The cut on Harv's hand had been from handling a panel that he was dragging into place to become part of their shelter.

Marcy opened her mouth to say something, but from the corner of her eye she saw Chow give the slightest of shakes of his head.

She took a breath and stayed quiet.

CHAPTER SEVEN

Natalie didn't wake the next day. Nor the next.

On the fourth day, her breathing was shallow and her heart was fluttering.

Broll started weeping. Chow could hardly walk in his abscessed foot. Thankfully Harv's hand was healing.

Birjette called Marcy aside.

The forest was filled with bird calls. It was like being back home, except that the songs were all different and odd. Clearly not of Earthly origin. Beautiful chimes and fabulous trills.

Birjette and Marcy stood in a small clearing. A tree had come down, tearing a hole through the forest. Lush ferns and saplings were quickly filling the space. A group of antlike creatures formed a line along the fallen trunk, carrying leaves and clods of dirt and other bugs.

"This is failing," Birjette said. Her face was streaked with dirt and sweat.

"Yep," Marcy said.

"You think there's a way out?"

"Not especially. But..." What did Marcy think? Not that they were likely to escape, but right now their situation was pretty poor. And growing worse day by day.

"Natalie's going to die," Birjette said. "I never lost a crew member."

Marcy didn't know what to say. Birjette was right. Natalie's condition was deteriorating. The wound wasn't healing. *Necrotic* was probably the word.

If they had the skills and equipment, they could have probably amputated. But then, if they had the *Puerto Limón's* medical bay, they could have saved the arm. And her life.

"And Chow," Birjette said.

"What?" Marcy said.

"Chow's not letting on, but his foot is ruined. Infected. He's been getting me to clean out the abscess. I say reassuring things, but he knows."

Marcy trembled. A shiver ran up her spine.

"We need a ship," she said.

"Yes we do. And we have to wait for help."

"Which we assume is coming. But we don't know."

"Exactly."

"You want me to scale the wall and go see what's out there?"

"I can't make you."

"I know. I want to. Even if there was a dry area. A cave. A clean... river... I don't know. Something."

"Any information is better than none. I've been too focused on surviving without further injury, but it's not working."

"I'll go," Marcy said. "I know how."

"I know you do. Harv and Broll can help you."

"Good. Now?"

"Maybe first thing in the morning. It's late in the afternoon now."

"I can be up on the wall in a half an hour," Marcy said. "Make a first recce."

Birjette frowned. "Have you been up already?"

"No."

"But you've got a means of scaling all prepared?"

"I have."

"Why does that not surprise me?"

Marcy didn't have a reply.

"What is it?" Birjette said.

"One of *Puerto Limón's* structural trusses. I used cord to pull it up a tree, then tied it on and let it fall out to connect the tree to the wall. Like a bridge."

"Right. Like that confidence course we did in early training."

"Yes." The course had been out in Adirondacks, with high-wires and flying foxes and mud crawls.

"All right then. Take Harv, at least. One recce now, and report back before nightfall. Then at first light you can go for a longer looksee."

"Sounds good to me, boss."

CHAPTER EIGHT

Insects buzzed around as Marcy, Birjette and Harv made their way to Marcy's makeshift bridge partway along the northern wall. The evening air was cooling, and the sun cast brilliant light through the trees and through the glass of the wall.

Marcy led them to the spot and put her hand on the rough trunk.

Tempting as it had been to climb even higher in the tree when she'd mounted the truss, Marcy had resisted. She'd been exhausted from the effort, it had been growing late, and she'd gone up the tree about as far as she safely could. The branches were thinner looked fragile, and when she'd been up there, getting ready, Birjette had already been expressing some anxiety about people getting hurt and sick.

It wouldn't do for Marcy to fall and kill herself. Or, worse for everyone, fall and be badly injured. Then they would be obliged to care for her, when everything was already a struggle.

At the base of the tree, Birjette looked up, casting her eye across Marcy's handiwork.

The truss was a little over six meters long. Made up of three long straight poles. Parallel, in a triangular box-form. They were joined by a zigzag of triangles, each about a half a meter on a side. Structurally very strong.

The truss stood at about a forty degree angle. The overlap at the top of the wall was about a meter. Marcy had anchored it with a cord, weighted at the end. The cord hung vertically from where the truss met the wall.

A bird stood about halfway along. Black wings with long, curly tail feathers. The bird bent and wiped its beak on the pole.

"Some effort," Birjette said. "It must have been pretty hard to haul that up there."

"The truss is carbon fiber and aluminum," Marcy said. "It's pretty light. I climbed the tree with the cord and looped it over a branch, then hauled the truss up from the ground."

"You must have had to climb several times."

Marcy shrugged. "I'm a good climber."

"All right then. And you believe that it's secured?"

"Tied on to the tree at this end, and weighted at the far end." Marcy had wound the cord around the trunk and into the truss, back and forth several times. There was enough flex in the bindings that the tree could move in the breeze without anything snapping.

"You're pretty brave," Harv said. "I could have helped."

"I know. Sorry. I kind of wanted to do a proof-of-concept before bringing anyone else in."

"Underhanded."

"I know." Marcy looked over at Birjette, whose face was a mask. Keeping her thoughts close.

A balancing act, being captain.

"All right," Birjette said. "Get to it. Don't fall out of the tree. Rope yourself to the truss. Tell me what you see from the top."

"On it, boss," Marcy said.

CHAPTER NINE

Harv complained about getting sap on his hands, but they quickly made it up and across the truss onto the top of the wall.

Marcy found herself peering over the wall as she came toward the upper end of the truss. Needing to know what was out there.

Would it be better for the crew? Did the forest run on endlessly?

Their observations from orbit had suggested that. Like Earth, Kirchall boasted all kinds of environments. Dry, dusty deserts. High barren mountains. Vast oceans. Polar caps.

And numerous tracts of vegetation. Temperate forests, prairie and savannah, humid jungles.

It seemed logical that the jungle they'd found themselves in would continue as far as the eye could see.

So when she got high enough, she was startled to find herself looking out at some kind of tan-brown rock outcrop. But it was far off. The top of the wall was at least ten meters across, as they'd surmised earlier. She didn't have that much extra height.

"Stop craning for a look," Harv said behind her. "Watch your footing.

"Thank you." They were both roped up, and had transferred the tie point away from the tree, into the truss itself, so if they fell they would, in theory, just pendulum, rather than slam back into the trunk.

But it wasn't exactly like climbing a ladder. The triangular structural became like badly-angled rungs, and the upward angle of the truss itself made it kind of a precarious trek.

So Marcy kept her head down, and focused on climbing.

Soon she reached the top, and she still didn't look. She reached back and helped Harv transfer from the truss to the top of the glass wall.

"Thanks," he said.

"How's the hand?"

"Sore. I might have opened the wound up again."

"Let's take a look." They'd both brought along small backpacks, and Marcy had a makeshift first aid kit with items pillaged from the camp medical kit.

Harv showed her his hand, and the wound, which kind of followed his life line. The wound was scabbed, but weeping in a couple of spots.

Marcy swung her bag around, got the medical kit and used a cotton ball to wipe away at the ooze.

"I'm going to tape it again," she said. "We never should have left it open."

"We need to save the tape though." They didn't have much of the tape left, not after Chow's foot and Natalie's arm, and a few other cuts and scrapes.

"No sense in saving it," Marcy said.

"What if someone gets hurt worse?"

"What if your hand drops off?"

"Oh."

Being judicious, Marcy taped off most of Harv's wound.

Birjette called up from below. "Are you all right up there?"

"We're good," Marcy called, waving out.

"Don't stand so close to the edge."

Birjette was like a mom in many ways.

"We'll be back soon," Marcy called. She turned to Harv. "Ready?"

"You bet."

Together they started across the wall. As they went, more of the outcrop and its surrounds came into view. There was some kind of a scrawny scraggly tree clinging near the top. White.

Harv came to a stop.

"What?" Marcy said.

"Look down."

Marcy did.

She was staring into the glass. It was coated with a thin layer of dust and grit. In a few places were splodges of gray-green growth, like some kind of lichen.

But there was something below. Down in the glass itself. Movement.

Within the glass.

Marcy knelt and rubbed away some of the grime.

Harv was doing the same. He scraped with a little piece of metal he must have brought along. Like a knife.

"People," he said. "There are people down there."

"People?" Marcy said, right away imagining some trick of refraction that was showing him the rest of the crew back at camp.

But it wasn't that at all.

There were people down there.

Bending their necks and looking up.

"They're odd," Harv said. "Aliens."

It was hard to tell through so much glass, but he was right. They weren't regular humans at all. Different hair, different gaits, different eyes.

They were perhaps five meters below. On a walkway.

"Exhibit," Harv said. "We're just an exhibit." He stood and started walking toward the far side of the wall.

"An exhibit?" Marcy said, still looking at they people. They had practical clothes in a variety of colors. There were different sizes. Adults and children. Bipeds. Hominids. Perhaps their skin was a little green, but then, that might just be an effect of the glass.

"Yeah," Harv said. "Come look."

Marcy found it hard to tear herself away.

"Come on," Harv said.

Marcy stood and joined him a couple of meters back from the wall's edge.

Ahead of them, a desert vista stretched out for kilometers. Rough and rugged terrain, with pits and gullies. There were a few patches of scrubby vegetation.

"I wish we had lenses," Harv said. "A decent pair of binoculars."

"Yep," Marcy said, looking back. She could see the tops of some of the trees of their enclosure.

How could that exist right next to the desert?

"We need to walk the top of the wall," she said. "We should have brought along more food."

Marcy looked back toward the truss. They would have to return and stock up.

Was it weird that she actually felt excited? After all this time just trying to survive, now there was a real mystery. Something to get her head around other than just staying dry and fed, and trying not to get hurt.

"Desert," she said, looking again into the area. She took another step forward.

"Yes. Keep away from the edge."

"I will." Marcy squinted into the desert. The sun was low, but bright. The air was dry. She could practically smell the sand.

Harv came up beside her.

"How far are we from the corner?" Marcy said. "I think we're closer to the western wall."

"Ah..." Harv looked away. "Maybe a couple of... oh."

Harv had seen what Marcy had just seen. There was another wall there. Bounding the desert. Running south to north.

There might have been more greenery beyond.

"More than an exhibit," Marcy said. "More than a terrarium. It's a whole zoo."

CHAPTER TEN

Through the time that Marcy and Harv walked west toward the desert's wall, the alien people below watched them. Some followed along, some actually pointed.

"I feel like I'm on show here," Harv said. "As if I should perform some tricks or something."

"I think that getting up here was a trick in and of itself," Marcy said.

They'd relayed back to Birjette what they'd seen and what their plan was.

She'd offered up some soft objections, but let them go.

"The sun will be down soon," she'd said.

"We know it. We're walking almost straight into it."

"Back here by dark, all right?"

"You got it, boss."

"I think you can stop calling me 'boss'. Birjette is fine, but 'Captain' if you're in trouble."

"I'm never in trouble," Marcy said, with a laugh.

"You are edging toward it right now."

"I know it. See you soon."

The wall that ran by the desert, leading off to the north, was at a crossroads, effectively.

The wall that Marcy and Harv were following continued on west, and the desert wall met their south-running forest wall.

The south west corner had more forest, but it was different to the one where the *Puerto Limón* had come down. There was more blue to the leaves and more variation in their shapes. The foliage was so dense that Marcy couldn't see the ground at all. Even straight down the walls' faces.

Something big was moving through the trees, but hidden by the foliage. The sounds of thick breathing, and heavy footfalls came through the forest. Was that the dinosaur thing Marcy had seen?

The north west corner was more like grasslands. Sparse and brown, with low, rolling hills.

"It's like South Dakota," Harv said. "I half expect to see signs for Wall Drug."

"We can relocate," Marcy said, mind whirring. "We're going to need more equipment. A way to transport things. We'll need a buggy of some kind. Maybe we can recce into the blue forest. Camping in the prairie is going to be a whole lot nicer than where we've been stuck... what?"

Harv was staring at her.

"What?" she said again.

"We can't move Natalie. And Chow ain't climbing any trees any time soon."

Marcy looked down. There were more of the alien people moving through the central part of the walls.

Why weren't they visible from below? Only from directly above seemed odd.

"I'm spit balling," she said. "Considering. We need a better long term plan."

"Dragging us to the prairie is a long term plan? Don't we even need to talk about these aliens inside the wall, whom we'd never even seen before? What about this whole grid of enclosures here? I'm assuming that this goes on a ways. Like... all around the planet? Oh, no, we would have seen that from orbit, wouldn't we?"

"You would hope."

"What if we're elsewhere? What if in the crash we were taken to another locations?"

"How?"

"How do you make walls of glass that are kilometers long?"

"To think," Marcy said, "that I was hoping we might find some answers up here. All we get are more questions."

"Come on, Marcy, how long have you been a researcher? You know that's the way it goes. That's science for you."

"I know it. But, still, I was hoping."

Marcy took a step back. She went to the middle of the intersection between the walls. Really there were no joins. The walls just continued on, crossing over as if stamped from a mold.

She knelt down, peering at the people below.

Some of them were watching her back.

"You know what we need?" she said.

Harv sighed. "No. No idea."

"We need a pad and some marker pens."

"Pens? What, are you going to give our alien friends here a *seminar*?"

"Communication. Wait. Do we have the old Pioneer plaque?"

Back in the early days of space exploration, a couple of probes had been sent out on a tour of Jupiter, Saturn, and perhaps other planets. The probes had kept on going. Maybe heading for Aldebaran.

The researchers, knowing that the craft would drift on away through interstellar space, had included a kind of a plaque with diagrams and images about humans, the solar system and other information.

With a kind of a binary way of breaking it down to be understandable.

"The Pioneer plaque?" Harv said with a shrug and a rolling of his lips. "Like the probes?"

"Yes."

"I guess in the *Puerto Limón's* databases."

"Then let's go find those." Marcy stood and started back toward her truss.

"Wait up," Harv said. "What are you thinking."

"I'm thinking we need help, and short of chiseling through the glass, I can't think of another way to communicate with them."

CHAPTER ELEVEN

Marcy spent three weeks scouring the wreckage again. Digging up cables and actuators buried in the mud, handing broken silicon drives to Broll to fix. Finding textiles caught in trees and saturated cushioning lying on the bottom of ponds.

In between, she made frequent visits to the top of the wall. Just to check that the aliens were still there.

Chow's foot got worse. Harv's hand wound opened up again and required daily attention. He was in a lot of pain.

Natalie died.

It sent a chill through everyone. As if bringing home their situation.

Nothing was improving.

Broll managed to fix a display and figured out how to power it with a battery. He began a search for the Pioneer plaque, but the drives were damaged and the information he could pull from them was limited. Very limited.

"I found some games," he said one evening at the campfire.

"I found the datasets and schematics for the *Puerto Limón*. Lot of use all that is with the ship scattered across our enclosure, right?"

"Pretty scattered," Marcy said. The days were growing cooler. Kirchall's angle of inclination was just fourteen degrees, so its seasons were more subtle than Earth's.

"So," Broll said. "I'm sorry about getting the Pioneer plaque for you. You've gotten us a whole lot of stuff lately. Looks better for us than it has for a while."

"Still going backwards," Marcy said. "We're not going to last long."

"It's getting better. Natalie notwithstanding, I think we've got a good shot."

"Maybe." Getting the Pioneer plaque had been a long shot anyway. As if it would make a difference.

"I think I can remember some of it," Broll said. "And I'm sure we can figure it out if we work on it together. The five of us."

"Remember it? The Pioneer plaque?"

"The states of hydrogen, and a way of explaining binary? A naked man and a naked woman. The location of the solar system. If you could understand the whole thing."

Marcy sighed. Her shoulders slumped.

"What?" Broll said.

"I got fixated on it. You know, a way of communicating with aliens. We don't need all that. You'd think my training would be better than that."

"To be fair, we never expected to be stuck in a terrarium with our ship more or less reduced to sand."

"Sure. But I should have been smarter here. We just need to make our own plaque, using our own ideas. Binary and language and what have you. It can be two way. I mean, the

Pioneer plaque was a one way thing. They never expected a reply."

"Couple of million years, I heard," Broll said. "Before it was likely to be found. At best."

"Right. But we can talk to these people."

Broll *tsked* with his tongue.

"So what do you need?" he said.

"Something to write with." Marcy looked over at the pile of panels she'd retrieved from the wreckage. "And I need to write big."

Broll held a stick into the fire. The end caught alight, flaring like a candle. He brought the stick back and blew out the flame.

"Happy birthday," Marcy said.

"Thanks. Not for a few months. Oh. I see. Blowing out a birthday candle. Right." He held the stick toward her. A tendril of smoke rose from the tip, twisting and winding.

"Oh!" she said, realizing. "Charcoal!"

CHAPTER TWELVE

Marcy climbed the tree and crossed the truss. Morning sun shone across the landscape, glinting on the glass and scorching the desert. The heat was actually quite wonderful through Marcy's seemingly perpetually damp clothes. Her skin tingled.

Using a length of cord she hauled the pre-written panel up the wall. Broll and Birjette guided the panel for the first couple of meters, then let it go and stepped away.

The panel was over a meter square. It clattered against the wall. Hopefully her crude charcoal drawings were big enough and clear enough that the people in the center of the wall would be able to make them out.

She'd drawn a picture of herself. Clothed, rather than naked like the woman in the Pioneer plaque. Wearing what she hoped looked like the roughened ship overalls that were still hanging from her.

They had been washed often during the time here. Dried in the sun.

She'd written the word 'Help' in English. Then added some crude images of herself eating, and one that she hoped looked like her dead. Lying at the bottom of the picture.

That could be seen as her, or as Natalie.

Would it work? Would it communicate to them?

At least she could erase it and try something different.

Maybe the hydrogen phase thing and binary language as in the Pioneer plaque.

Who knew?

The panel came up over the edge of the wall and Marcy stepped back to pull it right on up.

She took the edge and carried the panel across until she could see the people below.

They'd been there every time that she'd come up onto the wall. Adults. Families with children. All with their odd hair and odd gaits.

Many of them looking up at her.

Marcy hauled the panel into place and laid it face down.

She knelt beside it

Below her, the people were stopping and looking up. Some of them pointed.

This was a ridiculous idea. Pictures drawn in charcoal.

She needed a better way to tell the story.

Below, many people walked on by, not even looking up. Even though others were pointing.

"How does it look there?" Birjette called.

Marcy looked over. Birjette was walking across the top of the wall. She'd climbed the tree and crossed the truss.

Birjette had never come up before. Marcy and Harv had made three trips, and Broll had joined Marcy on one other, on a day when Harv's hand was just too sore.

"No better than anything else, I think," Marcy said.

They had tried other things to get the attention of the people below. Shouting at them. Miming distress. Nothing had worked.

Birjette came and knelt next to Marcy.

"At least you're trying something," Birjette said. "We need a change in our circumstances. Soon."

"I know it."

"Any other ideas?"

Marcy snorted. It made her nose run a little.

"What?" Birjette said.

"Move our camp up here, maybe."

"Say more about that."

"Well, it's exposed, which is a disadvantage. And we'd have to return to the forest fairly often to hunt and gather."

"Advantages?"

"Dryer, lighter. And we'd be right in front of these people all the time. They would see us up here."

"Other disadvantages."

"Restless sleepers might roll and fall off the wall."

Birjette actually smiled.

"And," Marcy said, "it would be colder at night. And we would always have to make recces for resources. Harv might struggle getting up here. And I don't know how Chow would, with his foot."

"We can make a travois. See how that would go."

"He won't like it."

"Maybe not." Birjette rolled her shoulders. "Keep going."

"Well, then there's the opportunity to explore the other regions. Perhaps we can find materials we can use. Perhaps there might be better game and vegetation."

"Hmm." Birjette stood and took a few steps, looking off into the desert area. "There?"

"It looks barren, but it has a vigorous biosphere." Marcy sighed.

"How can there be desert here and rain forest right back there? There must be a whole lot more going on."

"Yes." Marcy peered into the glass. The alien people kept watching her.

"All right," Birjette said. "Let's start exploring some more. After all, that's what we were sent here to do. And I'm feeling less confident of rescue."

"We're still within the time frames, though." Marcy stood, catching a glimpse of something in the corner of her eye.

Movement below.

A grouping of some of the alien people. They seemed to have a kind of machine with them. A blocky thing, with arms and straps. On wheels. Turquoise.

"There's something going on below," Marcy said.

Birjette came over.

The aliens were doing some kind of set up with the machine. Spreading out the arms, lowering them to the floor of their space.

"I know you told me about it," Birjette said, "but I still don't follow how they're within the glass, and we can see them from here, but we can't see them from the ground. I mean, it's clearly a corridor through the middle of the wall. And the wall is transparent."

"I guess they know more about glass and light than we do."

"Explain."

"They've made the corridor invisible. They can still see out into the area, but..." Marcy trailed off, looking back along the wall.

"What?" Birjette said.

"I hadn't considered it before, but the walls are kilometers long. Unless these people have a strangely different physiology to us. They're not walking all of that distance just to look into the trees and the desert and the other places."

"Perhaps it's a variation on the invisibility," Birjette said. "Maybe the length they travel inside is less than the external length."

"Okay, that's mind-bending."

"Yep. What are they doing down there?"

The people seemed to have their machine set up, and they were activating it. A kind of cylindrical part on the top started spinning. It might have been a couple of meters across."

"Step back," Birjette said.

Marcy stepped with her, moving away so they weren't directly above the spinning cylinder.

Out over the forest, one of the bigger birds was gliding along above them. The bird made wide circles, but stayed within the confines of the walls. As if the walls continued up invisibly.

This place just kept being stranger.

"Oh," Birjette said.

The spinning cylinder was rising now. And spinning faster.

Marcy and Birjette kept stepping back.

The cylinder burst through the top of the wall.

The glass didn't shatter. It kind of melted away. Drips of it splattered around. Marcy found herself jumping, but the glass wasn't hot. Molten, but more like ice water. As if this wasn't glass at all, but rather just water ice.

The cylinder kept rising. A meter. Two meters. Three.

Still spinning. The sound was quiet, but still piercing. A whine, with an underlying deeper drone to it.

The cylinder began slowing.

"They used it to cut through," Marcy said. "What is this about?"

"We might soon see," Birjette said, pointing. "There's a hatch on the side of it."

Marcy glimpsed the hatch as it spun by again. Human-sized.

The cylinder was still moving at a couple of revolutions per minute. Still slowing.

"Are they inside it?" Marcy said.

"Separate parts. The spinning exterior, and a fixed interior."

"The technology is just baffling. Why? How?"

"We'll get answers. In a moment."

The hatch swept around again. Once more, and the next time it came to a stop.

The whining, droning stopped. The machinery hummed. There were markings on the side that might have been lettering. The cylinder was rifled. Very tightly. A kind of a drill, but more like something for boring tunnels than for cabinet-making.

The hatch was inset from the rifling, and the top of the mechanism overhung the cylinder.

The hatch opened.

CHAPTER THIRTEEN

Three people stepped from the stationary cylinder. They were each a little taller than Marcy. Thinner builds, with high shoulders and multi-jointed arms. Their thighs were longer, and their calves were short. Their feet were wide and flat.

They wore loose, colorful clothing made from a variety of shaped panels. On their feet they had something like moccasins, and on their heads they had wide-brimmed hats with bright jewels all around the brims.

Their eyes were small and their noses were big.

"Hi," Marcy said, stepping forward, and raising her hand. "I'm Marcy."

"Hello, Marcy," the middle one said. "I am Turlenain. We are sorry for your situation. We have been working to come help you."

Marcy just about fainted right there. Turlenain's accent could have come from Alabama or Georgia. Their inflection was rich and rolling.

"You speak English," Marcy said.

"We received all of your ship's transmissions. We have received information on your survival issues in the forest. We hurried, but our resources are limited."

"Limited?" That seemed odd, if they were the people who'd built this complex.

"Limited," Turlenain said. "And fractious. Many of us believed that there was no reason to offer help. After all we are as trapped as you."

"Trapped?"

"It is a long story. I think that's the phrase you use." Turlenain looked at the other two aliens with them.

"I would use that phrase," Marcy said. "I want to hear more of that story, but right now we have people who are hurt. We're holding on by the slimmest of threads down there. Is there something you can do to help?"

"A moment, please." Turlenain and the other three stepped back. They talked quietly among themselves. There were clicks and buzzes in their language.

"This is troubling," Birjette said to Marcy.

"How so?"

"Turlenain said they were as trapped as us. But look at that machine. And the people below just walking around. Clearly their understanding of 'trapped' is different to ours. Their situation is quite different."

"We need to get to the bottom of that."

"Absolutely."

Then Turlenain's group broke. Without looking at Marcy or Birjette, the three of them returned through the hatchway in the cylinder.

"Turlenain?" Marcy called.

But Turlenain didn't turn. The hatch closed up and the cylinder began descending. Without spinning.

"What just happened?" Birjette said.

Marcy walked closer.

"They left?" Birjette said. "Without offering anything?"

"Cultural distinctions, perhaps," Marcy said. "They couldn't offer help, and so left. The conversation was over."

The top of the cylinder passed by Marcy's eye level. The top was rough and rippled. It looked like the pattern sand would make across a dune. Some interesting technology there, surely.

"Marcy," Birjette said. "Step back. We're done here."

"We're not," Marcy said.

"Yeah, we are. Let's talk some more about relocating. That prairie area might work well."

"It might."

The top of the cylinder passed by the level of the top of the wall. Around the edges of the hole, the level began forming up again. Little blobby pieces of the glass rolled into place. It was like spackle. Rebuilding itself.

Marcy jumped out. She landed with a thump on the top of the cylinder.

"Marcy!" Birjette shouted.

Marcy descended. It was like being on a freight elevator. The roof shivered. The air was cool. The reforming glass smelled of burning fabric. It was strange.

"Marcy!" Birjette called from the edge. The new glass had formed up perhaps thirty or forty centimeters, closing off the hole slowly. The glass kept building up on the inside of the shaft.

"It's all right," Marcy said. "I'm going to talk with them on their ground. See if I can convince them that we could work together."

She stepped back a little so she could see Birjette's face.

Birjette was clearly torn. Perhaps wrestling between jumping in too, and knowing that she had a responsibility to the rest of the crew.

"Stay," Marcy called. "I'll be back soon."

"I wish I could believe that."

Then she was out of view as the cylinder continued to descend and the spackle spread, closing up the top of the shaft once more.

CHAPTER FOURTEEN

The cylinder came to a stop with a sudden thump.

Only just below the ceiling of the wall's cavity. There was no way for Marcy to squeeze through.

The air was cool, with a metallic tang to it. Presumably if Turlenain and the other two had been able to breathe up top, then Marcy should be able to breathe down here.

Above her, the glass kept rebuilding itself. What kind of mechanism could that be? Humans were pretty clever with materials now, but there was probably no one who knew how to make glass reconstruct blob by blob.

Marcy lay down on the cylinder's rippled roof. The material was cold against her hands and belly. She peered through the gap. It was perhaps five centimeters from the bottom of the shaft to the top of the cylinder.

There were people out there. Walking around the machine's legs. Some of the people looked, but many just walked on by. Mostly they were in pairs, but a few were alone, and many had children with them.

Above her, the glass kept filling in. Quickly. If she couldn't get out of the hole, would the rebuilding descend and crush her? Or entomb her in glass?

The cylinder gave a quiet clank from the side. Marcy moved around and through the gap she saw Turlenain and the other two step from the cylinder.

She was about to call out, when the cylinder moved. It jerked back, sliding horizontally away from under the hole.

Which gave Marcy a gap right away.

She swung around and hung from the lip. She checked below, then pushed away and dropped to the ground.

All around her, the alien people stopped and stared.

The machine rumbled as it moved away.

The space was light. The corridor through the glass continued on away ahead for ages. Kilometers? Did it run right on through the wall?

"You should not have done that," Turlenain said, turning to her and taking a step forward.

CHAPTER FIFTEEN

They tossed Marcy into a glass cell, far along the wall.

The cell was spherical. Like an air bubble in the glass. A little over two meters across. There was dust in the base and the refraction of light made the surroundings quite surreal.

She could see back into the forest, but everything was bent up and lensed to the extreme.

The other way, in the corridor, there were very few people now. Only one or two going past every ten or fifteen minutes.

They seemed to be very distant, then swelled rapidly, reaching maximum size right outside, with their heads and legs apparently bent and stretched almost to the top and bottom of Marcy's sphere.

Clouds drifted through the sky, swelling and shrinking.

Marcy sat in the sphere's base, trying to get comfortable. You would think that there would be some kind of cushion or blanket.

It turned out that she didn't have to wait long.

A small delegation came along the corridor, dressed brightly, and without hats. It was Turlenain who opened the circular glass hatch and ushered her out.

"This is Brewellan," Turlenain said. "Brewellan does not speak your language, so I will translate."

There were sixteen in the delegation, with, presumably, Brewellan at the head. They were a little shorter and a little taller than Turlenain, with an aged look to their eyes.

Brewellan looked Marcy up and down. Muttered something quick and sharp to Turlenain.

Turlenain turned to Marcy, but Marcy spoke first.

"Tell me how you are trapped," she said. "You seem to be doing all right to me."

"Brewellan wants to know how you had the audacity to enter our area."

"Your area?"

"These corridors belong to us. We have been here for decades. No one has ever encroached into the space before."

"Is that how you're trapped?" Marcy said. "These corridors are like your enclosure. Like us out there?" She pointed toward the forest.

Brewellan muttered some more and Turlenain translated.

"Yes. We have been here some one hundred years. We are the third generation of our kind to have lived in these glass tunnels."

"Generations," Marcy whispered.

"Three. Some, here, are fourth generation."

"What do you eat? Where are your homes?"

"Elsewhere in the tunnels. It was hard for our progenitors, but they did have supplies. And the means to propagate foodstuffs."

"Farming. You're talking about farming in here."

"Yes."

"What do you use for soil?"

"Hmm. Perhaps we could say that it is a closed system."

"Closed! For a hundred years. That's some terrarium all right."

Marcy looked out through the glass into the forest. It still wasn't clear to her how she could see out and through, but not within.

"How often do you get out?" she said. "You drilled that shaft through the glass. Do you make other recces out into the world? Could your drill go sideways?"

Brewellan muttered some more words. Perhaps agitated.

"Brewellan says that you should focus on answering his questions, not asking more of your own."

"I haven't heard any questions yet. And I'm not sure that you people ask the right questions anyway. You should be looking for a way out of here."

"Brewellan asks why you jumped through the hole."

Marcy smiled. Sheer stupidity, perhaps.

"Spontaneity," she said. "You were the first contact we've had since we got here. And you were leaving. I didn't want to let you go."

Turlenain translated.

Brewellan said some more.

"You are a very odd creature, Marcy," Turlenain said. "Very odd indeed."

"Tell me about that drill, though."

"The drill, as you call it, is an old piece of equipment."

"You could use it to escape."

"You saw the glass," Turlenain said. "It remakes itself. Very quickly."

"We can help each other."

"How?"

"I don't know yet, but I know we can. Like, I can figure out how to stop the glass regrowing."

"You can? How?"

"As I said, I don't know yet, but I know I can. Do you have labs?"

"Labs? I am familiar with your language, but not that word."

"A laboratory. Where we can do experiments."

"We?"

"We can help each other."

"Do you think that we need help?"

"I do."

"What makes you think that?"

"I'll answer that with another question. How did your people get here?"

Turlenain did not respond right away.

Brewellan made a quick series of bird-like chirps. Turlenain touched their hands to their cheeks. Marcy hadn't noticed earlier, but their arrangement of fingers was odd. Five, but with many more joints than a human's. No opposable thumb, but it looked as if the fingers could splay and Turlenain could pick something up as easily as Marcy could. Perhaps more easily.

"What did they say?" Marcy said.

"Brewellan wants me to tell you the legend of our arrival. We were people of a ship that was journeying slowly through the cosmos. I know that you understand the speed of light, and that it is an absolute limit."

"Yes. Though our scientists have worked out how to go around that limit."

Turlenain touched their cheeks once more.

"Faster? Faster than light?"

"Not really faster. More like going around a different way. Like if there was a mountain in front of you. To get to the other side you could go over it, but if you went around, you'd still end up in the same place."

At least that was the analogy that one of the engineers had used to explain it to Marcy before they'd departed Earth.

Could that have only been a matter of months ago?

Turlenain said nothing for a moment, then turned to Brewellan and chirped.

The two of them went back and forth rapidly. A variety of expressions went over the faces of the delegation, but all completely unreadable.

Their language was complex, of course. They had taught themselves English from the *Puerto Limón's* transmissions, such as they were. Perhaps there was more to it than that. Certainly, these people had a far better facility with language than Marcy. Her own stuttering attempts to learn Italian had come to little more than *grazie* and *sì*.

"We had a generation ship," Brewellan said. How about that, they could speak English.

"So you were used to limited space?" Marcy said.

"Exactly. These tunnels seem spacious to us." Brewellan touched their cheek, as Turlenain had done. "At least, the tunnels seemed spacious to our ancestors.

"I bet." That same engineer, Damien, who'd used the mountain to represent the speed of light, had also talked about generation ships and the whole challenge of building those. They needed remarkable power plants, incredible recycling systems and launch profiles as good as the *Puerto Limón's*.

Marcy had spent many pleasant evenings down on The Cape with Damien, talking about the various challenges of the *Puerto Limón's* voyage.

"What happened to your ship?" Marcy said. "At least your ancestor's ship."

"It broke apart in the atmosphere. Most of the occupants died. The survivors found themselves inside the tunnels."

"With much of the equipment?"

"Enough for more than a thousand people. There were eighty-seven."

"We were just six," Marcy said. "Now five."

"One of your team died."

"Yes."

Brewellan turned then, and walked off. The delegation followed. With Turlenain.

Marcy hustled along to keep up.

"I don't like the way that you do that," she said.

"You don't like the way that I do what?" Turlenain said.

"Walk away in the middle of a conversation. Not just you. Brewellan too. It's as if everything has been said, but really it hasn't. Not even close."

"I do not understand. We were finished conversing. Perhaps we could take it up later, but there was no more to say."

"We should help each other. Have you had any contact with your people from the planet you left behind? Have you made any attempts to escape? To leave the planet here?"

"No."

Brewellan, still walking away, said, "We are safe and happy here. There is no need to leave. There is nothing else for us to do."

Alien minds, of course. Very different to humans. Natalie would have loved being able to interact with them.

"And," Turlenain said, "we lack the means to make contact."

Perhaps they, all of them, were making the best of a bad situation, the way that Marcy, Birjette and the rest of the *Puerto Limón's* crew were making the best of the jungle.

Since Turlenain and Brewellan and the others had grown up

in these glass tunnels, that was all they knew. And for all Marcy knew, the people aboard the generation ship had been leaving an untenable situation on the home planet.

There surely had been talk about that back on Earth, after all the damage wrought.

"We could help you make contact," Marcy said.

Brewellan came to a stop.

"You?" they said. "How could *you* help us make contact?"

Marcy sighed. It was a long shot, that was for sure.

"We're expecting rescue at some point. When our people back home do not hear from us, they will send rescue. Eventually."

"Eventually. These are hollow promises. Eject her. This is not productive. Do not return."

Turlenain took Marcy's arm. "This way," they said.

"You could help us," Marcy said, pulling from Turlenain's grasp. "You have the resources. We're trapped in there."

Unless they moved to the prairie. But would that be any better really?

"Eject her," Brewellan said.

Turlenain stepped in front Marcy as the others walked on.

"This way," Turlenain said, with a gesture back the way they'd come.

CHAPTER SIXTEEN

Turlenain used an odd device to open up a side of the wall into a tube just big enough for Marcy.

"You could help us," Marcy said. "And we could help you."

"You are mistaken."

Turlenain gestured to the tube. It was like a slide. Angled down. Leading out to the forest.

"Go now," they said. "The conduit will not last long. It will close. You would not want to become caught up in the glass as it seals."

"Give me the device," Marcy said. "Let me come back when I need to."

"I cannot." Turlenain looked away along the corridor. The way that Brewellan and the rest of the delegation had gone. "I cannot."

"Tell them that I stole it from you."

"They will come looking for it. For you."

"Good." Marcy didn't believe them, though. Their people were too caught up in living their lives in these tunnels.

"You should not come back."

"When our rescue comes, I want to be able to return. To farewell you. To offer again the opportunity for us to contact your home world."

"You would do that?"

"Of course. We can travel faster than light. In effect. If you can tell us where your home world star is, I can navigate to it. I can take a message."

"You would do that?"

"I would."

"Personally."

"If I'm allowed to. There's an enormous bureaucracy behind it all."

"Ah, there you are. Please exit now."

Marcy held out her hand. Open. Ready for them to place the device.

Again Turlenain looked along the tunnel.

"You won't know how to use it," they said.

"I'll figure it out."

Turlenain nodded. A very human gesture.

They placed the device in Marcy's hand.

"Go quickly." Turlenain again gestured to the tube.

"Thank you." Marcy got down and slipped into the tube. She slid quickly and found herself on the ground in the forest.

Looking back, she saw Turlenain standing at the top of the slide, looking down at her.

The glass was building itself up again. Blob by blob.

"Until soon," Marcy called.

Turlenain made no response. Just turned and walked away.

Marcy sighed.

Now she had to find her way back to camp.

CHAPTER SEVENTEEN

Ten weeks later, when a rescue skiff arrived from the orbiting vessel the *City of Marseilles*, Marcy and the others were camped in the prairie land.

It was a glorious thing, to hear the sonic booms and look south to see the craft speeding in, shining in the sunlight.

The prairie had proven much more conducive for survival. Drier and lighter, with game they could catch and a huge stand of bushes with tasty, if tart, red berries. The branches scratched arms when they went to harvest the berries. It was worth it.

Marcy and others had made regular recces into the jungle and into the desert to gather other resources. They'd almost reached the point where it felt that if rescue never came, then they would be able to survive long term. Perhaps even do better than survive.

The skiff was a thirty-meter long black and gold ovoid, with fins and antennas and wide, glistening cockpit windows. The hull ticked and pinged, cooling from its entry flight.

Right away the skiff's crew set to work with medical care for the team. Chow's foot was much better, but he couldn't put weight on it. Harv's hand still gave him issues. Broll had gotten a nasty cut from the berry bushes a few days previously and the wound was seeping.

Birjette and Marcy took the skiff's commander, Garry, up their truss ladder to the top of the wall.

"You were in that jungle there?" Garry said, pointing. He was Canadian and had a thick accent, leaning toward French. "Or that one?" He pointed to the one with the bluer leaves where Marcy had glimpsed the dinosaur-like creature. From up on the wall, she'd occasionally considered exploring. The sounds that came from it were off-putting, though. It was frankly irresponsible to go into it while their situation had remained so tenuous.

Birjette and Garry talked awhile, as Marcy looked into the wall.

The people were still there. Walking. Moving around. Sitting in groups. On other recces she'd discovered their farms in spaces within the walls. Lush and verdant. Almost jungles in themselves. Very well managed.

And other parts. Where they had hidden areas. They'd built shades to block out the sunlight. That had to be their homes.

Amazing that a people who would build a generation ship seemed to have so little interest in leaving their odd haven.

"A remarkable thing," Garry said. "How was it constructed? Where are the people who built it?"

"Those are questions for future teams," Birjette said. "Not for now."

"I'll come back," Marcy said, surprising herself.

"You would?" Birjette said.

"Certainly. First, though, I need to let them know that we're leaving."

Marcy had brought along Turlenain's device. She'd practiced a couple of times in discreet parts of the wall. It had taken a few goes, but she'd been able to make tube holes. Something about resonance frequency or something. Technically she should hand the device to Garry so it could be taken home and analyzed.

Still, there was plenty of time for that.

As Birjette and Garry watched, Marcy carefully cut an angled hole in the top of the glass wall. Right above the occupied areas.

"I'll be back soon," she said. She sat on the hole's edge and pushed off. She slid fast, then fell into the air.

She was ready for it. She'd practiced it in her head again and again.

She landed kind of like a superhero, into a crouch and leaning forward, one hand darting out onto the floor.

There were people all around her.

Marcy stood. "Hi," she said. "It's me. I'm back. Where's Turlenain?"

AFTERWORD

I have a natural tendency to write my stories at somewhere around the novella length, although some would call "Terrarium Blues" a 'novelette'.

In 2024, I found two of my longer stories, though, both appearing in the 'novella' category for a regional award (neither won)... one of the stories—"Daisy And Maisie, External Hull Maintenance Experts"—was around 7600 words (say a little more than half the length of "Terrarium Blues", and the other—"Wildest Skies"—was 22,000 words (as in, almost three times the length of the other story). Both were too long for the Short Story category (capped at 7500 words), and too short for the novel category, which had a bottom limit of 40,000 words.

I did have the good fortune that "Daisy and Maisie..." did win another award, the Analog Analytical Laboratory readers' poll award in the novelette category (7500 words - 17,500 words). Novelette in that instance, sitting right between short story and novella.

All of which rambling, I suppose, is to say that I often find my stories themselves rambling on (if you've made it this far, then perhaps my rambling in the story was compelling enough… I do try, inside of all of that, to write compelling fiction).

When I get started on a story, I often find that there's so much to tell that it does need to keep going. Perhaps I'm a novelist playing at being a short story writer, and my fingers and brain just want to stretch out into novel territory.

Suffice to say, I write a lot of novellas and novelettes. They're fun. My natural length.

I enjoyed writing "Terrarium Blues", though I'm sure when I had the thought of chucking the crew into a transparent box, I didn't know where I was going with it. It took them, and me, a while to figure out how they were going to deal with the situation.

I hope you enjoyed the story.

Thanks for reading.

Sean
January 2026

BIG STEPS

Ingrid stepped through the murky damp flax forest, unsure of her direction. Through the blades she caught occasional glimpses of a western crescent moon, cutting infrequent glints through layered cloud.

It was so easy to get turned around.

The ground was boggy. It squelched and gurgled with each footfall. Even her sturdy leather shoes struggled against the water. Her feet were wet and her toes were cold. The muddy damp was creeping up the cuffs of her jeans.

Not the kind of outfit to be wearing when lost out in the wilds. Boots, jeans, a tee shirt and a black vinyl motorcycle jacket. The jacket had red bands across the chest and a double way zip with domes. Great for the wind, not so great for the cold.

Stretching out her hand in the gloom, she touched the edge of a flax leaf. Sharp. The leaf was as broad as her hand with outstretched fingers. It shifted under her touch. Other leaves rustled in the light breeze.

The sounds could have been a soft lullaby—*shh, a-shhish, a-shish, aa-aaa, shh*—but in the cool dark the tiny sounds pushed at the edges, suggesting dangers and presences unknown.

Were there holes here she could fall into? Thick, gripping muds that might hold her in place? Might tear her boots from her feet?

Were there creatures abroad? Things with talons and fangs? With stiffly muscled legs ready to pounce? Ready to stuff her into their gullets?

Ingrid stopped. Took a breath.

She could be no more than a mile from the road. Maybe a mile and a half.

And she knew which way west lay. Ahead. The flickers of the moon.

All she had to do was bear to the right. Just a little. Keep it in sight.

It wasn't as if she was afloat in a dinghy in the middle of the ocean, trying to use a brass sextant to determine her position.

Toru Flax Forest was only forty or fifty square miles, wasn't it? Ten or eleven miles on its longest axis. No more than two at its narrowest. Hourglass shaped. Pressed between a curve in the river and the humps of old dunes.

New growth. Less than forty years old. A return to the old flax swamps.

And here she was. Lost.

At night.

Silly, really.

Stupid.

She took another breath.

Took another step.

From somewhere came the cry of an animal. Piercing at first, but descending into a growl. Something big.

East? Hard to tell in the maze of leaves.

Impossible.

Ingrid took another step.

Bartolemew cracked his knuckles and sipped from a beer. The brew was good. Full and rich and with just the right kind of tang.

The tankard was pewter and the table was wooden, and his motorcycle stood outside. The makings of a good evening.

Around him, customers circled the bar. Some staggered. Some swaggered. Some warmed their hands by the fire blazing in the central stone pit.

The floor was hardwood and the ceiling was high. On a shelf fitted just below the ceiling stood the detritus of ancient days, arrayed and displayed to bring some atmosphere to the place.

Magnesium alloy wheels. A big block of a wooden telephone with a winder on the side and a black speaking horn in the middle. A pedal car. A traffic light stuck on blinking red. A silvery coffee machine with spigots and spouts and handles and dials. A radiostereogram.

Bartolemew's table was in the back corner. Where he liked it. Where he could keep an eye on proceedings.

There were twenty-two people in the bar, as well as Silvya, the barkeep. Mostly locals. A couple from up north who'd ridden the highway on a recently refurbished Triumph Nine.

Bartolemew rode a Triumph, so he'd gotten talking to them.

The pair were now thoroughly soused and kind of slumped at a table two over from Bartolemew.

Ah, people. He took another small sip from his tankard. It would last all night, which suited him. Suited Silvya, who was counting on him to keep trouble at a minimum. Saturday it could get a bit boisterous.

The door opened, admitting a new arrival.

Stoke. Ingrid's father.

Stoke looked around the bar. Spotted Bartolemew.

Hurried over.

The mud squelched. Ingrid stepped around another flax. They were close together here. In places, jammed in one against the other. And that all seemed to make the bog worse. Stickier.

Something snipped at Indrid's finger. A sharp jab. She recoiled.

Stumbled backward.

Glimpsed the glitter of a spiderweb in the moonlight. Shimmering in the light wind.

Her finger throbbed.

Had she been bitten?

Wouldn't that just cap off the night?

Bartolemew gunned the Triumph's engine. The beast fair hummed along. Some of the roads around were still in good shape. Peter and Jenni got out with hot mix from time to time and filled holes. The patience of those people.

Of course, they did all right with grateful locals who brought them fruit and bread and, sometimes, a carcass.

Stoke clung on behind Bartolemew, clearly terrified.

The wind whipped their hair and tugged at their clothes.

"She had a fight with Melissa," Stoke said over the clatter of the engine. "I just now found out."

"They fight all the time," Bartolemew said. It was true. Sisters, huh? Never can agree.

"Melissa said Ingrid raced off," Stoke said. "On her bicycle."

"How old are they now?"

"Twenty-two."

"Should be well over that kind of nonsense, you ask me."

"Should be. Aren't."

"You're sure she's gone to the forest?"

"No. But anywhere else she'd just come home. Or be easy to find."

"Yep." That was right. No one should go into the flax forest after dark.

Ingrid sucked on her finger. There was a lump. She ran her tongue over it. Maybe hoping to find fang holes. Or worried that she would.

But she didn't.

Could be anything.

Still, the finger throbbed.

She needed to get out of here. Go home and either slug Melissa across the chops, or make up with her.

No telling how it would go.

Ingrid pulled herself up. She was wet now. The back of her jeans soaked through. Water crept up her tee shirt.

She clambered higher, pulling up into one of the flaxes. Right into the bole.

It was soft and insubstantial and bent under her weight. But maybe if she could get some height, she could get her bearings a little better.

Again there came the cry of the animal.

Closer.

It sounded bigger than she'd first thought.

The last section of road, off the main strip, was rough gravel. Potholed and covered with runnels large and small. Few people came this way. Mostly just picnickers with horse and cart, coming down to the meadows at the edges of the flax forest.

Bartolemew took it slow.

The Triumph's electrical headlamp blazed through the night. Shining off the old signs and posts and rusted out vehicles. Somehow the discards ended up just a little out of sight from the main throughways.

"I don't like it out here," Stoke said over the clatter of the Triumph's engine.

The sickle moon was popping in and out of jumbles of cloud.

"What's to like?" Bartolemew said. "There's a job to do."

And there it was. Picked out in the beam from the headlamp.

Ingrid's bicycle.

Leaning up against a low wood pole fence.

Right by the entry to the old boardwalk.

Ingrid hunkered in against the lower stems of some big flaxes. The smell was earthy and organic. Rich and full. And usually it would be reassuring.

Something was moving nearby.

Could have been a boar, or one of the bigger cats. Either way she was in trouble.

"Ah, Melissa," Ingrid whispered. "Look what you've got me into now."

Truth was, she'd got herself into this situation. No one else to blame.

Things fell quiet for a moment.

Ingrid waited.

The quiet lay across the flax forest.

No cries from the animal.

Ingrid could hear her own breathing, and the sough of the wind. The tiny chirps of crickets and low croaks of the small brown marsh frogs.

She waited.

Waited some more.

Perhaps she could make a break for it. After her quick look-see she was sure that she was close to the end of the boardwalk.

She waited some more.

Maybe it had gone. Passed her by.

If she could reach the boardwalk she would be fine. Scramble back up onto the solid platform. Run back to her bicycle.

As she moved, something snuffled nearby.

Ingrid stopped. Became rigid.

It was right there.

Just around behind the flax bush right by her.

Bartolemew trotted along the boardwalk. Stopped ten yards in.

The light was bad, even with his kerosene lamp.

Stoke came up behind him.

"There are spirits around," Stoke said. "Bad energy."

"If by spirits you mean wild boars and pumas, sure."

"Those too. But we're not supposed to toy with the forest. We know that."

"Yet you let your daughter—"

"Stop," Stoke said. "There's no 'let' involved in the raising of my daughters. They do what they need to do. Were I to ever try to stop them from anything, it would simply double their resolve."

Bartolemew held up his hand.

"What?" Stoke said.

"Quiet," Bartolemew said. "I think I heard something out there."

He shone the lamp around.

"What did you—" Stoke fell silent as Bartolemew clapped a hand over his mouth.

There was something moving in the flax. If it was Ingrid, then he should call out. If it was something else, well, he needed to stay silent.

Some of the things that inhabited this place, it would kind of be better to just get back on the motorcycle and hightail it. Wishing Ingrid the best of luck, of course.

Bartolemew kept shining the lamp around.

The flax blades shone in the light. Their fat, fibrous leaves fat and brown-green. Tall flower stems stood up from some, black, with golden drooping bell flowers. Many were gray and white. Last year's. Dead, with their seeds long dispersed.

Bartolemew dropped his hand from Stoke's mouth. Moved along the boardwalk. His footsteps seemed loud. Echoey.

Stoke came right up by him. Whispered in his ear.

"We need to shout for her."

"And attract critters? I think there are more subtle ways."

"Like what?"

"Eyes and ears. Let's head for the end of the boardwalk. I have a feeling about this."

"A feeling."

Bartolemew turned to face him.

"Stoke. You asked me to help. Let me help. From the end of the boardwalk there's the trail. We'll see her footprints."

Possibly they would see her footprints. Bartolemew wasn't hopeful, but Stoke needed to hear something.

"All right," Stoke said. "Lead on."

Ingrid backed into the cover of the flax bush. In places they almost knitted together, forming canopies and hollows. The twists and curls made the forest so dangerous.

They'd explored as kids, her and Melissa. Around the fringes. Never deep. Never at night.

Something was breathing nearby. Waiting.

Then, voices.

People trying to be quiet, but nearby.

To her right.

Were they in the forest too? The boardwalk was the main way through, she'd just lost track in the dark. But wasn't it on her left now?

How turned around had she got?

She could stand and find the moon again. That would tell her where she was.

Because if she was close to the boardwalk, then maybe, just maybe, she could make a break for it.

The thing snuffled. She heard the sounds of it pushing through the leaves.

And a growl.

It wasn't a boar. The sound was wrong.

Had to be a puma.

The thing could tear her apart in a second.

Bartolemew cast the lamplight out across the rough path that led through the flax. The path had been cut years ago. Someone's idea to extend the boardwalk right out to the river. Ambitious. Never happened.

People were happy to come this far. Besides there were plenty of other places to access the river. Especially upstream.

A sound came from behind. Scuffling.

For a moment he thought—hoped—it might be Ingrid.

But it wasn't.

The lamp picked out a toothy big cat. Tan hide, with subtle stripes. A puma.

On all fours it stood as high as his waist. The thing had to weigh a hundred and fifty pounds. Maybe more.

Stoke swore.

The animal had gone.

Ingrid leaned from her little hideout.

Gone.

For sure.

In fact she could hear it moving away.

Moving to her right.

Toward where she'd heard the voices.

She followed.

Bartolemew backed away. One of the boards creaked under his boot.

The puma pulled its lips back in a snarl.

It was maybe fifteen yards back along the boardwalk. Halfway between them and solid ground.

"Get behind me," Bartolemew told Stoke.

"No. Let me stop it."

"You're not going to stop it. That's just a killing machine."

"I've heard that, but then how can they be so very different from house cats? They look so similar."

"House cats have fires to lie by and their tummies tickled whenever they want. Food delivered twice a day. They're not feral."

The puma advanced on them. One slow step at a time.

It wasn't taking chances.

"We should have brought a gun," Stoke said. "A pike or anything. Any kind of weapon."

Bartolemew put his hand on Stoke's shoulder. Pulled him back. Stoke was trembling.

Something else moved at the edge of the boardwalk. Climbing up like the puma.

Not another cat, though.

A person.

Ingrid.

Ingrid rolled onto the boardwalk. It was higher right here than most parts. The muddy ground below burbled at her. Thanking her, perhaps, for the boot it had kept.

Her foot was cold and the boardwalk felt rough under her sole.

She stood.

The animal was there. A big cat. Tawny. Its fur glistened in the light someone farther along the boardwalk held up.

Two shadowy figures hidden there in the light's backwash.

The cat turned.

Ingrid took a step away.

A puma. A big one.

The cat snarled at her.

"Ingrid!" someone called.

Stoke.

Her father.

What was he doing here?

The cat turned again. Faced into the light.

"Get out," Stoke called. "While you can, Ingrid. Get home."

"Don't run," another voice said. Bartholemew? Of course he would be here.

"We'll distract it," he said. "Get home safely."

Ingrid stayed right where she was.

Bartolemew stared back along the boardwalk.

The puma looked ferocious. It would easily turn Ingrid into mincemeat.

"Hey!" Stoke shouted, waving his arms. "Hey, cat! Over here!"

He took a step closer.

Bartolemew put his hand on Stoke's shoulder again.

"You've done enough." Bartolemew pulled him back.

The cat advanced.

"Ingrid!" Stoke shouted. "Get! Go!"

Ingrid stayed where she was.

"Don't let it get you too!" Stoke's voice broke. He was just about beside himself.

"Come," Bartolemew said, pulling again on Stoke's shoulder. "Let's lead it away."

Bartolemew turned the lamp. Lit up the empty stretch of boardwalk beyond.

Ingrid stood still. Her throat clenched.

They couldn't do this.

It was her fault.

They would be mauled and it would be all her fault.

The puma followed them.

Ingrid took a step after it.

She shouted.

The cat ignored her.

"Quiet down, love," Stoke said. "Get going. It won't stop with us."

He sounded so sad.

Melancholy.

"Dad!" she called. Yet she'd never called him that.

"Ingrid. Go."

They were slipping away into the dark. Him and Bartolemew.

Bartolemew.

That was how they'd gotten here! Of course. Stoke would never ride a bicycle. Would never bring a horse out after dark.

Ingrid turned and ran.

Her boots thumped on the boardwalk.

She didn't even look back.

Bartolemew reached the end of the boardwalk. The builders had constructed a wider platform with a small roof, kind of like a band rotunda. There was a railing, and a long octagonal bench seat all the way around.

All around, the flax swayed in the breeze. Crickets chirped and the little cusper frogs croaked.

"Wait," Stoke said. He ran by Bartolemew and scrambled around on the bench seat. Stood right up on the railing.

Reaching out, Stoke grabbed one of the flower stalks. The things were stiff and more than ten feet long.

The puma was still striding along after them. No hurry. It knew that it had them.

Bartolemew considered how he might smack it with the lamp. He'd get one shot. That would be all.

Stoke wriggled the stalk back and forth.

It gave a crack.

The puma's ears pricked up.

From the distance came another sound. An engine.

Bartolemew had no time to concern himself with that. He swung himself back. Around. Over the seat. Over railing.

Dropped the the ground.

Lithe and agile, the puma followed easily.

Ingrid found Bartolemew's motorcycle right near the boardwalk entry. She flung herself onto the saddle and kicked the engine to life.

She wasn't going home.

She was going back after them. Along the boardwalk.

Bartolemew was so proud of the machine. He kept it oiled and polished. Once a year he took the thing apart and reassembled it. Fascinating how many pieces it took to make up a machine.

He'd shown her how to ride.

But she'd never actually driven it before. Three times she'd been a pillion, so she knew how to lean into the corners.

In principle she knew the gears. Knew to twist the throttle.

Knew where the brakes and other things were.

With her left hand clenched over the clutch, she clunked the motorcycle into gear. The engine thrummed.

She turned the throttle a little above idle.

Let the clutch out slowly.

The motorbike leapt away. Got out from under her.

It went careering into the flax.

Before Bartolemew had even landed, the Puma swiped at him. Knocked him down.

Spinning, he slammed onto the muddy ground.

The puma landed astride him. It bent its head down toward him. Its breath was fetid.

The lamp had spun away. It came to rest shining back into the puma's eyes. They glowed, like little lamps themselves.

"Look out!" Stoke called.

He came racing in from the side of the platform. He had the flax flower stalk. Holding it out like a lance. Like a polearm. As if he was some jousting medieval knight.

The puma looked over.

The end of the stalk lance struck the puma's shoulder.

The puma yowled.

The stalk broke with a meek cracking sound.

"Get up!" Stoke said.

"You didn't hurt it." Bartolemew sat up.

The puma had stepped away, but it was still watching them. Perhaps a little more wary.

"I didn't want to hurt it," Stoke said. "I knew I never could. Not with this. I just wanted to surprise it."

"Good that was—"

The puma pounced.

Arms wide.

It collected both of them. Threw them to the ground again.

The puma slashed at Stoke's stomach.

Ingrid retrieved the motorcycle. It had been lying on its side. In the mud. Draped against one of the big flax plants.

Mud dripped from the chassis. She got the motorcycle upright again.

Got on it.

Kicked the starter.

The motorcycle bucked.

Forgotten to take it out of gear.

She fixed that. Kicked again.

Pulled in the clutch.

Kicked.

Felt the thrum.

She revved the engine.

I'm coming back.

Gearshift.

Clutch.

Easy.

Easy now.

She eased it out.

Slowly. Let it grab hold.

The bike began moving.

She rode forward.

Turned.

Bumped along.

Headed for the boardwalk.

The motorcycle seemed to know where to go.

She was but its guide.

Bartolemew found himself wrestling with the puma. Trying to get it off Stoke.

Stoke lay groaning. Bleeding.

Thick. Heavy blood. Right from his gut.

Bartolemew was too.

It wasn't a fair fight. The puma was designed to inflict damage on its prey. Claws like blades, teeth like awls.

All his work went into trying to avoid a mortal slash.

He heard his motorcycle again. Drawing closer.

Ingrid could barely hang on. Hard enough to be riding a motorcycle, but riding it along the narrow boardwalk was ridiculous. Every time she corrected it felt as if she was going over the edge.

The motorcycle's headlamp flickered. It cast terrifying

shadows through the flax forest.

The tyres drummed on the boards.

Despite her speed, the boardwalk seemed longer than she remembered.

Perhaps it was the dark.

The whole situation.

A puma.

Attacking Stoke.

And Bartholemew.

Ingrid gunned the engine. It felt like the only sound in the universe.

Then, ahead, the boardwalk's end.

The platform with the seats and roof.

And, at the edges of the motorcycle's light, movement.

Off the end. Beyond the little set of steps she'd taken earlier.

"I'm coming!" she shouted.

Words lost to the wind.

She slowed before the end. The motorcycle bumped down the steps. Slid on the muddy ground.

But she stayed upright.

The puma reared up. Back.

It roared at her.

Ingrid grabbed the clutch. Gunned the engine.

Louder than the puma.

Bartolemew was there.

Stoke was on the ground.

Ingrid started to get off the motorcycle.

"Stay there!" Bartholemew shouted.

The puma was on all fours now.

Prowling. Staring at Ingrid.

As if it wanted to eat her.

Bartholemew grabbed Stoke up from the ground. Staggered over.

"Shuffle forward," Bartolemew said.

There was so much blood. On his face. His arms. All over Stoke.

The puma roared. Lunged.

Bartolemew swept Stoke around. Put him astride the saddle. Right behind Ingrid. She edged farther forward.

Bartolemew climbed on himself. Behind Stoke.

"Go now," he said.

Ingrid let out the clutch as fast as she dared. They didn't need for the motorcycle to take off out from under them.

The puma moved back on its haunches.

Preparing to jump.

The motorcycle hummed. Moved forward.

Bartolemew's fingers dug into her sides as he clamped on. Holding Stoke in place.

Ingrid drove as fast as she dared. The headlamp showed the way ahead.

The little set of steps. They seemed huge.

Three people on on motorcycle.

"Lean back," Bartolemew said.

"But..." She leaned back.

They bumped up the steps. The motorcycle chugged. The back tire spat and jerked on the edges of the steps.

They came up to the platform.

Instinctively, Ingrid leaned forward.

The puma appeared. Leaping. Landing right there on the platform.

Ingrid twisted the throttle.

The motorcycle took off. The puma swiped at her.

Then it was gone. Left behind.

The bike's engine bellowed, as if taunting the animal.

Bartolemew held on tight. Ingrid was a natural. The boardwalk whipped by below.

They came to the end and she didn't stop. Just barreled on along the rough road and onto the highway.

Without him having to say a thing, she made straight for Doc Millerton's place. Parked the bike. Even put the kickstand up. They carried Stoke inside.

The house was warm and smelled of frangipani, and Doc brought them straight through to his little front room surgery.

"He'll be all right," she said, pulling on gloves and arranging medical things. "Stitch him up and he'll be out digging post holes in no time."

Ingrid sat in a surprisingly comfy chair in the corner of the little surgery. She must have slept, some, because already whiskers of light from a rising sun were working themselves through clouds visible through the window.

Glass-fronted shelves stood along one wall, filled with medical equipment. Brass and steel and old plastic. There were benches and drawers and an iron sink with a big spigot.

Stoke lay on a bed in the room's centre. He had a sheet over him and he was breathing regularly.

Doc brought her a glass of milk and went and looked at Stoke. Touched his clavicle.

Doc turned to Ingrid.

"He's awake. You can talk to him."

Ingrid came and stood beside Stoke. Took his calloused hand.

He stared into her eyes.

"My girl," he said. "You did great."

"I did lousy. I ran off. I should have just gone and made up with Melissa."

"Well, you can still do that." He smiled.

He was right, of course.

"Also," he said. "You ride a mean bike. I'm proud."

Ingrid swallowed.

She nodded.

"Thanks Dad," she said.

And he smiled even more.

AFTERWORD

Each year our town's public library curates a collection of local writing. Titled *Versions* it's now seen publication of six annual volumes. As a way of encouraging creativity in the local community, it's a wonderful initiative.

Full disclosure—I am one of the volume's editors.

Each year there is a 'prompt' which is designed to get those creative juices flowing. Last year the prompt was 'Home' and the previous year it was 'Earth', though there have been lengthier prompts in earlier years.

Of course, the prompt is not mandatory. It's just a starting point for those who need it. The library's intent is just to stimulate creativity in our local community.

Each year I myself also write a story to submit (sanctioned of course by Craig, the co-editor), and as with many times when I'm working on a story for one anthology or another, it takes me a few shots to get at the right story.

And the right length.

I've written in other afterwords and elsewhere about how I

do struggle to write shorter (some might say, that my stories do go on a little, and I should get to the point), and that happened with 'Big Steps'. I was writing this for the 'Earth' prompt. and looking to stay well under 3000 words. But Ingrid's story had legs and there were things she needed to get done and it ended up half again as long.

So I put 'Big Steps' aside and wrote another story for the anthology. That story 'Petersen Farm Volcano Response' was quite different (as you may be able to tell from the title), and was much shorter (and sillier).

But I still like 'Big Steps', in it's odd, slightly removed world. I'm not sure if it's fantasy or post-apocalyptic, but I enjoyed writing it. I hope you enjoyed the read too, and thank you, of course, for picking it up. I appreciate it.

Sean
January 2026

AUTHOR OF TERRARIUM BLUES

SEAN MONAGHAN

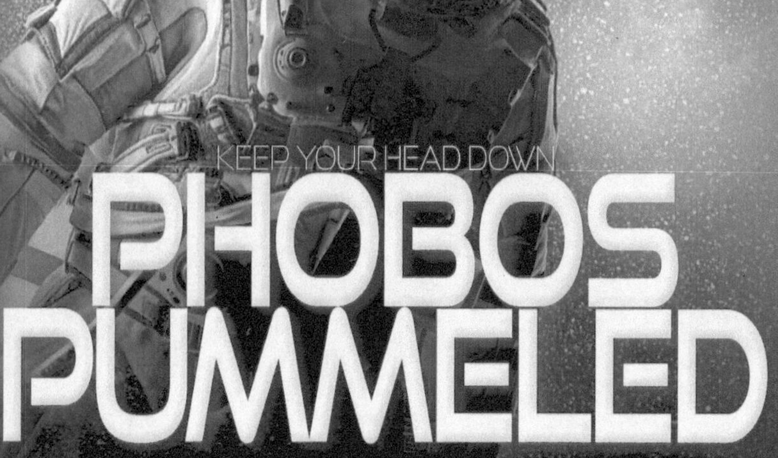

CHAPTER ONE

Sula Morgan smiled to herself as she turned the last locking ring on her worn old EVA suit. The thing stank of vinyl and dust. It dug into her right knee where some burr in the lining fabric had gathered over repeated use. One of the helmet fans chugged and griped a little, well past its replacement due date.

But it was reassuring. A little spaceship for one. Protection against the vacuum out here on Phobos. Protection against the solar rays and micrometeors.

She was twenty-eight years old, divorced for five years already, stationed out here in Mars's orbit for the last two years.

Wouldn't trade it for the world.

The inner face of her helmet's visor lit up with its cute little series of telltale dots. Green for integrity, green for air, amber for power. Amber for heating-cooling too. And another amber for water.

Once, probably before she'd been born, any one of those

would have been grounds to abort stepping out of the station. Or a ship. Or landing vehicle. Or whatever.

Forty years ago, when Candace Kildare had first landed on Mars, she'd set the precedent for just getting on with the job. It was written so deeply in the histories.

With a fried telemetry chip, and glitching vitals, the wise people back in Houston had told her to abort. Abort and reassess and repair.

Too bad that by the time the message arrived—the speed of light is pretty fast, but radio waves still take many, many minutes to travel fifty million miles or so—she was already on the ground, claiming Mars for all humankind or something.

She'd had a scripted speech—along the lines of "One small step for a man"—but that got lost in her pithy response to mission control.

"I'm getting the job done," she'd said. "We didn't spend months in a can to wait around for approval."

Sula liked that. The whole get on and do it attitude.

Of course, when things went wrong, they could go wrong catastrophically.

Sula's suit had a patch kit and external power and air sockets, exchangeable chipsets and batteries. The whole thing was designed to be repaired ad infinitum.

Sula stepped into the station's east airlock, waiting for the old equipment to cycle through the settings. Sucking out the air, the pumps groaned away.

She wore weighted boots. Phobos's gravity was miniscule. People would even make jokes about jumping high enough to put yourself in orbit. Completely impossible—Phobos's escape velocity was around eleven meters per second. Forty-one kilometers per hour.

Even without weighted boots there was no way even an Olympic high-jumper could jump that fast.

But still, it was easy to jump a little too high, which could be inconvenient. The weights came in handy.

Her helmet radio crackled at her.

José, the station's comms and rotor guy. He kept the machinery going. He jokingly called himself a hammer hand, with a PhD.

There were four of them in the little outpost. Minders for a cluster of eight slowcoach mining machines extracting water and other volatiles, metals and everyone's favorite, silicon, from the regolith and deeper. There was nothing fancy about their jobs. They were all essentially support crew for Tepou base below—or above, depending on how someone thought about it—on Mars.

The other two stations, I and II—so imaginatively named—were little more than simple pods, used by the very first arrivals as outposts. Set up as beachheads. Establishing human presence. Long abandoned.

Phobos Station III might have been cramped and compromised, but it was positively luxurious compared to what those places had been.

The radio crackled again.

"Hello, José," Sula said. "Please don't try to tell me that my task sheet has changed here."

She had a list of ten different items. Starting out with running a manual check on one of the miners. The machines were little bigger than her Uncle Steve's SUV and they brought themselves around to the station every five days for maintenance checks.

They had plenty of on-board telemetry, but there was nothing like hands-on visual and manual inspections to pick out things the sensors missed. She was the station's tech spotter, though her ability to code mostly got pushed aside with the day to day needs of maintaining a little mining outpost.

"I think we should pull your whole sheet," José said.

"What's that?"

"Shut down the cycle and come back inside the station."

The airlock's external hatch flashed a green light at her. Ready to open.

Sula undogged the hatch and stepped out.

"No, no, no," José said. "Don't go out. Stay in."

"Something's happened?" Sula stepped out into light. From this distance, the sun was bright, but little more than just the largest star.

She looked up at Mars, its wispy dusty atmosphere was gorgeously enticing. That was why she was still here after two years, really.

Nothing compared.

"We have meteors," José said. "Lots of meteors."

"Meteors?"

"Listen closely. Come back inside. We need to get into the bunker."

"The bunker?"

Phobos Station III was mostly above Phobos's base surface level. A series of alumino-plastic tubes and spheres in a vague starfish pattern. Loose regolith had been piled on top to diminish radiation and protect them from micrometeors.

Below, dug into the bedrock before the station's modules had even been placed, was a small rock chamber. Little bigger than a regular bathroom, it had bunks, supplies and a bucket for toileting.

Nothing elegant or private about it.

Designed for their protection during solar flares, primarily.

In theory the four of them could occupy the space for two weeks before supplies grew tight.

Though by then, the stench of their own waste might have killed them.

"Meteors?" she said.

"Imminent. Get back in."

"Copy that."

CHAPTER TWO

When she'd been young, maybe twelve or thirteen, after her folks had passed on, Sula's Uncle Steve had taken her out to the desert to watch meteor showers.

He'd had a motorhome then, and he had bumped it across rough and rugged dirt roads as if it was a monster truck.

He would cook up a delicious chili so they could have tacos, and he would play ancient Coldplay songs way too loud. He had a guitar and would strum wildly and sing along.

Way overcompensating in terms of trying to raise an unexpected child alone.

She got to sleep in the insect-free, warm comfort of the motorhome's interior, while he set up a one-person inflatable tent nearby.

He would set an alarm and come and wake her. A fire would be blazing and he would tell her not to look at it.

"You need to keep your night vision."

He'd put out blankets ten yards from the fire and they would lie on their backs under an extraordinary panoply of stars.

Billions of them, though only some millions were visible.

The thick, almost purple, cloudy band of the Milky Way would stretch out, as comfortable as they were on the blankets. Uncle Steve would point out the ones he knew. Polaris and Achernar and Wolf *something*.

"Planets," he would say "Almost all of them have planets."

And then the show would start.

The Leonids or the Perseids. The Earth passing through the remains of a shattered comet, regular as anything.

Two AM was always the best time to watch, apparently. And they had to be patient. Sometimes the sky would be clear for minutes at a time, then two or three might streak by in thirty seconds.

They would see dozens.

Long, brilliant streaks as the icy rock—or rocky ice—fractured and atomized in Earth's thickening atmosphere.

It was just glorious.

"Meteor showers," Uncle Steve would whisper. "There's nothing better."

Perhaps that was a whole big part of why Sula had ended up out on Phobos. Those nights looking away from the Earth, out into the endless universe.

CHAPTER THREE

Instead of stepping back to the airlock hatch, Sula leaned and looked skyward.

As if she would see any meteor.

At orbital velocities—tens of thousands of kilometers per hour—she wouldn't see a thing. Not at all.

Back on Earth, that thick atmosphere protected most everyone and everything from all but the biggest of bolides. From time to time there would be one that shattered windows and blasted down trees. On very rare occasions, one might be a *planet-killer*. Sula always imagined those words spoken as if by someone who did the voice-over for a movie preview. *Coming soon. Miss it... if you dare!*

"Inside!" José said.

"But..." Sula took another step.

The miner stood nearby. Its six knobbly wheels were worn and dusty, and its hopper stood high and tipped up, as if it had just dropped its load of spoil.

"Sula!" That was Miranda. Station chief. Do not tangle with

her. She and Val, the fourth member, were both geologists, though in reality, they worked just the same as Sula and José—keeping the place running.

"Coming," Sula said, still looking up.

Mars.

There were people down there. Dozens of them.

"Now!"

Far off across Phobos's surface a sudden plume appeared. Dust thrown skywards.

Rising from beyond the close horizon.

A moment later the ground shook under Sula's feet. The miner rocked on its suspension.

Through the helmet speakers, José swore.

"We're getting pummeled," Miranda said.

Sula charged through the airlock hatch.

CHAPTER FOUR

Down in the chamber, Sula released the rings and started getting out of her suit. The chamber's air was cool, and there was a soft hum of machinery.

José was at the end, up on the ladder rungs, dogging the access hatchway closed.

"You're lucky you got down here," he said. "Your suit's so bulky and the shaft is so narrow."

"But I'm not gangly and inelegant like you."

"Ouch!" He stepped off the ladder and kind of drifted to the floor.

Dust from her suit swam around in waves. The scrubbers would be gathering it up.

Not a great thing. The airlock, antechamber and suit room were designed to keep dust out of the main part of the station. Now she'd traipsed it all through. Even though she'd only been outside for a moment.

Three of the bunks were folded up against the wall, and the lower one was set up with cushions, like a sofa. The opposite wall had a bench with a small sink, and cupboards below with the supplies.

The walls still had their chiseled rocky shapes, but there was a translucent layer of plastic lacquer coating them.

Miranda stood at the end opposite the ladder, and Val, the fourth team member, sat on the cushions with his knees drawn up to his chest and his arms wrapped around his shins. He was tall and lanky, so it was odd seeing him so compact.

Miranda was working on a portable display. Almost feverishly. Sula kept working on getting her suit off, trying not to bump the walls or equipment or anyone else.

The others were all wearing standard dark blue station overalls, with moccasins on their feet.

Sula shucked the suit and stowed it as best she could in a locker back by the ladder. There wasn't space for the helmet.

"What happened?" she said. "I thought that clusters of meteors were tracked? We know where they all are."

"Apparently not," José said.

"This is known." Miranda looked up from her display. "Meteor shower TM-16. Supposed to be small. In an eccentric orbit, so it rarely intersects with Mars's orbit."

"That sounds far fetched."

"See for yourself." Miranda reached and handed José the display.

"Doesn't matter if it's far-fetched or not," Sula said. "It's clearly here. Did you see the impact out toward grid nineteen?"

"I saw it," Val whispered. "On the feed. Smacked right into one of the mines."

"We're safe here, Val," Miranda said.

"You tell yourself that."

"As safe," Sula said, "as we can be. Besides, it won't last long."

"Couple of hours, maybe," José said. "Looking at this data." He waved at the display.

"How are they doing on Mars?" Sula said. "Are they experiencing impacts?"

"There's no word." José passed her the display. "But plenty cameras are watching. See?"

Sula looked at the display.

It showed a view directly down toward Mars. From one of the satellites.

Circular balls of dust. Billowing high into the atmosphere.

"Near the base?" she said.

José reached and pointed to one of the plumes.

"They're right there."

CHAPTER FIVE

Down in the rock chamber below Phobos Station III, Miranda got Val to set up the little stove and make them all coffee. Not real coffee, of course, but near enough.

And it gave Val something to do, rather than sitting on the bunk brooding.

"I think Tepou is gone," José said. "That dust. Right there. That was some impact."

With a seven hour orbit, Phobos had left the base behind, but there were still satellite feeds coming through. Mars had on the order of fifty satellites now. Some of them little more than historic antiques, but plenty of them functioning.

Data-gathering proceeded at pace. Sula and the others were little more than a scouting team really. They said that in another decade there would be more than a thousand people down on Mars's surface.

"We don't know until we hear from them," Miranda said.

"Or don't hear from them," Val said.

"Fair point," José said. "But next time we're overhead, the dust might have cleared. We might see what's happened."

"If it clears."

Despite the thin atmosphere, dust storms on Mars could last for weeks. The particles were so fine.

This was different, though. Not due to atmospheric conditions.

"When can we go up again?" Sula said. "Meteor showers don't last so very long, now do they?"

"Couple of hours," José said.

As if to confirm that, the walls shook.

Another impact.

Val swore.

"Yeah," José said. "I'm with you buddy. Phobos is pretty vulnerable. Unconsolidated. The place could fall apart."

"You're not helping," Miranda said. "I need you to focus on making contact with Tepou, and getting comms going with Earth."

"I can do that." José leaned back on the cushioned bunk and worked on the display.

Val leaned in to the little cooker and sniffed. The coffee scent was beginning to fill the chamber. Reassuring, really. As if there was a little normalcy going on.

"Phobos isn't going to fall apart," Val said. "We've dug up enough of it to know that its consolidation is sufficient to hold it together for another fifty million years or so. Any rock big enough to do any real damage would be well on our scopes."

The walls shook again, and something rattled in one of the lockers.

"Sounds as if they're trying real hard, though," José said.

"José," Miranda said. "How about just focus on your work."

"Hard," he muttered, "to focus when there's a bolide onslaught." He glanced over. "Sorry. Shutting up now."

"Good."

Sula rolled her shoulders. She sat on the bunk next to José and focused on her breathing. It could get real boring real quick down here. At least it wouldn't be for so long. Once they'd passed through the shower, they could head back up and see what, if any, help Tepou needed.

"Almost done here," Val said. "Everyone? Who wants a latté and who wants cappuccino?"

It was an old joke. Coffee, such as it was, came black or with milk—creamer—or not at all.

José laughed. "I'll take a—"

A bigger shake cut him off.

The lights in the chamber flickered. From somewhere above, something groaned.

Val swore. Worse than before.

The chamber was still shaking. A crack appeared in the rock opposite Sula. Over top, the lacquer coating stretched.

"Sula," Miranda said. "Put your suit back on."

CHAPTER SIX

Sula watched José as he worked through the display, trying to bring in data.

They'd lost all the connections. Not just to the satellites, but also into Phobos Station itself.

The buried chamber had its own separate air system, and its own separate power. Even if the connections to the station got damaged, they wouldn't lose those utilities.

But the flicker of the lights was concerning.

Every second, though, that Sula worked on getting back into her crusty old suit, she worried. She was the only one with a suit down here. What if something fractured and the chamber got opened to vacuum? The lacquer ensured that it was airtight. The rock walls were strong, but it was impossible to tell where they might be porous. It wouldn't take much of a hole for all the air to drain out, considering that the station was essentially in vacuum.

"Sealed?" Miranda said. Her voice was staticky through the helmet speakers.

"Sealed," Sula said.

It was weird standing there, looking back at the other three. Val's face was an odd mask, but José was clearly scared. Miranda moved around, poking and prodding at Sula's suit, checking it.

It was good to be back in the familiarity of it, but too strange in these circumstances.

"All right," Miranda said. "I need for you to get back up into the station and recover three suits for us. In the first instance."

"Three suits, copy that."

"What use are suits?" Val said.

"Pipe down," Miranda said.

Sula smiled to herself. Miranda was a great station chief. For the most part she just participated in the running of the station. She barely ever gave instructions and never gave orders.

But here she was being direct.

The situation required it.

"Once we're suited up," Miranda said, "we can make a full evaluation of the situation up top. I'm assuming that given the loss of feeds, and the obvious damage down here, that we could be dealing with a loss of integrity to the station itself."

Sula tried not to think about that.

José stepped up the ladder and opened up the hatch. It tipped down.

"Careful as you're going up," he said. "Remember, the shaft is narrow."

"I remember."

"Good luck."

"Thanks." Sula started up the ladder.

CHAPTER SEVEN

In Phobos's minuscule gravity, it was easy ascending the shaft from the emergency chamber. Even in her suit.

Sula's suit lights played on the facets of the rock wall and lacquer. The ladder rungs were spaced widely. Her life-support pack bumped against the wall and she found herself having to concentrate to stay close to the ladder rungs.

The helmet fan glitched and chugged. The telltale lights flickered between green and amber.

"After this," she said, "we should put in requisitions for new equipment."

"Yeah," José said. "Some of those new Skin31 suits are amazing. Practically standard issue on the Lagrange stations."

"I know it."

Sula reached the upper hatch. A circle of gray steel alloy with a simple wheel that ran three levers, locking it in place.

It was awkward getting herself around, but there was a second bracing rung and she stood on that. She took the wheel in her hands.

"Are you sealed down there?" she said. Imagine if the station itself had been punctured and evacuated.

"Sealed," José said. "Go ahead. I'm getting your suit feeds. You look fine."

Sula tugged on the wheel, but it didn't budge.

"Ah, I have a problem here," she said. "Just a second."

Sula tugged again. The wheel moved this time.

"Got it," she said. She kept turning and the levers slowly moved out of their recesses.

"I see that," José said. "Now, take care as you open it that it doesn't swing down on you."

"Copy that." Sula tugged on the hatch's handle. The hatch didn't budge.

She braced her knees in and pulled some more.

Nothing.

"On Earth," she said. "Or even on Mars, I could just swing from it and pull it down."

Up here she, even with her suit on, she weighed about as much as a small apple.

"Yep," José said. "You are a classic ninety gram weakling."

"Hey! Who's a weakling?"

"Stand by. I'm going to evacuate the shaft."

"You're what?"

"If the station's been punctured, then it's vacuum on the other side of the hatch. There's no way you can open it against air pressure."

"Copy that."

"Your suit's good?"

"Yes. Go ahead."

A moment later the suit shifted around her as the external pressure decreased.

Another moment later, José said, "You should be good to go ahead now."

"Copy that."

Sula tugged again on the hatch. It didn't budge.

She tugged a little harder and it jerked down. She easily held it in place, and lowered it gently.

Some rubble tipped off it and floated down past her. Dust too.

Some kind of rod was lying across the opening.

"I have debris," she said.

"I see it on your feeds."

Sula moved on up carefully, and pushed the rod aside. She kept going and pulled on up out of the hole.

She stopped, with just her head and shoulders above the hatchway.

Around her lay wreckage.

Phobos Station III had been practically obliterated.

CHAPTER EIGHT

Sula stood stock still in the center of the scattered parts of the station.

Torn and bent metal. Ripped apart equipment. Shattered glass and plastic.

"We got lucky," she said.

"Repeat please," José said. "Your feed is getting jittery."

"It's a mess up here. We could have been buried." Just a few meters away lay one of the station's structural support members. Two meters of aluminum girder thicker than her thigh. Technically not so much to lift in the light gravity, but how would they have shifted a pile of it?

How would *she* have? The others weren't coming up out of the chamber until she got suits down to them.

Sula took a couple of steps, not even sure how she was oriented.

She looked up at Mars.

Night side. Just coming up on morning. Phobos was always racing along ahead of the planet's rotation.

She took a step away from the hatch.

"Can you see this?" she said. "José?"

"I'm getting a feed, but it's lousy. Weird. Your suit should just be sending to the hardline antenna."

"Yeah, there's no antenna anymore. I'm surprised you're getting my voice feed."

"Please repeat, you're breaking up a whole lot."

Sula turned and crouched to the hatch.

"I'm going to have to figure some stuff out up here." She reached in and pulled the hatch closed. Dogged it.

"What stuff?" José said.

"Tell you later."

Sula stood and moved through the rubble. Chunks of regolith had been tossed through everything.

Where would the airlock and suit room have been?

She couldn't even line up on that miner that had come in for maintenance. It was gone.

Clearly blasted away in the impact.

There were few landmarks.

But she was still on the night side of Mars, so she had stars.

The cloudy drift of the Milky Way gave her a bearing. Kind of.

Quick calculations told her where she was, and where the suit lockers would be.

She walked across, and her guess was confirmed. The twisted remains of the airlock's inner hatch lay there. Still attached to the seating. The seating was still attached to a section of floor.

Which meant that that pile just there was where the suit locker had been.

She pulled away a couple of rocks. Shifted a sheet of plastic.

A helmet. Visor shattered.
She pulled it out. Dust and sand fell from it.
"We lost the suits," she whispered.

CHAPTER NINE

Ten minutes later, Sula had dug out two suits. Both of them ruined. Holes, and bent joint rings. Smashed up life support packs.

Working fast, she pulled out umbilicals and cables and linked the pair together. Plugged in the helmets. Powered up the working pack.

She hauled the amalgam over to the hatch.

"Comms check," she said. "José? Are you reading?"

"Copy that," he said. "I've got twin signals."

"Good. I'm using two other suits as a relay here. An aerial."

"What?"

"I've got to go for a walk."

"What? Just bring the suits."

"Yeah. A little bad news on that."

Sula looked around the remains of the station.

Uncle Steve had once lived in Kansas, before Sula had been born. Back when the tornadoes were getting bigger and more frequent. He'd shown her pictures of his neighbors' house that had been destroyed.

"The twister just licked right on in and smashed their place to smithereens. And the only damage to my place was a couple of broken windows and some chips in the paint. All caused by pieces of their house escaping the vortex."

The station looked like his neighbors' house had. Smithereens.

"Bad news?" José said. "Spit it out."

"There is no station."

Silence. Presumably he'd heard her.

There was rock debris from the impact. Hard to say how close it had been, or how big. Big enough to tear down the station was all that mattered.

"José?" Sula said.

"Still here. We're kind of trying to process that right now. No station?"

"It's been destroyed by the impact."

A beat. Then, "We have limited supplies here."

"I understand that." Sula spotted the inverted miner and started over. "I'm in the same situation."

"Copy that."

"When can we expect help?"

Another beat.

"Six days," José said. "There's an ore carrier en route."

The ore carriers came and collected the big containers of processed material the miners had dug up. Some of it was further processed in orbit, and some of it was just slung back toward Earth. One day Phobos would be filled with holes like a sponge, and then one day there would be nothing left of it.

The ore carriers also brought in fresh supplies for the station. While Phobos Station III was essentially a closed loop system, they still needed fresh scrubbers and food and water and rubber seals and other station essentials. Things they couldn't manufacture themselves.

The ore carrier also had a habitable section. Rigged up well enough to get them back to Earth if that was required.

"Six days," Sula said. "And what's the rating on the chamber?"

"Technically two weeks for four occupants. In practicality, with the shake up, probably less."

"Less."

"Don't make me estimate."

That was clear enough.

Maybe less than six days.

"I need one of the other miners brought over," Sula said.

The inverted miner's chassis and hull were bent and scarred. It had left a gouge across the surface.

"Miners?" José said.

"Yes. I need transport to get to Phobos Station II."

"Copy that. Bringing one over now."

"Thanks."

Station II was closer to Stickney, Phobos's great big crater. A whole lot simpler and more compact than Station III was—than Station III *had been*—but it was still functional and equipped.

And it had suits.

CHAPTER TEN

It was night when Sula arrived at Phobos Station II after an uncomfortable ride in the big old miner's nominal cab. The things ran themselves and it was almost as if they resented having to carry a passenger.

The miner's lights played across the station's exterior. It looked like it was in worse shape than Sula had expected. Unlike Station III, it had never been buried in regolith, so the station just stood proud on the surface like big tanks up on low stilts.

The windows were dull and dark, and the silicon-aluminum exterior was patinated and pitted. Various pieces of abandoned equipment lay around. Barrels and drills and tool benches. Handcarts and long poles of rebar and a small three-wheeler transport.

Sula cycled through the lock. There was still atmosphere, but she wasn't confident enough to remove her helmet and breathe. How long since the place had been occupied?

"Four years it's been empty," José said through the comms, as if reading her thoughts.

"Four years. Yeah, I'm keeping my helmet on."

"Can you replenish your air there? I'm cognizant of your suit's limitations."

"I'll figure that out." On paper the suit should be operated for up to four hours, but technically, there were easily eight hours of air in the tanks. Plenty of time.

Except that there was no way to replenish back at her own station.

The station's lights didn't come on, so she just had her suit lights. They cast eerie shadows across the old table and chairs. This was where the crew would have eaten, had meetings, and even conducted some of their assay work.

How could four people have possibly functioned in here for months on end?

There was the table and a small kitchen at one end, bunks at the other. In between were the airlock, bathroom and tiny machine shop. Little more than a closet space, the machine shop had the suit locker.

Two suits. Helmets and gloves racked above.

"Two suits," she whispered.

"What's that?" José said.

Sula took a breath. "There are only two suits."

José cursed.

CHAPTER ELEVEN

When Sula got the Phobos Station II suits down and checked them, there was damage to one. An underarm seam that had frayed away. Perhaps it had gotten caught on something or just worn out with use.

She knew as well as anyone that things got pushed to their limit out here. Space exploration was littered with inventory exceeding its design life.

Everyone celebrated when it was a rover or a probe still functioning years after a ninety-day primary mission had been completed. Woo-hoo.

But all too often it was the workers—the astronauts—who were dealing with constant improvisation to keep things running. Highly motivated since if the thing didn't keep running, they would die.

"Good news," José said. "I've managed to figure out a relay to Earth. Thanks for positioning those ruined suits."

"You're welcome."

"They're putting a burn on one of the ore carriers. Getting it here faster. Four and a half days."

"That's great."

"In a way."

"What do you mean?"

"That shake up it's, well, it's punctured something. We're losing air here."

A chill ran through Sula's core.

"How fast?"

"Fast."

Her mouth was dry.

"Be precise," she said. "Minutes or hours?"

"Oh, definitely hours."

Sula muttered something Uncle Steve would not have approved of.

She told José about the ruined suit.

"That's fine," he said. "Miranda wants to speak with you."

"Go ahead."

Some clicks and quiet thumps came through the helmet speaker.

"Sula?" Miranda said. "Make sure you drink something."

"Yes Mom." But Sula leaned forward and took a sip from the helmet's tiny drinking straw. Some kind of spirulina-papaya mix. It was actually pretty tasty.

"Can you confirm that there is just one functional suit?"

"Yes. I'll bring it over right away."

"I want you to stay put."

Sula took a moment to parse that.

"I can be back with you within an hour," she said.

"It's not going to work. Not with a single suit."

"I can ferry you. One at a time."

There was no response for a moment.

"We've talked it over," Miranda said. "You're safe now. Reboot the station. Use its equipment to stay alive. You might get hungry, but you'll last the four days until rescue arrives."

"I'm sorry, you're breaking up. Did you say to come rescue you right away?"

"Stay put."

"Copy that. On my way now."

"Sula. Listen. You can't save us. You—"

"I'll save you," Sula said. "Or I'll die trying."

CHAPTER TWELVE

As the miner trundled over Phobos's surface, Sula used a screwdriver from Station II to jimmy open the control box in the little cab. She'd found an old portable display in the station and with a simple plug interface, she broke into the operating system.

Jiggered up the speed overrides.

There was good reason for limiting the speed of a miner on Phobos. Big as they were, it didn't take much to bounce them up off the surface. Not that they would be likely to tip or launch very far, but in reality there was no hurry, and every bump or jolt made for more maintenance for machinery that was already very high maintenance.

And still it took over thirty minutes to make it back to the ruin of Phobos Station III.

It looked interesting, really. Would future archaeologists come out here to investigate? Would tourists come the way they flocked to ruins in Greece and Cambodia and other places?

Sula's helmet had a row of amber lights. She'd been able to

recharge her air at Phobos Station II, but there were still issues with the water and the heating-cooling.

"How are you doing in there?" she asked.

"Well," José said. "Miranda's pretty mad with you. Val's ambivalent and I guess I'm kind of the same, maybe."

"The same 'mad' or the same 'ambivalent'?"

"Either, or."

"You're so funny. I'm going to open up the hatch and lower the functional suit to you. I'll stay topside. You can open the inner hatch and retrieve it. Careful not to bump the helmet."

"Copy that. Miranda wants a word."

"I bet she does." Sula got out of the miner and retrieved the old suit. She bounced across to the chamber's upper hatchway.

"Sula?" Miranda said. "I wish you would have listened."

"Shut up. I'm giving you a chance here."

She set down the suit, and pushed aside the damaged linked suits. She undogged the hatch.

"One of us," Miranda said. "You're asking us to draw straws."

"No. I'm asking for patience." Sula got the hatch undogged and lowered it on its hinges.

"Someone has to climb out of here while the other two watch."

"We came out into space knowing the dangers. And listen, they don't climb out. They wait."

"Wait! While the other two asphyxiate. Sula, I know this is hard but you've—"

"Listen, Miranda. I'm not waiting here for someone to get into their suit and climb out." Sula pushed the suit's boots over the edge. She lowered the whole thing. Let it settle on the lower hatch.

"Not waiting?" Miranda said.

"While they're changing, I'm going to be on my way over to Phobos Station I." Sula had a cord and she lowered the helmet.

"Phobos Station I?" Miranda said.

The helmet touched the suit and Sula let go of the cord. She grabbed the hatch's upper wheel and pulled it into place. She turned to wheel to dog the hatch shut.

"Sula?" Miranda said.

"Trust me."

CHAPTER THIRTEEN

Sula didn't even know if she could believe it herself.

This was blind faith.

Trusting that Phobos Station I would have two functional suits. Trusting that she could make it back in time on her makeshift transport.

The miner bumped and jerked across the regolith. The sun was rising. Tidally locked to Mars, Phobos's day matched its orbital period. More or less three and a half hours of sunlight, three and a half hours of night. That meshed poorly with the human body clock.

"Sula?" José said in her helmet speaker. Quieter than earlier.

"Problem?" she said.

"Yes. We got the suit fine. Now we're all just standing around looking at it."

"Do you need me to pick who gets in it?"

"It's too small for Val."

"I can choose between you and Miranda. That's easy."

"You joke too much. Look, I've pulled up the records on

Phobos Station I. When it was decommissioned, there weren't any suits left behind."

"Really?" Usually decommissioning a base just involved walking away. It cost too much out here to try to recycle gear. Even from Phobos, there was a cost to weight ratio when it came to launches.

"Really," José said. "So, you might as well stop."

Sula kept driving. She was only fifteen minutes away from the Station I. More or less. Phobos was small.

"Do something for me," she said. "Check the records on Phobos Station II as well."

"Why? You already raided it."

"Check."

"Just a minute."

The miner kicked up dust behind it. Sula was getting jostled around and she had to hold on to the little cabin's frame to stay upright.

"Huh," José said. "How about that?"

"What?"

"Phobos Station II records show that there were no suits there either. Nothing at all, in fact. The place was stripped."

"According to the records."

"Yes. You found two suits there."

"I did. Though only one was functional."

"Yes. But someone falsified records. Or was just plain lazy."

"Easier to tick boxes than to drag everything into a freight compartment."

"I guess. Gives me a little hope that there might actually be suits at Station I."

"A little hope goes a long way."

CHAPTER FOURTEEN

Soon, Phobos Station I came up over the horizon. The station was simpler even than Phobos Station II. No windows. No stilts. No style.

Just a pod standing on the surface.

Sula slowed the miner and stopped ten yards from the open airlock hatch.

That wasn't good.

If the outer hatch was open, then maybe the inner hatch was too. Which meant maybe a whole lot of dust and contaminants inside. Assuming there were suits in there, years of exposure like that wasn't great.

Sula jumped from the miner, letting Phobos's minuscule gravity tug her down. She landed right at the airlock. Stumbled inside.

She activated her suit lights.

The inner hatch stood open too.

Inside there was a coating of dust over everything. Phobos Station II had seemed like an exercise in compactness, but here was a whole other level. The work bench was horizontal, with two bunks folded against the wall. If the occupants needed to sleep, they would have to fold the bench out of the way. The entire crew occupiable space was maybe six or eight square meters. The size of small bedroom back home.

Papers and a plate and utensils lay, dust-covered, on the table. Fascinating. There were whole stories in here.

Sula didn't have time for archaeology.

She turned to the other end of the station. A closet with machinery and a tiny work space. A bathroom which combined the shower with the toilet. And lockers.

Three suits.

There was no time to check them here. She gathered them up and tied them together with cord from another locker.

She hustled back to the miner. She laid the suits out on top and shuffled around into the little cab. She tapped on controls to turn around.

Nothing happened.

The old display flickered. Came back on strong and clear.

The connection had been lost.

She pulled out the plug and jammed it in again.

Nothing.

This was what happened when stuff got jury-rigged.

She unplugged and plugged in again. Still nothing.

With some clicks and swipes, she got the display to reboot. It was running off power from the connection to the miner. She just needed to get the controls operating.

While the display went through its boot cycle, she took the miner's regular controls. Levers that overrode its internal automatic systems. Simple and easy to operate.

She pulled the levers back.

Nothing.

"José?" she said. "Are you seeing any telemetry from the miner?"

There was no response.

"José? Come in."

Still nothing.

She shoved the pair of levers forward. Pulled the left one back. That should initiate a turn to the left.

The miner didn't budge.

The display's display flickered to life again. She swiped through to the makeshift control system and tried again.

Nothing.

The miner was refusing to cooperate.

"José?" she said. "Miranda? Val? Someone there?"

No response.

How far was she from Phobos Station III?

In frustration she yanked on the levers again.

The miner jerked. Moved backward a half a meter and came to a stop.

The display shut off.

Sula looked behind. Back toward the Station III.

Maybe two kilometers away?

The miner's tracks made a trail leading directly there.

Sula gathered up the ungainly bundle of suits.

She jumped.

CHAPTER FIFTEEN

The arc of Sula's jump carried her high and over the long tracks left by the miner. She saw Mars above. Half dark, half light. The terminator drove an almost straight line north to south. Lightning flickered on the dark side. She didn't see that often. Something to do with the impacts sending up dust plumes?

Then Phobos's surface was rising toward her. She braced for her landing.

Left foot. Right foot. She stumbled. Almost fell.

Kept her balance. She skipped along.

One of her telltale LEDs flickered between amber and red. Cooling.

Not great. If she was going to run all the way back to the station, she was going to get hot.

Ironic. Out here where heat was scarce.

She jumped again. Felt light as she went. Floating. Flying.

She came down. Left foot. Right foot. Caught her balance.

Jumped again.

"José?" she said. "Come in."

A little burst of static came back, but no words. Was there something up with the suit relay she'd left behind?

Best to think that was the problem and not anything else. Best not to think of them in trouble.

Left foot. Right foot.

She jumped again.

Got it wrong this time, turning as she progressed through the arc.

She came down sideways. Staggered.

Fell.

The bundle of suits spun from her grasp.

They bounced away. The cord snapped and they spilled out separately.

Sula rolled over. She knelt, with her hands on the surface. As if she was going to crawl the rest of the way.

She was breathing hard now. Her heart was pounding.

Sula stood. She looked back.

The miner didn't seem so far away. As if she'd hardly made any progress.

She closed her eyes. Steeled herself.

She gathered up the suits. Tied them once more. Held them above her head.

Jumped again.

She was going to do this.

Or die trying.

CHAPTER SIXTEEN

There was liquid on her right leg. Warm.

Either a heating-cooling tube had gotten a leak, or she was bleeding. The burr there in the suit, digging into her. She'd almost stopped noticing it.

And she'd lost count of how many jumps she'd made. A hundred? A hundred and fifty?

She'd developed a good rhythm. She was covering twenty or thirty meters at a time. Conservative. She could jump farther if she wanted, but she needed to keep too many things in mind.

Landing, for one. She'd fallen another six more times.

The poor suits were getting a little beaten up.

And she needed to make sure she didn't overheat.

Another jump.

Landing. Left foot. Right foot.

Another jump.

Phobos Station III came into view. So close.

A little gasp escaped her.

Phobos's size meant that the horizon was remarkably close. She was just a few more jumps away.

"José?" she said. "Come in."

Nothing.

She walked the last thirty meters. No sense in risking it all so close.

She kept calling for José, but he wasn't responding.

Setting the suits down, she moved the two original, linked, smashed-up suits from the hatch.

And right away saw another issue.

The shaft was narrow. It had been hard enough for her to make her way down just in her suit. Now she needed to get all these other suits—even the smashed-up ones—down into the chamber below.

"José?" she said. If there was a response, she could dump the suits all down into the shaft and they could open the lower hatch and just gather them.

But there was no response.

"José? Please come in."

Still nothing.

One at a time, then. Like so many activities out here.

One thing at a time.

CHAPTER SEVENTEEN

Sealed in, Sula moved the hatch at the base of the shaft. She'd tugged down one of the suits. It now hung above her, one glove tucked into a rung.

She used the electric system to cycle the lower hatch.

Dropping through, she found the other three standing there staring at her.

There was dust in the air, picked out by her suit lights.

The lights in the chamber were all shut off.

Sula took off her helmet. The air stank. It was thick and cloying.

"We lost power," José said. "About an hour ago."

Sula glanced back. "How did I open the hatch then? How did I cycle the shaft open?"

"Separate battery," Val said. "Isolated system."

"Okay. I have suits. I'll drop them down the shaft. You open up. Get what you can. We'll make our way to Phobos Station II to wait it out."

CHAPTER EIGHTEEN

The process took an more than an hour. Back topside, Sula worked on trying to call up another one of the miners to come to transport them.

There was no response.

What she did manage to get hold of was the little three-wheeler transport she'd spotted back at Phobos Station II. It showed up as a menu item on the display that José had given her.

The three-wheeler still had power. It was big enough to transport one of them easily, with some gear. Maybe two at a pinch.

With some prodding into its system she got it trundling on its away to her.

It arrived just as José poked his head up out of the access shaft.

He cursed, looking around.

"Yeah, I know," Sula said. "Yet here we are."

José climbed out and Miranda followed.

"Val's not liking the suit," she said. "Says its compressing his spine."

Then she swore.

"Easy," José said. "All of this is getting relayed back to Earth."

"Who cares? How long until the rescue vessel gets here?"

"Four days, give or take."

"Well, that's... what is that?" Miranda was looking at the three-wheeler.

"Our chariot," Sula said. "It will take us to our new home."

"Our new home? You mean Phobos Station II?"

"You think our place was cramped? Wait until you see this."

CHAPTER NINETEEN

Phobos Station II turned out to serve them remarkably well. They had to jury-rig plenty to get power and heating and air working right, but it became livable.

Sula told herself that it was only for four days, really.

Tepou Station, down on Mars, had taken a hit from the meteor shower, but they'd lost just a single module, and no personnel. The station was bigger and more robust that anything on Phobos. And on the surface, they had the advantage of a little bit of atmosphere to buffer them.

On the third evening, Sula was sitting alone at Phobos Station II's little table, with a cup of distilled water and a handful of tasty nuts. There were enough supplies to last them the four days, but not for much longer.

"Hey," José said, appearing from the little bathroom. He'd showered with water that had already been drunk and peed out. Probably multiple times. The purification system was getting a good work out.

There had been talk of a jaunt to Phobos Station I to see if they could recover other supplies, but that was really only in case something broke down.

"Hey yourself," Sula said. "You still stink."

"Yes, but I stink less than you." He was wearing just a towel around his waist, and he pulled on tee-shirt as he made his way to her.

Miranda and Val were both in the narrow bunks at the other end, sleeping. All four of them had been working intensively to get the little station running right and to a point that they felt comfortable.

"Good job," José said, sitting across from Sula.

Sula smiled. "Meaning?"

"Meaning trekking around Phobos and getting us here and safe. That took something."

Sula shrugged. "Just doing my—"

José held up his hand. "Don't brush it off. We'll be rescued soon, and we wouldn't be here if you hadn't gone off and broken every protocol we have."

"Not every one. I looked at the document, and there are a couple on page eight hundred and sixty that I didn't go near."

José laughed. He reached out and touched her hand.

"Emergency chambers should have suits in them," Sula said. "That's what I'm putting in my report."

José smiled.

"Thank you," he said. "Your uncle would be proud."

"My uncle?"

"Your Uncle Steve, who kind of raised you. Took you out to look at the stars."

"You know about him?"

"Of course. You and I have had conversations before, you know. You and me. I enjoy your company. I'm proud of you too. Honored to know you."

He took her hand and shook it, and winked at her.

Standing, he said, "I'd better go get dressed. I'd hate for the towel to fall off."

As he walked away, the towel did fall and she got a view of his butt.

"Idiot," she said.

But she smiled to herself.

Uncle Steve would have been proud. And if she would admit it, she was proud of herself too.

AFTERWORD

I love writing near-future, near solar system stories, and Sula's tale was one of the most fun writing times I've had. She's a tough customer, even if she has to deal with team mates who have other opinions.

The idea of surface bases being vulnerable to space rocks is nothing new. With thin atmospheres, or no atmospheres at all, those likely bodies for our near-term exploration and occupation —primarily the Moon, Mars, Mars's two moons Phobos and Deimos, and even the asteroid Ceres—have surfaces revealing eons of impact craters.

I'm under no illusions that the danger is real, but also cognizant that the chances are remote. Sure there are plenty of floating rocks out there that can swirl unexpectedly into a planet's or moon's gravity field, but this story is very much at tale of being in the wrong place at the wrong time.

Yeah, I like writing those kinds of stories too.

I have a blast writing survival tales. Throwing my characters into desperate situations and watching them tough it out.

Sometimes they surprise me with their resourcefulness. Of course, as a writer, when they do that, I have to toss them another curveball. And Sula proved up to the task.

Thanks for reading. I hope you enjoyed 'Phobos Pummeled'.

Take care.

Sean
January 2026

CHAPTER ONE

The pyramids in the place were tall and skinny as if built by people with far better senses of height perception than humans. It's always been a thing that we humans are pretty good at estimating horizontal distances and lousy with vertical distances.

Some kind of old *survival on the Serengeti* thing, maybe.

Try it. You'll see. Take a look along the road, or across a field and figure out how far it is to walk. Then go walk it. No trouble, right?

Then go to a hill. Some steep incline you've seen from a distance. Go to the bottom. Walk to the top. *Whew*, how about that? Not so easy. It looked like it was maybe a hundred and fifty feet, but it was more like three hundred and it *felt* like six hundred.

Or maybe that's just me.

I had a friend, Egret Palm, who loved rock climbing. She would take on the half dome without ropes and laugh at all the other climbers. Dead now, but that's the case with most of my friends. Don't cry for me, I'm the one still alive.

And here I am digressing and I haven't even started in on the story, which is what you all are really here for, isn't it?

About the time when we discovered the first sentients and it freaked the living pajamas out of me and my boss and my boss's boss and right on up the chain to the *New York Times* and *Chicago Post* and *Le Monde*.

Of course, who reads those venerable institutions now, after hundreds of years? Me for one. My daughter Kadie, and she would know, being of that generation what understand the world, they would think, and bring a certain element of annoyance about the state of things and the mess we're leaving them.

Same with every one of the generations since Gutenberg, I guess. All of us kind of with our back up about perceived wrongs in the world that need righting.

And then, turns out, after hundreds of searches and investigations and hooptie-what-illions of petabytes of data analysis, that there actually are other sentient lifeforms in the galaxy.

That put a capybara among the pythons for sure.

And me, Peter Jaimble, the guy who found them.

Wish I never had.

CHAPTER TWO

There was a time, and I don't know the exact history, when the civilizations of Central America had been lost, but their pyramids and cities were later rediscovered. I think it was Tikal in old Guatemala or Belize that was one of the most famous.

As someone who is now studying these things out on Wilderun IV—don't you love how they number planets?—you'd think that I would know a little more. At least would have gone and done some reading.

But really, I'm just a drone jockey.

Before I was born—cue age jokes—some bright sparks in the remnants of NASA sent out something like one *trillion* kernel bots.

Mostly forgotten, after all, this was about 2100, 2150, something like that. Hundreds of years back. Those people knew more about the dark ages than we know about their time.

These things they sent were state of the art for their time. The size of a clenched fist, enclosed in some kind of bubble and fired out into the vast unknown.

The historians all agree that it was an automated system, built out around the moons of Jupiter, self-building and self-directing. There have been archeological expeditions to the moons to look over the old workings. There are books about those, if you care to read them. Lemm Colwin's one is my favorite—filled with remarkable and well-framed photographs. Ruined conveyors and sifts and stampers with the crescent of Jupiter hanging on the horizon. Fabricators that look like gigantic beached animal carcasses.

Anyhow, these kernel bots were like little fabrication machines themselves. And they got accelerated to something like eighty percent of the speed of light. Ninety percent? I forget those details.

I heard the most of them were sent to the nearby systems. Alpha and Proxima Centauri. Ten year trip or something, when you account for acceleration and deceleration.

Story goes that there were people willing to sign up to go if the boffins could figure out a reliable vessel to keep people alive for ten years. A decade in a can. No thank you.

But it was just as well they didn't go. When the data came back, those places were not so hospitable. Everyone would have had to stay in the ship. And come back. *Twenty* years in a can.

Just nope.

Those kernel bots landed themselves on moons and asteroids and got to work building better bots. Mining the local resources to build satellites and telescopes, atmospheric drones—the kind I was watching through on Wilderun IV—and ground platforms, and vast dishes for sending the data back.

That data took four years—so, including all that build time, over fifteen years from departure—and it was all quite wonderfully rich. Filled with extraordinary imagery of the system. Comets and asteroids. Gas and ice giants. Dwarf planets.

And of course, rocky planets. Basically, you got a couple of Mercuries, a small hot damp Venus, a big baked dry Mars and an Earth-sized dead world.

Scientists were thrilled. Of course.

Media, not so much.

But then, over the decades, more and more of the datasets came through as those kernel bots established themselves in more and more distant systems.

For a long while, they were all dead.

Until Ollatine.

And here I am jumping around all over the place. Really you need a nice crisp narrative that tells you about Wilderun, since I was the first on the scene. You know, the Nell Armstrane of my time.

I wish. Really, I was just the guy in the seat when the data came in.

And you need background. About the program. About the history.

Otherwise none of it makes sense.

Or perhaps all this is just me trying to make sense of it for myself.

And Kadie would tell me that would never happen.

CHAPTER THREE

So I'm going to ask a little more of you here. Because it's important to getting to the pyramids and our understanding. If I'm going to understand the implications, I need to run through all this, and if I'm going to be clear, I need to be clear with myself.

I've been a lousy father.

I'm sure that fathers have been saying that since time immemorial. People will say that it's the ones who say they're lousy are the ones who are just regular fathers making missteps along the way, and that the fathers who really *are* lousy don't acknowledge. They just plough on through, working late or vanishing, or beating up their kids' mothers, justifying everything.

But there was me. Working late.

Because of Wuscha.

Because I allowed myself to become entranced by that delicate soft artificial voice.

And I allowed it to draw me away from Kadie.

When she needed me.

I'll circle around.

My job, at the institute, was to sit in the drone chair at the receiving station and watch the live feeds from Wilderun IV, Pasteur, Omigoggle, Selter II and III, Happenstance, Granite, Billshakes, T9-45ald, Top, Cleopatra and a half dozen other worlds.

Lurching back and forth in the shell as the feeds come through. Keeping my eye out for anything interesting.

Four hours a day. Four days a week. It's long hours, I tell you.

Meanwhile, Kadie was busy winning climbing contests and endurance races. Twelve years old.

Mother in the ground.

Let me take a breath there. Ease out of the anger at Belinda leaving us like that.

And the anger at myself for dealing with it so poorly. As in leaving the kid to raise herself.

Circling again. Amazing to think that I make my livelihood as a data interpreter and I can't even put all this down in a straight line.

Maybe what you do, dear reader, is run this through your system and have it reorder things to create a linear narrative.

That's what we've wanted since the Serengeti, isn't it?

Bral was hunting an antelope and threw his spear but missed and the antelope ran off. When Bral retrieved his spear, a lion spotted him and gave chase.

Bral raced up a tree and hid for a while, but the lion stuck around until after nightfall. And when the lion slipped away, and Bral climbed down the tree, a branch broke and he fell and twisted his ankle and jabbed himself with the spear tip.

His blood attracted hyenas, and he had to limp away as fast as he could, throwing rocks at them. He swiped with his spear, but it broke.

He ran again. Just two hundred steps from the safety of the village, his ankle gave out and he stumbled. He could see the light from the fire.

The hyenas swarmed him.

But Bral still had hold of the spear tip. As the alpha hyena stood over him, Bral stabbed upward. Into the hyena's neck.

The animal collapsed. The others ran off, distressed.

Bral dragged himself along the rough ground, hauling the carcass with him.

Soon he was back with his hungry family, with a new story and food aplenty.

That's it. A nice linear story. You're unlikely to get that with me, but with luck I'll be able to pull off that moment of the hyena's jaws snapping at my throat.

But of course, it will be a looping path.

CHAPTER FOUR

Ollatine's Earth-sized world was covered with a huge range of lush forests, and wide deserts, polar habitats, prairie, savannah, steppes. Huge deltas brimming with mangrove and cypress swamps.

The drones and aircraft flew themselves. The systems were smart, for sure—and getting smarter—and they offered commentary with the data.

Primeval.

Another step back, in case I need to explain that a little more. Most people are concerned with their home's air systems and backed up water, and all this stuff happening light years away is off the scopes.

The kernel systems operated as if there were people present. Made decisions. Built mechanisms for scientific examination of star systems people would never visit.

And those systems allowed us to visit them virtually. Albeit years upon years after the datasets had been sent.

Live-feeds were hardly the tennis ball match from Barcelona

or wherever, delayed by milliseconds. These were delayed by decades, many of them.

Ollatine was exciting. The first direct imagery of off-world life.

Then there were others.

Then it became dull, almost. Routine. More trees with purple leaves and birds with twin wings and insects with proboscises that could bore through the shells of rhinoceros-sized land mollusks.

Perhaps all this destroyed our sense of wonder.

What little we had left.

Is that enough background on the program? Feel free to ask questions at any point. Fire them off and I'll try to reply, when I get time.

As you might appreciate, though, I seem to have precious little time now, what with the Wilderun IV discoveries.

People are interested all over again.

CHAPTER FIVE

An aside here. One for all the parents among you. I managed to have dinner with Kadie. It was nice. She has a new beau. Some guy working on genetic redressation systems. I think that means making plants less dependent on us again. He explained it, but I lost track about three sentences in.

She seemed kind of bored too, and I wondered if she'd only brought him along as a kind of a buffer between us. So we didn't have to talk the whole time. Someone to fill the awkward silences.

The restaurant was nice. Decorated with a kind of glittering undersea theme. Whales and gulls, bumphead parrotfish and hermit crabs. They wandered the deep blue walls in slow animation.

The waiters cranked around on uniwheels, delivering an array of seafood fresh from the vats.

"So," Miki—the beau—said. "You're *the* Peter Jaimble."

"I'm *a* Peter Jaimble." The family name has grown to be

fairly familiar, when once it was unusual. From a line of the family that had changed its name, from James, when a politician had soured things for his brother and sister. They were protecting their kids.

"But you're the Peter Jaimble who discovered the sentients on Wilderun IV," Miki said.

Really, I was just the person watching the show at the time. Celebrity, though, can be massaged through.

"I am," I said. "I logged the details. They could hardly get me out of the pod when I reached the village."

"Extraordinary." He stared at me. For a moment, I thought he was going to ask for my autograph.

"Also," Kadie said, "he plays a mean game of jai-alai. Put out another guy's eye. Broke someone's arm."

To be fair, that guy had taken exception to an umpire's call and attacked me. It was all self-defense.

Miki looked around Kadie, as if she'd told him stock prices were going down, or that she was thinking of changing her hair again.

I could tell it wouldn't last. Maybe not even beyond the end of the meal.

Which arrived then. Jambalaya for them and a delicious looking thick ceviche broth for me. The smell was heavenly.

"Are they coming?" Miki said, ignoring his plate and looking at me again.

"Coming?"

"The sentients? Are the coming to us? Maybe they have faster than light technology. They might give it to us."

I looked at my daughter and she had the slightest of smirks on her face, but she locked eyes with me. We understood each other right then. This guy was a bozo. A scientist who read the popular press and simply forgot that you can't go faster than light, even if you're a six-fingered, four-eyed, gray-skinned alien who builds pyramids shaped like church steeples.

CHAPTER SIX

All right. Family stuff out of the way, now I can give you the details on the mission.

On that moment.

When I saw the Wilders—what else could we call them?—I was both astonished and relieved.

The drones and fliers and whathaveyou have a built in rudimentary intelligence. They make their own decisions. Choose what to look at. Remember, we're dealing with tech that's a couple hundred years old. Ancient stuff.

But solid. *Rock* solid, as they say.

The trick is that they're ninety-eight years away. All the data, all the feeds, are ancient.

These images that I've been watching were sent from Wilderun IV before I was born.

The discoveries were made. The systems' intelligences made their inferences and deductions about things and sent them along with the information streams.

If we want them to do anything, it will take a hundred years —yes, I'm rounding up—before they hear from us, and another hundred before we hear back and see the results.

I'll be dust. Kadie will be dust, but I don't want to think about that, of course.

We are but passengers. Observers. Almost like we're just watching a documentary film. You know, something about genetically rebuilt lions being released into the Kalahari. It's been filmed and now we just watch.

So I was in my pod, six weeks back, enjoying watching the flyover of the pyramid fields. As I said, they were tall and spiky. Church steeples. They stood way above the tops of the forest canopy.

In case you haven't come across them, my pod is egg-shaped, with a seat in the center, and display all across the internal walls. This is lumeric display, so there's a depth to it. The facets track my eyes so each retina receives a slightly different image, so it's as if I'm sitting on a flying carpet, whispering along above the jungle. There are sounds, of course, birds calling and animals grunting and the rustle of the wind through the leaves. No smell, which I suppose is no surprise, and feeling of the wind—this is not a theme park ride, but a scientific mission.

The pyramids' stone was worn and a weathered. Ages old. Vines crept up parts of them. There were glyphs and imagery carved into the sides.

Everything was being diligently recorded. The bots and the boffins were developing datasets for deeper analysis. It was already a huge tasks—thousands of planets with the kernel bot results pouring in—but adding in the Wilders just multiplied the requirements.

You might ask what my role is, and it would be a fair question. As in, am I just along for the ride? If that data is a hundred years old, and the feed is just a simple, solid reel of radio waves coming in endlessly, there's nothing I could do to change it.

Not like when Melanie Aitch spotted that rock on the surface of Mars and went off program to go and retrieve it. You'd think that technically there was nothing I could do to assist.

Thing is, the human eye is pretty remarkable with what it can assess. Sure, those drones out there on Wilderun IV are loaded with intelligence and decision making capacity. Theoretically smarter than any human. Than any ten.

But for all of that, there's an element of intuition.

That sense of knowing something when the data doesn't quite point to it. I've always considered it a holographic way of observing the world. Something that, despite holographic neural networking, the machines have never quite closed up.

And so it was me, floating through the jungle, virtually aboard one of the flyers, who spotted the movement at the base of one of the pyramids.

A Wilder.

The first.

Walking along with its odd slow, looping gait—think about one of those lackadaisical cartoon characters—carrying a bow, and with a small dead animal over its shoulder.

Within the pod, I turned my head. Watched it until it was out of sight.

The Wilder had been watching me too. I bet, wondering what the hey kind of a bird is that up there, and whether it might be a viable meal.

Of course, I couldn't do anything about retracing my steps. Circling or anything.

The flyer just kept on moving with its gridded sweeps.
So right away I flagged the contact.
And the institute's settings suddenly ramped up.
Me in the middle of a maelstrom.

CHAPTER SEVEN

There's an old saw about information flow coming at you like a fire hose. Chances are you don't even know what a fire hose is, right?

So, back in the day, from most of the time between Bral running away from the hyenas and Nolex launching the embryo starship and destroying its own credibility at the same time, things humans built used to catch fire. And catch fire with alarming frequency.

Trees and plastic and other materials with all this potential energy and they made their houses out of it.

So, to reduce the potential of property loss and people burning to death, there was a whole huge system of water piped in all around the cities. High pressure. People in helmets and heat-proof jackets would race around in sleek, loud vehicles and blast the offending blaze with the water to douse every last flame and cinder and spark.

Dead serious with the water, right?

That's the metaphor for how data comes in from Wilderun IV. And all the other places.

Sheesh, I can go on, right? Someone will probably parse this later and get it down to twenty or thirty words.

Data transmission from all the automated exo-explorers is at a level beyond requirements.

Anyway, a firehose of data. Imagine your daily feeds, you know, movies and conversations and all and we're talking about terabytes and petabytes. The stuff coming from the stars comes in exabytes. Or tens of exabytes. Or zettabytes? I lose track of those numbers.

A firehose of data. And we're trying to get it through a drinking straw and into a glass.

So plenty of the data is lost.

Gone forever. We just don't have the storage capacity or the receiving facilities.

So right away I flipped a switch. Opened up the Wilderun IV drinking straw into a massive funnel. Turned the glass into a gigantic vat.

And I set the systems analytics onto it.

CHAPTER EIGHT

All of which—firehose data and me in the pod *intuiting* what's important—cycles us back around to Miki's question.

"Are they coming?"

That's the scary thing and that's the thing that the institute and the government and everyone wants to keep quiet.

Which is a heck of a thing, let me tell you.

Back in the early days of space travel, there was a whole broad swathe of people caught in some kind of information loop with the belief that *We Never Went To Mars*. As if the Martian landing, and Melanie Aitch and her crew, had never existed. Or that they were faked.

These people had all kinds of evidence. Too expensive. Too hard to do. Focal length of some of the photos wrong. Someone who'd been to Jordan and taken photos, saying that it all looked as if it had just been staged there.

Of course, all of those could be easily explained with some simple logic. But one of the kickers was that the effort took hundreds of thousands of people over millions and millions of hours, so how come not one of those went to the media? As one wag said, "Anyone trying to build that kind of house of cards conspiracy would just give up since it's actually easier to just go to Mars."

But us here, now, with our firehose of data, trying to answer the question *are they coming?*

So that was me. In the pod. Simulating and running through the extrapolations.

And that was when it got real bad.

See, the pyramids were like just one isolated part of Wilderun IV.

You know how there are still indigenous peoples who maintain distance from us so-called civilized folks? You know, they still hunt and gather. And we leave them alone, which is a whole lot better than it used to be.

Well, that was like the Wilders near the pyramids.

When I looked over the data for more areas of the planet, I found industrialization.

On small, but very advanced scale.

Shipbuilding yards.

Space-capable ships.

CHAPTER NINE

So the spiky pyramids were just in a few corners of Wilderun IV. You might ask how come the global surveys didn't show up the industrialization right off the bat and that's a fair question.

Maybe it was because the datasets were still being parsed. Maybe because the cities and yards were so very different from anything we would build—as if the Wilders had never heard of a straight line. Swirls and curves, all integrated into thick forests and bayous and harbors.

Maybe it was just my sheer laziness.

You know, I love flying around in the pod, exploring new worlds. Maybe rather than laziness it could just be a certain kind of jaded-ness. After a while things start the blur, perhaps.

Still whatever the reason for not picking up on the data right away, we did pick up on the data.

Now, there are sixteen of us, all riding through the data that's still coming in. Building up extrapolations. Working with what we have.

We've sent instructions to the kernel systems to have them examine the cities and the yards more closely. Asked them to ramp up their asteroid construction bases to build more fliers and drones and get them on site.

It'll be a hundred years before they get that message.

A hundred more years, and then some, before we start getting clearer, directed and more useful data.

But it's clear enough to me what's going on right now.

Taking pieces of the drone data, of the satellite data and extrapolation sets, we're starting to get a full picture.

A huge bell of a ship.

Size of one of those old football stadiums.

Now, the drone and flier systems had figured out by this point that there were interesting things happening there—in a way it made my 'discovery' of the first Wilder almost moot; these cities would have been found anyway.

But it meant that there were more focused data coming in.

And, it meant that the Wilders, the ones with the cities and the ship-building capacity, were taking notice.

Some drones got shot down. Some got caught.

Those ones sent back data for a while as they were examined and broken apart.

I got called into a meeting.

The brief was a simple *please explain*.

Which is mostly what you've got above.

So from that I got a request for solutions. That meant a bigger meeting with a team of people.

I won't bore you with that.

But Miki, he was well-keen on getting bored with it all.

CHAPTER TEN

It was another restaurant. *Aftrican Fusion*. All black beans and thick, doughy breads which are so delicious, but at my age simply make a beeline for my waist.

And still it was good to be with Kadie and Miki. There were only about fifteen tables, and the whole place was set on a gently bobbing raft in Turner Swamp which is basically just a big algae farm outside of Nuku Alofa.

Between the entrée—brittle crab—and the main—beans and dough for me, swarmbeef for the other two—Miki pumped me for information.

"There's not much to tell," I said. "It's all been in the papers."

Papers. Such a quaint term. The idea nowadays of pulping trees to make sheets of paper sounds positively barbaric.

"They're building a ship," he said. "That's all we know."

"Ah, so it is a little interesting then." I leaned forward. "They're not *building* a ship. The *built* a ship. A hundred years ago."

"Ninety-eight," Kadie said. She was energetic and smiling. She had a glint in her eye. Just as well I now kind of approved of this Miki bloke, otherwise I'd be getting concerned.

"Yes," I said. "Ninety-eight years ago."

"So they could could be almost here by now," Miki said. "We'd never know."

"They can't go faster than light," I said. "So factor that in. And now we're already scanning to see if they did launch their ship and are on their way."

Miki squinted. He put his hand to his forehead.

"Let me help," Kadie said. "We *will* have some warning. No matter how fast they're coming, we'll see them first."

"What?" Miki said, looking around at her.

There were condiments on the table. Pepper and chili flakes, in cylindrical ceramic containers. Kadie picked up the pepper and put it against my plate across the table.

"Dad's plate is Wilderun IV," she said. "The pepper is the ship."

"I'm not a child," Miki said.

"Yet to be proven. So if their ship leaves, traveling close to the speed of light, somehow, the light is still faster."

She moved the pepper closer to her own plate.

"Earth," she said. "We can see it coming."

"It might only be a year or two away," Miki said.

"Sure. But the key is that we'd see it."

"The data would get here before any ship," I said. "And if they've somehow figured out how to evade the limit of the speed of light, then—"

"Impossible," Kadie cut in.

"—then they would be here already."

"Ray guns blasting and city-killer bombs exploding," Kadie said.

"Fishbowl helmets on their heads," Miki said. "Since they breathe liquid."

Kadie laughed. And I did too. Despite my misgivings, I was warming to Miki.

The meal was good, with no more talk about possible invaders from Wilderun IV.

Plenty going on in my head about it, though, let me tell you.

CHAPTER ELEVEN

Right after dinner, I hit the transport and wound up back at the institute. Shut myself in the pod right away. Started reviewing all the visual and audio data.

Looking hard.

Should have been obvious and yet, here it was, a connection revealed to me by my daughter's current beau.

If the Wilders are building starships, then maybe there's a thing or two we could learn from them. What kind of propulsion systems are they exploiting?

I got the system on it, working overtime to extrapolate every piece of data it could. What were those coils for? Why did that copper and glass apparatus look different a few days later? Were they using something biological in that tank?

Our systems are remarkably smart, but there were things the Wilders were building that we'd never come up with.

But things we could use.

Suddenly I was beyond being a researcher. I was an espionage agent.

Mining that data and sending it back to our engineers. Who knew what would come of it, but you know, I had something in mind.

Which makes the tale here circular in a way. I'm told you should never withhold information from your reader, but there's a better way to tell it than just baldly listing it here. More fun and, well, bear with me I suppose.

CHAPTER TWELVE

Kadie, bless her, had built a cabin up in the mountains. Now when I say cabin, most people would think of it as a mansion. Six bedrooms, six bathrooms. A landing pad that could accommodate ten vehicles. The entire fourth floor was given over to one wide open space filled with sofas and easy chairs and low tables from which visitors could sit and admire the wonderful, thick beech forest climbing the surrounding hills.

The air filled with their succulent scent and the day was warm and bright. The fifth floor had a balcony and I was sitting out on that when Kadie flew in. One of those little rental flitters that will wait all day, or all week, if you like.

"You're doing well," I told her when she found me on the balcony.

She shrugged. "I guess." She was wearing black leggings and a sports top, with blobby shoes, as if she was planning on running the mountain trails.

I filled a glass of wine for her from the bottle I'd brought along. A Bordeaux-cross. Something. Sweet and alcohol free. I had one myself.

"What's this?" she said. "A celebration?"

"No Miki?" I said.

"Miki is long gone. I told you."

"That's right." It was hard to remember the comings and goings of people she hooked up with.

"Celebration?" she stepped forward and took the glass.

"I guess," I said, echoing her, and seeing in the moment that she echoed me, really. Inflections picked up from when I was attempting to raise her.

A tui flew by, white throat feathers shining.

"Miki was in part to blame," I said. "Or credit. So I suppose the same goes to you."

"Credit?" she said. "Or blame?" She took a sip. "Oh! That's good."

"It is, yes."

"So. Tell me."

"The Wilders. You remember that—"

"I know what you do, Dad. Get to the point."

"They were building ships. In our hundred-year old feeds. So we looked closer. Saw that they had seen us. Believe that they know the source of the kernel bots. Know that we were observing them. Also, we know that they captured some. Deconstructed them. Used the technologies."

"Oh my. That doesn't sound good." Kadie stepped to the railing and leaned over. The wind whispered through the trees.

"Maybe," I said. "Maybe not."

"Is that why you got me out here? Is an invasion imminent? Are they going to come blasting. Like Miki said, with ray guns and city bombs? Are we trying to be all survivalist against the aliens."

"No. I asked you out here because I wanted to say how proud I am—"

"Sheesh, Dad!"

"I am proud of you. And I know that I haven't always..." Well, I trailed off. No sense in being all maudlin. "From what we talked about, I did some deconstructing of my own. Ran through the data. And we're building ships too. Big ships. Sending them out using their tech. Trying to meet them halfway."

"A little less than halfway, I'm guessing." Kadie took another sip. "After all, they have a head start."

"Sure. The estimates vary, but we're imagining a rendezvous about twenty-five light years out. Communication will just about be possible as we draw closer. There are already signals underway. Trying to figure it out."

"Smart. They'll give you a medal and a raise."

I licked my lips. My mouth was dry.

"What?" she said. She stared at me. Set her glass on the railing.

"No medal," I said. "No raise. But they are giving me a seat on the ship."

Kadie blanched.

And that was all I needed.

"But I'm not taking it," I said.

"No," she said. "You should. This is your life's work, after all."

I laughed.

"Sure. But I'm too easily distracted and I waffle on, and... no. What I mean is, and I know it sounds twee, but sitting in the pod or riding the ship is not my life's work."

"Good grief, Dad. Don't tell me that *I'm* your life's work."

A chill ran through me. It did sound wrong, but despite

everything, my life's work was right here. Maybe not in the pod, and definitely not Kadie—she was a piece of work all right, but all of her own invention—but my life's work nothing more than to be here.

I looked away, unable to look at her.

"I was thinking that you need a caretaker out here," I said. "Your cabin. Vulnerable to the elements and all."

I leaned on the railing and stared out at the lush forest.

"There are bots to do all that Dad." She moved closer. Picked up her glass. Leaned too, right by me.

"But yeah," she said. "Yeah I think it would be good to have you right here. Where I can keep an eye on you. Make sure you're not calling down raining hellfire from alien hordes."

I laughed and she put her arm around my shoulders, and I knew I'd made the right decision.

AFTERWORD

As I was preparing "We Are But Passengers" for publication, I wondered to myself if it was as much an exercise in voice as it was a story. One of my readers said to me something like 'Peter is a really *voice-y character*'. It was meant as a compliment. I think.

One of the things I've found myself doing more and more, in my writing, over recent years, has been writing a story for an anthology or in a series or even just to send out on submission to the top magazines, and discovering that the story didn't hit the marks I was expecting. This is kind of bothersome when I need to cover certain bases for an anthology.

Of course, the solution to that is to write another story. One that will hit the marks. Or at least come closer.

In this process, I'm ending up with a bunch of story pairs. The same ground, the same topic, sometimes even the same character. I think it's a good process for my learning and development as a writer. I always like to think that I'm getting better (of course, you, dear reader, are the judge of that... assuming you've read earlier, or later works of mine).

I guess the point of that digression is that with "We Are But Passengers", I felt like I hit those marks right off. Peter's voice is his own, and he told the story he needed to tell. There was no need for me, the writer—or in this case kind of just the stenographer taking down the story for Peter—to come back and have another shot.

The story here is the story as it stands.

Then, of course, there's the question of those other story pairs (and even some triples) and where they will show up. The trouble being that I generally like *both* versions, for different reasons. I suspect that it will come to publishing them together in little volumes with both or all three contained. Paired, I suppose, like, to create a bad metaphor, left and right socks.

Oh, that gives me an idea too; since I'm getting my act together and putting out more collections now, wouldn't a collection titled something like *Twins* or *Duos* or similar work? Then readers could pick for themselves the version they prefer.

Hmmm, I'll muse on that for a while.

As always, thanks for reading, I appreciate it. See you next time.

Sean
February 2026

AFTERWORD TO THE COLLECTION

Thanks again for reading the stories contained in this little book. I hope among the pages you found something entertaining and engaging. As I mentioned in the introduction, I have a lot of stories.

And I'm writing more all the time. I'll keep sending them off, and I'll keep publishing them like this, in collections and as standalone volumes. It's fun.

I'm told that I'm a prolific writer, but as I've noted previously, I just write at my own pace. There are plenty around who are far more prolific than I will ever be. I'm driven, perhaps, but not quite *that* driven.

My goal for the next year or so is to write more novels, but I know that I will keep mixing it up with stories too. It feels as if the adventures are just beginning.

Thanks once more. Cheers.

Sean
February 2026

ABOUT THE AUTHOR

Award-winning author, Sean Monaghan has published more than one hundred stories in the U.S., the U.K., Australia, and in New Zealand, where he makes his home. A regular contributor to Asimov's, his story "Crimson Birds of Small Miracles", set in the art world of Shilinka Switalla, won both the Sir Julius Vogel Award, and the Asimov's Readers' Poll Award, for best short story.

He is a past winner of the Jim Baen Memorial Award, and the Amazing Stories Award.

Sean writes from a nook in a corner of his 110 year old home, usually listening to eighties music.

www.seanmonaghan.com

instagram.com/seanmonaghanauthor

facebook.com/seanmonaghanauthor

OTHER BOOKS BY SEAN MONAGHAN

CAPTAIN ARLON STODDARD ADVENTURES

Asteroid Jumpers

Ice Hunters

Ship Tracers

Core Runners

Desert Creepers

Underworld Climbers

Island hoppers

Mist Drifters

Dead Ringers

Tramp Steamers

Cradle Robbers

Margin Dwellers

CAPTAIN ARLON STODDARD Shorts

Ortanide Steppers (novella)

Sea Skimmers (short story)

Dark Behemoth (short story)

KARNISH RIVER NAVIGATIONS

Arlchip Burnout

Canal Days

Eastern Foray

Guest House Izarra

Jackpot Kingdom

Liquid Machine

Night Operations

Persephone Quest

Rorqual Saitu

Tombs Under Vaile

Waxing Xebec

Yesterday's Ziggurat

THE JUPITER FILES

Book 1: Deuterium Shine

Book 2: Tritium Blaze

STANDALONE SCIENCE FICTION

The Ergs

Raphael Marooned

Hanging Vines

Raven Rising

Athena Setting

The City Builders

The Cly

Gretel

SCIENCE FICTION SHORT STORY COLLECTIONS

Balance

Balance II

Balance III

*Un*Balanced

Listen, You!

OTHER COLLECTIONS

Arms Wide

One Degree Below Freezing

Landslide Country

STANDALONE THRILLERS

The Courier

Ice Fracture

Rotations

Taken by Surprise

EMILY JADE SERIES

Big Sur

Glass Bay

COLE WRIGHT THRILLERS

The Arrival

Measured Aggression

Hide Away

Slow Burn

Scorpion Bait

Zero Kills

Not Above The Law

Hard Ground

COLE WRIGHT COLLECTION

No Lack Of Courage

COLE WRIGHT NOVELLA

Cold Highway

COLE WRIGHT SHORT STORIES

Dark Fields

Schedule Interruption

The Forest Doesn't Care

The Handler

One Little Broken Leg

Cardinals

A Steep Climb

What Do You Say Gus?

Stillness

Much Too Familiar

Peruser

SHORT MYSTERY FICTION

Lake Summerfield Incident

Ghost Beats

Uninvited

Off Into The Night

The Man With The Hat

SCI FI COLLECTIONS

The Blaze of Pollux

Chasing 'Oumuamua

In Custody

Listen, You!

Dreamhaul

SHORT STANDALONE SCIENCE FICTION

The Molenstraat Music Festival

Barrens

Aelonee

Little Voices

Designated Driver

Cami, Metta and The Cube

Dangerous Machines

Fubrelli's Ghost

Lydia's Mollusk

Load Bearing Member

A Cultural Exchange

Life Span

The Film Adjuster

Problem Landing

The Chule

Sail Man

CONTEMPORARY SHORT STORIES

Single Branch, With Blossom

The Umbrellas of Tokyo

Concentration

CONTEMPORARY NOVELS

This is the Perfect Way To Wake

Steel Wagons

MORGENFELD

The Mapmaker of Morgenfeld

The Stairs at Cronnenwood

The Chimneys in Atterton

The Wintermas Paintings

The Bergeron Sculptures

The Ingersal Ballet

MORGENFELD Short stories

The Quiet Hours

Brevelmeister and Kirrinder, Stationers

The Duchess, The Maid and the Ocelot

COPYRIGHT NOTES ON INDIVIDUAL STORIES

Chasing Fox Palton

Published by Triple V Publishing

Cover art by © Grandfailure | Dreamstime.com

Paperback isbn: 9798278652236

Err: Internet Disconnected

Published by Triple V Publishing

Cover art by © Tatyana Khanko | Dreamstime.com

Paperback isbn: 9798241525970

Becca And The Ghosters

Published by Triple V Publishing

Cover art by © Grandeduc | Dreamstime.com

Paperback isbn: 9798242360983

Terrarium Blues

Published by Triple V Publishing

Cover art by © Nexusplexus | Dreamstime.com

Paperback isbn:9798242376526

Big Steps

Published by Triple V Publishing

Cover illustration © Philcold | Dreamstime.com

Paperback isbn: 9798243015547

Phobos Pummeled

Published by Triple V Publishing

Cover illustration © Nexusplexus | Dreamstime.com

Paperback isbn: 9798243344555

We Are But Passengers

Published by Triple V Publishing

Cover illustration © Luca Oleastri | Dreamstime.com

Paperback isbn:9798243473903

Published by Triple V Publishing

www.ingramcontent.com/pod-product-compliance
Lightning Source LLC
LaVergne TN
LVHW041055080826
845145LV00007B/1577

* 9 7 8 1 0 6 7 1 3 5 0 1 0 *